The Slovakian

The Slovakian

Thomas J. Lipovsky

Library of Congress Control Number: 2007908930
ISBN: Hardcover   978-1-4363-0267-8
                 Softcover   978-1-4363-0266-1

This book was printed in the United States of America.

To order additional copies of this book, contact:
Xlibris Corporation
1-888-795-4274
www.Xlibris.com
Orders@Xlibris.com
41961

"To My Mother"
1914-1995

PART ONE

ACROSS THE SHINING SEA

CHAPTER 1

Jon Valen arrived in the United States of America from Europe at the turn of the twentieth century. His money supply was meager and his academic education was minimal. He was a carpenter by trade, a skill that was in great demand in the burgeoning industrialization of corporate America. Both unskilled and semi-skilled labors were in demand. The steel mills and coal mines in Pennsylvania were salivating for the cheap labor the immigrants would provide. They needed muscle to do the heavy lifting required to build bridges and raise skyscrapers across the United States where cities were growing as fast as the railroads could transport. Jon was determined to be a part of this great undertaking and get a piece of the action, but even more, he would be a free man and so would his family and sweetheart, who were depending on him to succeed.

Austria-Hungary was where he hailed and where he was eventually driven from. He had the misfortune of being Slovak, a minority of people within the midst of the empire. They were treated as the name Slav, implies slaves, the bottom of the social barrel, nothing new to the Slovaks who had been under the boot of some conqueror since the time of the Romans. Finally the diminutive twenty-year-old boy would endure no more, so with the extreme sacrifices of his older brother and father, he scraped up the passage fare to America. The ocean voyage was for the most part comfortable and swift. He sailed from Hamburg, Germany, December 28, 1900, on the Deutschland, the fastest passenger ship of its day, afloat with 2050 passengers. Although it was built for speed with the latest quadruple expansion engines, twin screws and service speed of 22 knots, it was plagued with mechanical problems. This voyage would be no exception, causing arrival time in New York a day late.

It was New Year's Eve, the third day at sea, when the Deutschland faltered and slowed to a crawl. No one seemed to notice. The passengers were partying hard at bringing in the New Year, singing, dancing, and drinking. First class was served succulent dinners with quality French champagne and an orchestra clad in tuxedos playing waltzes and dancing into the New Year. Second and third class peered through the multi-lighted supported chandeliers suspended from a dome shaped black-painted ceiling creating a mirage of stars sparkling in a night sky. Steerage located in the belly of the ship was cramped with close to a thousand immigrants from central and southern Europe. The majority were Slavs, Italians, and Greeks. They had no fancy orchestra and no fine French wine, but still, they partied with wild abandon, drinking wine from fermented grapes grown in the foothills of the Carpathian Mountains and from the semi-arid lands of lower Europe. The music switched back and forth from the fast-moving Slavic tempos to the nostalgic romantic songs of the Mediterranean.

Jon Valen was shy by nature, but after several drinks saluting in the New Year with some of his countrymen, he joined in the festivities full steam until the songs and dancing melted into the dawn.

Jon was awakened by a ray of early morning sunlight that poured through a porthole that rested on his closed eyelids like a laser beam. He swung his right forearm across his eyes to shield them from the annoying intrusion. He pressed his hands against the floor deck and pushed himself up to a sitting position. The ship, not at full speed, was being tossed about by angry waves from a distant storm. This rocking and rolling did little to ease the nausea that threatened to push last night's food and drink from his stomach through his gagging throat onto the deck. He struggled to his feet and dashed towards the stair ladder that would bring him to fresh air on the second-class deck. He reached the deck rail, leaned over, and evacuated all the contents from his growling stomach into the churning sea below.

The Deutschland steamed into New York harbor at top speed January 4, 1901, 6:00 AM. They were greeted by an ensuing winter storm, making debarking an arduous task. In 1855, the New York State Legislature had established Castle Garden, formerly a military installation, located in Lower Manhattan as a processing station to facilitate immigration entrance. They were required to give their birthplace, occupation, and then after a cursory medical examination; they were passed through Customs and then had their name registered as having entered the country. In 1892, a new facility was built on Ellis Island in the middle of New York harbor, bringing stricter entrance regulations. The thousand immigrants from the ship gathered in the Registry room also called "The Great Hall"; many were totally exhausted from this ordeal and fell sound asleep on whatever baggage they had to rest their heads.

Some women were attending to their young children, changing diapers and removing wet clothes that had been drenched by the swirling snow and sleet that lay thick on their clothing; other women were breastfeeding their babies in an inconspicuous dimly lighted place away from the windows. The sun outside was imprisoned in the bowels of a raging storm that funneled down the Hudson River into New York Harbor, leaving the Statue of Liberty a blur.

After a long day and long lines, Jon Valen planted his feet on American soil on January 4, 1901. There he stood, all five-feet-five-inches of him with his dark brown hair disheveled from the bitter cold wind that blew through New York Harbor. Although he was short, his body was erect, muscular, and his high cheek bones coupled with his steel blue gray eyes and square cleft chin revealed a man who was also strong of will. His mettle would soon be tested. The immigrants usually had friends or kinsmen from their village or hometown already established in some community in the New World. Jon had cousins who had migrated to the coal mining regions of Pennsylvania. They were to meet him at Castle Garden after staying with other friends from their village, who were residing in Jersey City, New Jersey, just across the Hudson River. The storm had dismantled all means of communication and transportation, making it virtually impossible for his sponsors to cross the river by ferry. Jon waited countless hours for their arrival, but to no avail. The sun showed its face for only a moment and then was swallowed by hungry black clouds in the western sky bringing darkness and desolation into the heart and soul of Jon Valen. There was no moon; there were no stars to help him navigate his way through the unfamiliar streets of Lower Manhattan. His only companion was a cloth bag that was slung over his shoulder that contained all his worldly possessions. The evening was growing late, but people were still milling about the streets, going about their business, ignoring the brutal weather that surrounded them. From time to time, he spoke with other immigrants who were stranded, but all he could do was make them aware of the thieves and con artists that preyed on the new arrivals with promises of jobs and lodging. The con men would take their money and disappear. The streets were a cacophony of foreign languages, horse drawn vehicles, clanging trolley cars, and the crunching sound of footsteps on the steadily falling snow. The streetlights were shut down by the storm leaving only white snow glistening with sleet to illuminate the dark streets. The wet heavy snow that was already rising above his knees forced Jon to walk at a slow pace. He made attempts to speak to people, but he was passed by as if he were invisible. When he finally did get someone to stop, his inability to speak English left the courteous gentleman nonplussed and Jon fled apologetically. It was late in the evening when he found a bench to sit on and in spite of the cold; he was warm in his woolen clothes that were designed for the Carpathian Mountain winters that often held snow on its peaks far into the spring. The streets were quiet now, and only a few people were moving about with purpose. Others were wandering aimlessly, looking for food and shelter. A dog was gnawing at something it snatched from an upset garbage can that was blown over and rolling out of an alley spewing all its contents over the street. Jon watched passively as the garbage can and all the flying debris vanished into the dark street a block away.

Exhaustion took hold of him and forced his mind into a state of semi-consciousness. The snow turned to sleet and rain and then evaporated in the rising temperature. The wind calmed, bringing large, soft descending snowflakes that covered the sleet and rain with a deep white blanket that hid the treacherous footing below. Jon's mind was now trapped in his soul. He envisioned his precious Stasha swimming naked in a cool mountain lake in the Carpathians that was formed during the Ice Age. It was just an hour's climb from their village birthplace. The summer sun was bouncing off her wet, dark hair with a hue that matched the color of the deep blue water. He watched her swim to the lake's edge, where it was shallow and she was about to emerge and display all her sensuality that nature bestowed on her. That was a day in the past that he kept locked in his heart and soul. That moment he knew that their marriage was as inevitable as the sunrise.

He started to reach out to her, when his dream vanished into a scream of reality. "Fire! Fire!" His eyes began to focus and suddenly he was on his feet scanning the area. He didn't understand the language of the plea, but he sensed from the tone that it was a call for help. The snowfall was still dense, making visibility poor. A tall building began to materialize across the street with black smoke billowing from the second-floor window. As he got closer to the building, he could see people poking their heads out of the first- and second-floor windows. The fire apparently started on the first floor and was sending flames and smoke through the ceiling to the second floor, forcing people on both floors to run for the safety of the ledges outside of the windows. Extreme pressure was being created from the growing inferno, causing windows to blow apart, sending a shower of glass, wood, metal, and bodies to the cobblestone pavement below.

Jon spotted a light blue canopy with *Hotel Royal* printed in bold white letter on its front flap. The canopy stretched from the street, across a wide sidewalk, to the main entrance. As he ran under the canopy, he could hear the particles of shrapnel that were being hurled from the exploding building raining down on the canvas covering. When Jon arrived at the door, he found it slightly ajar. He squeezed through and found himself in an immense room with high ceilings and large paintings framed with royal blue curtains hanging ostentatiously on gold-papered walls. To his left was a curved shaped dark brown desk counter with geometric designs carved into its surface. While Jon was surveying the area, a man came running across the lobby floor in blue overalls with the name *Hotel Royal* printed across his left shirt pocket. The employee asked Jon to follow him and once again he did not understand the words, but because of his hand gesture, he knew what he had to do. The lobby ceiling was beginning to show signs of the fire; smoke was seeping through cracks made by the intense heat on the first floor.

Time was of the essence as they headed for the stairway that was located in the far right corner that led to the first floor. By this time people were rushing down the stairway, pushing and shoving, making it difficult for them to reach the top of the stairway. When they arrived at the top, they entered into a long wide corridor that ran parallel with the street in front to the corner of the next street that intersected. It divided the building in half and it was the front that was ablaze. The immense width of the corridor was helping to keep the fire from spreading to the rear. There were four more corridors that ran parallel to one another from the front of the building to its extreme rear. The employee led Jon to the first corridor where each took a side and knocked on the doors from one end to the other until they covered all four of them. The employee then instructed the guests to go to the back of the building where he was sure they would be safe from the fire. They checked the corridors quickly one more time to see if they had missed anyone and then returned to the front of the building. By the time they arrived, the stairway was beginning to catch on fire. The smoke was starting to overpower them. Their only recourse was to try and save themselves. They raced down the stairway with flames challenging them every step of the way. Now they too were looking for refuge on the street.

When they reached the lobby floor, the ceiling started cracking from flames knifing their way through from the first floor. Soon smoke would follow, making it impossible to stay. They turned together to take one last look and watched another mad rush of people stumbling down the stairway that was now engulfed in flames and collapsing underneath the rage. Bodies began piling up at the bottom. They could smell the stench of their smoldering clothes and burning flesh and the agonizing screams of those who survived the fall but were unable to move from injuries they sustained. Some rose from the ashes, slamming their hands against their burning clothes and found their way through the glass doors to the street. The main doors were wide open now, allowing a full blast of wind to blow through the lobby, fanning the fire that was sneaking through the ceiling into a frenzy of flames gone mad.

Without hesitation, Jon and his new found comrade raced to the door and quickly grasped the two huge door handles and in unison slammed it shut, blocking out the invading wind and calming the flames. They both turned and directed their attention to the stairway that was now impassable. Jon heard a desperate cry for help somewhere to the left of the stairway. He moved his eyes quickly toward the sound of the voice and saw a woman holding a young boy in her arms on a balcony that overhung the lobby. The flames were closing in on them. There was little time to waste. Jon scanned the lobby for something—anything that could aid in rescuing them. He looked for something he could stand on that would raise him closer to the outstretched arms of the woman. There was nothing in sight, and then he glanced down at the floor and spotted a throw rug lying in front of a long fancy sofa. He snatched it up with both hands and stretched his arms above his head until the rug stood full length in front of him. He determined that it measured five-foot by eight-foot. He motioned to his partner to hold up the other end until it lay horizontal between them, and then he walked towards him making the rug form a U shape. The woman watched and she knew now what she had to do to save the boy. They moved directly under the rail and looked up and watched the woman hug and kiss the boy, and then she leaned over the rail while flames were licking at her body like sharp razors inflicting excruciating pain and dropped the boy cleanly onto the rug, driving both men to their knees. Jon scooped the boy up, looked up at the balcony for the woman, only to find that she had vanished behind the mass of flames, smoke, and smoldering debris.

There was nothing left for them to do but to run out of the burning building to the safety of the street. Jon found his way to the bench where he had been resting and reminiscing about his lovely Stasha when he had heard the cry "Fire!" The snow had stopped, making the hotel clearly visible. The scene before him was sheer chaos; would-be rescuers were running about trying to help hotel occupants who were shimmying down bed sheets and blankets that were tied together and fastened to bedposts lessening the jump to the pavement. Some of them reached the ground unscathed. But others didn't fare as well, crashing to the pavement, splitting their heads and breaking limbs. Jon looked down at the boy who was in his strong embrace. The boy sobbed and said that he wanted his mommy. A gust of wind blew, bringing a swirl of snowflakes and tears to the eyes of Jon Valen, and in the distance he could hear the clanging of bells. The firemen had arrived.

CHAPTER 2

It was July. Jon had been gone for six months, and Stasha Ondreas was celebrating her sixteenth birthday. The lower Carpathian slopes overlooked the festivities in the plush green valley below where the village square was crowded with people of all ages. Some of the young men and women were dressed in traditional garb and were dancing passionately to the Slovakian folk music that dated back to the sixth century A.D. Stasha, exhausted from the dancing, eating, and endless conversation, retreated unnoticed into the labyrinth of cobblestone streets and narrow passageways that laced their way between stone houses and found their way to open countryside that was alive with fields of wheat, rye, barley, sugar, beets, corn, and vegetables of all varieties. It wouldn't be long before Stasha, her family and most of the villagers, would be bending their backs, plucking the vegetables and scything the wheat by hand.

Stasha watched the jagged mountain peaks slice the sun in half as she approached a mountain path that led to the ledge that cast its eyes over the valley like a sentinel. She arrived just in time to see the village below disappear into the night while the molten sun melted the tar roof of heaven on a paling sky. She shuddered as she gazed at the exploding universe that was engulfing her senses. Slowly she fell to her knees, freeing herself gradually from the trance that captured her. She saw the village in the distance that was now dotted with points of light. The square was lit dimly with gaslights and tar-tipped wooden torches. She could see the dancers vaguely and could hear the music faintly as the party carried on into the late evening.

"No one seems to know that I left," she thought. Stasha was painfully aware that her beloved Jon was gone. She remembered the last evening they spent together right here on the ledge that harbored all their childhood secrets—the first time they kissed, and then Stasha blushed thinking about the first time they touched. Her body began to tingle and grow warm and she could feel wetness between her legs. The moon was high in the sky, shining on Stasha's oval face that was adorned with coal black eyes that slanted slightly upward away from a perfectly shaped nose. Her pale tinged skin and blue-black hair that fell to the small of her back was a gift from the marauding Mongols who had slipped through the dangerous Carpathian pass, trying to escape the black death that was decimating most of Europe in the thirteenth century. They stayed only a year, but in that short time they plundered and raped, spilling blood and their sperm like no other invaders before or since.

The night air began to cool, sending shivers throughout Stasha's warm body and making goose pimples rise on her exposed arms that were hanging delicately from her sleeveless blouse. She stood up and smoothed down her skirt with the palm of her hands until it hung neatly at her ankles.

The mountaintops were a show of celestial lights. The peaks were sparkling from the luminous new moon that skirted the Carpathians and then suddenly disappeared behind the mountain, leaving the sky a black velvet cloth with coruscating diamonds pinned to it from horizon to horizon. Stasha turned her eyes from the night sky, still breathless from the sight, and turned her attention in the direction of the village. The square was no longer visible. The party was over, reminding her of how late it was.

"My mother must be sick with worry," she thought. She headed for the path and scampered down it as fast as she could. There was no moonlight to guide her, but still she did not stumble, lifting her skirt daintily as her nimble feet found their way instinctively to the bottom. As she approached the field she heard a voice shouting her name from the other side. She stopped momentarily and saw a shadowy figure slip out of the wheat field.

"Stasha, Stasha," the voice shouted, out of breath.

"Stefan," she said in a whisper, finally recognizing him, "what are you doing here?"

He took a step back away from her, looked into her eyes, hesitated for a moment until he caught his breath, and said, "I came to be with you for your birthday."

Before he could continue she snapped, "Don't you think you are a little late for that?"

"Well," he stammered, "you know how the army is."

"No, I don't," she replied, "but what I do know is that Jon would not approve of you being here with me. I told you time and time again that Jon and I are to be married as soon as he gets settled in America."

Stefan looked her straight in the eyes and said, "I don't give a damn what Jon approves of. As long as you are still not his wife, I will pursue you until that day!" He removed his hands from her face and gripped her hands and said, "I was sent here by your mother to come and find you and bring you home."

She pulled her hand away from his grip and said, "I can find my own way home thank you!" She turned and walked in the direction of the village.

CHAPTER 3

On January 6, 1901, the New York morning edition headlines printed in bold letters "Slavic heroics under fire." The article told of the story of Jon's recent arrival at Ellis Island from Europe and his plight through the streets of Lower Manhattan, and how he accidentally came upon the scene of the hotel fire. More amazingly, how the rescue of the hotel guests was accomplished without speaking a word of English. What was even more remarkable was that the employee who was a maintenance man at the hotel was also Slovak, and not knowing that Jon was a countryman, spoke in English.

It wasn't until Jon was sitting on the bench with the boy after escaping from the fiery building that the discovery was made. The employee had lost sight of him and the boy sitting on the bench across the avenue and made his way through the deep crusted snow that was glazed on the surface from the cold morning wind. As he came within earshot, he heard Jon say, "Jesus, Mary, and Joseph" in Slovak, which was a response often used for divine intervention and in some context a form of cursing or when caught in surprise; which in this case it was surprise—prompting the employee to respond with, "Jesus, Mary, and Joseph" in Slovak. Jon looked up slowly, a smile forming on his face that belied the tears that were streaming down his cheeks. Jon set the boy aside and stood up, brushing the tears from his eyes with the back of his hand. For a moment he couldn't move, and then the employee thrust out his right hand and said, "My name is Lucas Zatko."

"And I am Jon Valen," Jon responded joyfully. They embraced in Slavic fashion, alternating a kiss on each cheek. Then they stepped back and faced one another. Lucas spoke first and said, "I am from Kosice."

"My God," Jon responded, excitement growing in his voice, "I am from Dubovica, not so very far from Kosice in the adjoining county of Saris. I just arrived in America late last night."

Before they could further their acquaintance, the nerve-racking sound of an ambulance bell interrupted, reminding them that their work was not finished. Jon motioned the boy to stay, and then hustled back to the turmoil. As they crossed the avenue, a gilded and decorated steam engine drawn by three-matched white fire horses arrived with bells clanging and hoof beats pounding on the ice-covered snow. Following close behind them was the hook and ladder carriage drawn by three black matching horses. A horse drawn black sleigh was already parked with "Fire Chief" emblazoned in red and yellow on a silver metal shield.

They approached the fire chief, who was methodically giving orders to the firefighters. Lucas introduced himself as an employee of the hotel and gave a full description of where and how the fire started, and how he and Jon attempted to rescue the hotel patrons. He also told him how Jon, who was newly arrived from Europe, only by chance came upon the fire, and without hesitation joined in the rescue attempt. He told them about Jon's courageous rescue of the boy. The fire chief, after listening to the description Lucas had given him about the wide corridor that divided the hotel into two equal parts, ordered his firefighters to place their steam engines around the corner on Forty-first Street, and direct their water hoses in the area of the corridor on the first floor. More fire engines and more ambulances began to arrive on the scene, bells clanging, horses clopping on the hard snow, firemen and medical personnel scurrying about, and people leaping and being blown out of the inferno onto the cobblestone pavement below. This was surely "Dante's Inferno" incarnate.

Jon and Lucas joined the firemen and some of the guests who had exited by the rear of the hotel and circled the block to help the firemen and medical people. The fire was out of control. A blast of orange red flaming heat gushed through like molten lava from an erupting volcano. "The description that Lucas had given me of the hotel interior not only saved lives but also acres of real estate with their courage and quick thinking," the fire chief was quoted as saying to the newspaper reporters.

Splashes of blood stained the white snow-laden pavement from bodies that were strewn from the main entrance down to the corner of Forty-first Street. Doctors, medics, and nurses were swarming everywhere, looking for injured who needed the most attention, and checking to see who were dead. After laborious hours of moving bodies both dead and alive into some semblance of order, the fire chief observed Jon and Lucas' exhaustion and ordered them to stop.

"You both have gone far beyond the call of duty," he added with sincere admiration in his tone. Before they left, he insisted that they get their burns and cuts that were inflicted on them during their dangerous rescue work attended to.

The East River was already bathed in the sunrise when they returned to check on the boy, only to find he was gone. They were questioning some of the firemen of his whereabouts, when a police sergeant overheard them and said the boy was turned over to a gentleman claiming to be a relative. Jon was visibly upset, but the policeman assured him that the boy was in safe hands. Lucas looked at Jon, shrugged his shoulders, and raised his eyebrows as if to say; "We did all we could do." With that said, Lucas motioned Jon to follow him.

The sun was pulling itself out of the East River, dripping with rays of azure and orange red as they crossed Chambers Street where most of the immigrants lived in squalor. For the most part they were ignored by the most prosperous, until Jacob Riis, a New York journalist, published a bombshell study in text and photographs of New York City slum life, "How the other half lives." This publication opened eyes all across the nation, bringing effort to reform deplorable conditions that sat on the "better halves'" conscience like a boil ready to burst and spread its infection into their neighborhoods.

The political philosophy of this era (populism) was the juggernaut that pressed the privileged and big money men to share some of their power and wealth with the everyday workingman. Jon wasn't aware of it at the time, but it was this force that would facilitate his quest to be a member of the elite.

They reached Fulton Street and crossed Broadway, where the smell of fresh-cut fish permeated the clear morning air. The Fulton Fish Market was alive with activity, preparing fish for the local restaurants.

The sun was blinding in the clear blue winter sky and the air was cool and fresh when they entered the tavern at the corner of Fulton and Pearl Streets. They found a table close to the bar and collapsed like dead weight on the armed wooden chairs. Jon leaned forward, resting his chin on his folded arms that were spread across the edge of the round mahogany table. Lucas moved his head back while massaging the nape of his neck with his right hand, and at the same time brushed his hair back with his left. Jon raised his eyebrows and looked across the table at Lucas who he surmised was in his early forties. His hair dark brown like Jon's, except for a sprinkling of silver that laced through it as if painted by an artist's fine brush. His eyes were deep set in large diametric sockets and his nose was thick and reddish with flaring nostrils that complemented the deep lines in his face and forehead. Lucas placed both of his hands on the rim of the table and said in a gentle voice that belied his rugged appearance, "What would you like for breakfast, Jon?" Before he could respond Lucas said, "How about some Irish coffee to start off with?"

Even though he was speaking in Slovak, Jon had no clue what Irish coffee was and not to appear stupid he nodded.

Lucas smiled, showing two full rows of yellow stained teeth and then turned to face the bartender who didn't have the slightest notion as to what they were talking about. After all, this was Jim Clancy's Irish Pub, and Slovak was blarney to him.

"And what will you have?" he asked in a thick Irish accent.

"Why, we'll be having some of your strong Irish coffee," he answered in his best-broken English Irish brogue.

"Coming up," he answered in his pure Irish accent as he placed two coffee mugs on the bar. He turned and reached back to a shelf finding a metal coffee pot and carried it forward with his right hand and began pouring its contents into the mugs one at a time. Jon watched intently as the bartender finished filling the mugs and then was astonished when he reached for a bottle of whiskey and poured a shot into each coffee mug. Lucas noticed his puzzled look and asked, "Is there anything wrong Jon?"

"No, no." Jon lied. "I guess I'm just tired."

The bartender had made his way over to the table and noticed their bandages and other cuts and burns that were covered with ointment.

"Why, you two lads look like you've been to hell and back!"

Lucas laughed, and then said, "Well, I guess you could say that." He invited the bartender to sit down and join them while he told the story of the fire and their part in it. The morning was growing late, bringing patrons into the tavern at a steady pace. The bartender, Jim Clancy, who was also the proprietor, excused himself and went behind the bar to wait on demanding customers who were looking for a "Pick me up" shot of whiskey before they went off to their jobs where the hours would be long and labor tedious and backbreaking. In spite of the noisy mixture of foreign tongues and tobacco smoke filtering through the tavern, Jon dozed off with his head drooping forward, his chin resting on his breastbone as Lucas retold the story to newly arrived customers. Jon was drifting in and out of sleep from the numbing effects of the Irish coffee and the monotonous droning of Lucas' voice, and then he slipped into the timeless slot where reality is put on hold.

CHAPTER 4

Everything was quiet when Stasha and Stefan arrived at the Ondreas house at the south end of the village away from the mountain slopes. The morning sun would soon display a seemingly endless vista of meadows and grasslands where cattle and other livestock grazed. Stasha reached out to open the front door, but the quick, firm hand of Stefan intercepted her. She attempted to make a vocal protest, but was silenced while Stefan's lips pressed heavily on her partly open mouth. She tried to back away, but the closed door and the strong arms of Stefan prevented her. Stasha's body stiffened, as his lips grew gentler, but hungrier as his tongue slipped between her teeth and found her moist soft tongue. Her mind and body were a tug-of-war—her mind pleading no, and her body starting to heat up stirring the prurient juices that lay dormant deep in her sexual core, waiting only for Jon to rekindle her fire. Stefan's hand was on her breast, massaging slowly and ever so gently. Her nipples rose as she felt the hardness of Stefan pushing against her. Now her mind was no longer in the struggle as it surrendered completely to the unquenchable fire in her body. Her tongue began to play back to his. Thrusting and sucking and then instinctively, her hand reached down and grasped his thick pulsating hardness, inducing Stefan to moan while all the dreams of Stasha came oozing out in spasmodic spurts, relieving his aching heart and soul.

"Stasha! Stasha!" a voice cried out from behind the door.

"Yes mother?" Stasha answered, her voice shaking. Their bodies slowly disengaged with the scent of sex emanating from their sweating bodies.

"Stasha, are you alright?" her mother pleaded.

"Yes, I'm fine, I'll be right in."

"I sent Stefan to look for you."

"He is here, Mother, and was kind enough to walk me home."

"From where, child? I was worried!"

"I'm sorry. Now let me say good night to Stefan and then I'll tell you where I was and why." Stasha turned her attention once more to Stefan who was standing there like a man waiting to be sentenced to death.

"Forgive me, Stefan, I don't know why this happened. I love Jon, I really do!" She began to sob, and her crying became hysteria. "Stefan, I'm sorry," she repeated over and over until he could bear no more and turned abruptly and disappeared into the sultry summer night

Stasha stood silent for a moment to calm herself. She brushed the tears from her eyes with her handkerchief and then opened the door where she found her mother waiting impatiently ready to reprimand her, until she noticed she had been crying. She spread her arms apart to cradle Stasha. She balked for a second and then found refuge in her mother's gentle embrace.

"What is it, child?" she asked with deep concern.

"Nothing"

"Well, why are you crying? It's about Jon, isn't it?"

"Yes," she answered hesitating, not wanting to tell her what really happened, "I miss him."

"Of course you do." she answered sympathetically. "Be patient. Just think how much easier your life will be when Jon finally brings you to America. No more sweating in the fields. You two will be given the opportunity to move ahead and have a more comfortable life and there will be no Emperor to tell you what you can and cannot do. Here we work to eat, keep a roof over our heads, and to keep warm in the winter. The pay always stays the same no matter how hard we work. You don't remember, but I can still see your grandfather being hanged at the square and then being set on fire while he was still alive. All because he proclaimed that Slovaks were also God's people. For a thousand years, we have been fighting for that recognition, but to no avail, so now we must find freedom in America like the Jews did in the bible. America will be our promised land. So be patient, Stasha! Our long wait is nearly over."

"You make it sound so easy . . . you don't know."

"What don't I know? Is there anything you haven't told me?"

Stasha hugged her mother and said, "No, everything is fine. Good night. I'm sure everything will look better after I get a good night's sleep."

It was late morning when Stasha was awakened by the ringing of the village bells. She opened her eyes and sat up slowly, waiting a moment until her eyes focused and the cobwebs diminished in her throbbing head. She swiveled her body, directing her feet from the side of her homemade woven bed to the wooden floor. The bed was set flush against the left rear corner of the oblong shaped room, which measured about nine-by-fourteen. Nailed to the right wooden wall was a shelf with a wooden framed mirror hanging above it and an armless wooden chair setting in front. Stasha moved across the room and stood in front of the mirror. Her eyes were bloodshot from crying herself to sleep. Her dark hair fell in uneven cascades on the front of her shoulders and lay on her bare breasts. She pulled her hair back with her fingertips, exposing her breasts and began to visually examine them and then touch them, remembering Stefan's gentle caress and how it had aroused her and drove her to touch him. She was bewildered at her behavior . . . impure thoughts were one thing, but impure acts . . . my God.

"What will Father Marin say when I confess my sins?"

"Stasha!" an urgent voice called. "Are you awake? You must hurry or you will be late for mass. It's the last one, so be quick."

During the Great Moravian Empire that was created in the first half of the eighth century, Irish missionaries from Bavaria sought to Christianize the Slavic pagan tribes, but they were only granted limited success among them. Ratislav, the ruler of Moravia, was getting pressure from Louis the German whose influence was weakening Ratislav's control over the empire, and in order to curtail his movement, Ratislav asked Rome to create an Ecclesiastical Province on Slav territory. He importuned with Pope Nicholas to send teachers who were familiar with the Slavic tongue. Rome procrastinated, so Ratislav turned in desperation to Byzantium, requesting a Bishop. Two Greek brothers by the names of Cyril and Methodius, known to this day as the apostles of the Slavs, arrived in eight sixty-two AD. In eight sixty-three, Cyril devised a Slavic language alphabet. The Slavic state in the ninth century did not survive, but the memory of Cyril and Methodius remained spiritually evident in the souls of Slovaks for generations giving them the strength to overcome a thousand years of bondage and servitude.

Father Marin completed the offertory of the mass and then stepped up into the pulpit. He paused momentarily, scanning the congregation with a slow deliberate gaze. Everyone froze in their place, waiting for him to speak. After some time, with a deadly silence, he began, "Dear friends in Christ, today I would like to speak of loyalty. Loyalty to God, of course." he said in a rasping whisper, and then, raising his voice an octave, he continued, "But also loyalty to friends, family, and country . . . Country," he emphasized. "In the past ten years, our towns and villages have diminished in population. Our people are leaving in droves for western nations, particularly America." Father Marin paused once more and then repeated, "America, the land of milk and honey. Is that what you think! Is it!" he went on, his eyes moving in all directions.

"Well, you are mistaken. You owe all your allegiance to the Empire. The Magyars came here centuries ago when our ancestors were primitive people living in caves and they civilized us, and then brought Jesus Christ to us. With all that, and more, you want to betray your emperor? Remember the Israelites were led back . . . led back," he repeated, "to their mother country by Moses from bondage in Egypt. That was the natural course to take. Freedom comes from God when you do what is right. Loyalties, to God and your country, and to people you love. This is the proper way to behave."

The congregation did not stir as Father Marin removed a handkerchief from under his sleeve and wiped his sweat that poured down his forehead from his thinning silver hair. His pale gray eyes had the look of a man in pain as he finished his excoriating sermon. He composed himself for a moment, and then softened his voice and continued, "The Emperor has decreed that this coming school semester, twenty hours of the Magyar language will be taught in the Slovak elementary schools, and a love for the Magyar nation will be instilled. Teachers who neglect to conform will be summarily dismissed." Father Marin paused and then said, "Let us pray and ask God to give us the strength and determination to fulfill what our emperor expects from us. One last thought, remember what Christ said, 'Give unto Caesar the things that are Caesar's and to God the things that are God's.'" After reciting the "Our Father," communion was served and the mass ended with the words, "Go in peace."

CHAPTER 5

After six and a half months in New York City, working at Clancy's, Jon's English was improving with the help of Lucas and Clancy. His progress was impeded because he spent more time conversing with the Slavic-speaking customers that included Polish, Czech, Ukrainian, Lithuanian, and Russian, not to mention Hungarian that was light years from the Indo-European languages that interlaced one another. Yes, Jon had a knack for learning, that's why Clancy kept him. But he had a penchant for being less than civil to hunkies, a disparaging handle given to them by the Anglo-Saxon community. Later, that label would be placed on immigrants of Slavic ancestry, much to the chagrin of the Slavs, especially the Slovaks. On several occasions, Jon had to be restrained from getting physical with "The Magyar Menace," as he referred to them.

For the most part, he was busy waiting on tables and keeping the tavern clean and fixing anything that broke including the plumbing and electrical systems. He learned to repair by trial and error. His mental capacity to follow diagrammed instructions came gradually but accurately and still amazingly fast for a man with so little education. He also shared in the cooking with Clancy, a job he became well acquainted with after the early death of his mother.

After a long day's work, the tavern closed, and with everything quiet, Jon would open the windows and let the cool breeze that sailed up the East River into the hot smoky confines of the tavern. He would sit back on one of the table chairs and daydream of his future as a builder and the owner of property. From his eight dollars a week earnings, he was able to save six dollars a week. After six months, that added up to the sum of one hundred and forty dollars . . . not a paltry sum for turn of the century wages. It was a start. His goal was to save a thousand dollars and then move with his cousins to the anthracite coal regions of central Pennsylvania where the population was growing faster than houses could be built to accommodate the deluge of immigrants.

Jon's cousins never made it to Jersey City to meet him as planned because they too were trapped in the embrace of a blizzard that encompassed the mountainous coal regions with snow so deep that even the powerful train steam engines were laid helpless in their tracks. Several days after reading about the fire, Jon's friend from Jersey City, with the help of the New York newspaper that ran the story, traced Jon's address to Clancy's and paid him a visit. Their intention, of course, was to bring Jon back to their home temporarily until he was financially able to move on to Pennsylvania. It soon became obvious that the job situation at Clancy's was probably much more lucrative than anything they could arrange for him. In the coming months, Paul Malik and his wife Ana would visit Jon on their way to shop at the Fulton Fish Market that was located just a few blocks from Clancy's at the foot of the Brooklyn Bridge.

It was the last Sunday in August, and Jon was on a ferry crossing the Hudson River to New Jersey where the Maliks were waiting for him to arrive to spend two days at their New Jersey row home, whose backyard appeared to be a handshake with the Statue of Liberty. When Jon arrived at the ferry terminal on the Jersey side, the Maliks were waiting for him with a horse cart that they engaged to transport them home. The weather was hot and humid, discouraging the Sunday streetwalkers from moving at a fast pace. There was no semblance of order or destination. This was Jon's first time out on the streets at daytime, except for a few errands he ran for Clancy from time to time. The masses he encountered disturbed him. In Slovakia, people were impoverished. But at least they had plenty of space to move about and clean, fresh air to breath. The factories and refineries were contaminating everything in their wake. "Have I made a mistake?" he asked himself over and over. When they finally arrived at the Malik residence, he revealed his discontent.

"Jon," Paul answered with encouragement, "don't let these things upset you. Most of the people you saw today are not refugees. They have jobs and those who don't will soon be employed with the help of those who do. Their situation is exactly like the arrangement we had with you. The problem is that people are immigrating faster than proper accommodations can be made available for everyone. Be patient, Jon. People are being transported by the hundreds every week by trains to all parts of the country where work is waiting for them. You have seen the building going on all over New York City. It never stops; skyscrapers, bridges, elevated trains, paved streets, and now they are making plans for an underground railroad in New York City and plans to tunnel roads underneath the Hudson and East Rivers. Jon, I know that the streets are filthy and the air is dusty. There is debris everywhere, but you know Jon, that rubble you see represents our progress. It is a symbol of the blood, sweat, and tears of the immigrants that came here looking for freedom and self-esteem. It is a beginning of a dream that will spread across the country like wild fire. Take my word for it, Jon. I have been here for five years and in that short time, I have a reasonable paying job as a stevedore on the docks. I have a home. Sure, I work long hard hours, but it is still better than what I would have had back home. I know what you are thinking Jon. How hard could I have had it teaching? Well, let me tell you how hard. I was forced to teach what the Magyars deemed the truth. I was coerced into being a part of a conspiracy that would contribute to destroying the will and spirit of the Slovaks. I could no longer be a part of that and there didn't seem to be any remedy to the problem. Do you think that was cowardly of me, Jon?"

"No, Paul, that was exactly why I left. There was no way to improve your life. There was no future. Now, hopefully, I will be able to build a better life for my family."

"Yes you will, Jon. Right now there are people in the government working to get better wages and living conditions for us because they need us to fill all the labor jobs so that the rich can get richer. At least we will have a piece of it with an opportunity to make more if we are willing to sacrifice and work for it." Jon sat still for a moment, mesmerized by the passionate response to his discontent.

"Well I guess that settles that," Jon said, feeling a little ashamed of himself. "You are probably right. Anyhow, it is too late to turn back."

"Believe me Jon; you will never regret your decision to come to America."

After a scrumptious Slovak meal of cabbage stuffed with ground meat and rice, prepared by Mrs. Malik, they retired to the backyard and sat on picnic chairs and sipped red wine that Paul made from grapes, not from the Carpathian range, but from the grape-growing region of central New York State.

"Not bad," Jon said, taking a few sips after being informed of the wine's origin.

"See Jon," Paul said laughing, "things can't be that bad in a country that grows grapes for wine as good as you are drinking now."

Jon smiled and said, raising his glass, "A good point, Paul, I will take your advice and be more patient."

Paul set his glass on the picnic table and said, "Jon, after you hear what I have to tell you, you will be more confident about your decision to leave Slovakia." He turned his head in the direction of the kitchen door and shouted to Ana, who was busy at the time cleaning the dishes.

"Yes Paul?" she answered while pushing the screen door open. Ana was a short woman, a little on the plump side, but her round-shaped face centered with a pug nose and laughing green eyes made her appearance pleasing.

"The letter Ana—the letter from my brother. Would you please bring it to me?"

"Yes, of course," she answered. She disappeared into the living room and seconds later the screen door swung open with Ana holding an envelope in her right hand. Paul stood up to meet her as she stepped down onto the grass and snatched it from her outstretched hand. He turned and faced Jon, anger now showing on his face and his tone.

"Here, read this!" Paul snapped, handing the letter to Jon. Jon slipped the pages out of the envelope onto the picnic table and began reading the contents of the letter.

"My dear brother, it seems that every time I write you, it is always bad news . . ." The letter went on telling about Father Marin's sermon in relation to the Emperor's ultimatum. "Of course," the letter continued, "everyone was upset with the ultimatum, but as usual no one voiced their opinion, except Andrew Valen. This is why I am informing you of the incident because Andrew and some of his friends had a secret meeting in his barn where he keeps his prize bulls during the winter. Somehow, someone got wind of the meeting and informed the authorities, and they got caught red-handed. They were arrested and taken to Sabvinov where Jon's brother Jozef is chief of police.

Jon interrupted Paul, seeming shocked, and said, "Not my brother! He didn't have anything to do with the arrest."

"No, no, no, Jon. According to my brother, he was completely surprised by the whole affair. He is going to do everything he can to free them. Apparently they are taking the word of an informant . . . one whose identity they refuse to reveal. Jozef has been asking a witness to come forward to release the men. Jon, you know that Jozef is respected by the Magyars. This is why he was promoted to chief of police in the first place. So far, he has managed to keep both the Slovaks and the Magyars from taking drastic measures in volatile situations. Don't worry, Jozef will find a way. Anyhow, there is nothing more we can do now but wait for word from home."

Paul poured the final contents of the bottle into their glasses and then stood up and faced the Statue of Liberty, raised his glass with his outstretched arm and said, "To the lady whose guiding light will always be an inspiration to all who come here seeking a better life."

"I'll drink to that," Jon said, rising from his chair and finishing his wine with one final gulp. Suddenly, he fell back on his chair feeling light-headed.

As usual, the wine made him drowsy and he soon excused himself and retired to a makeshift guest room that served as a sleeping quarter and a study. Paul never lost his love for books and learning. His goal was to be financially secure, master the English language, then earn an American college degree and become a teacher. Jon collapsed into a deep sleep, exhausted from all the months of long working hours and sleepless nights, missing Stasha and yearning for her soft lips and body.

It was still dark when Jon was awakened by Paul shaking his shoulder gently. "Sorry," Paul said softly, "but we have to get you to the ferry terminal and then I have to be off to my job at the dock."

"What time is it?" Jon asked, rubbing his eyes with the knuckles of his index fingers.

"It's five o'clock."

Jon sat up, stretched his arms, yawned, and said, "Jesus, Mary and Jozef."

Paul handed him a bath towel and said, "Go wash up and get dressed. You'll find a shaving brush and razor in the bathroom."

A half hour later they were out the door and just in time to catch the trolley car that transported them to the ferry terminal. It was 6:30 AM when Jon boarded the ferry and bid Paul goodbye. The sunrise was less than spectacular as its glory was shielded by an impenetrable steel gray sky. A cool wind raced up the river, bringing large raindrops tapping on its surface. Jon stood on the front of the deck, oblivious to the ever-increasing quantity of rain that fell like rapid gunshots on his body that was aflame with passion and anger. Paul's advice was "all you can do is wait for word from home."

"Easy for him to say."

It was raining hard when he got off the ferry at Battery Park near the Castle Garden building, where he had first set foot in New York City. The incessant rainfall was slowing the activity on the streets like it did when he arrived in the snowstorm at Ellis Island. But as before, he ignored the inclement weather and trudged on through the rain, running under the facades and canopies of buildings along the way. He was soaked to the skin when he arrived at Clancy's about 8:00 AM. The tavern was already bustling with impatient customers looking to be served. Clancy had a look of relief on his face when he saw Jon making his entrance, looking like a drowned rat.

"Welcome home," Clancy said with a broad smile on his face. Then, that quick his smile changed to a stern, commanding stare and he shouted, "Get the hell to work."

"In a minute," Jon answered as he disappeared out the backdoor that led to the outside steps to his room. Less than five minutes later he dashed through the door with a change of clothes and his wet hair slicked back with a part in the middle, which was becoming the hair style for men in the new century. He inched his way behind the bar and picked up his apron and moved out into the dining area to wait on tables. It rained all that day, cutting back on business and making the hours drag. At the day's end, Jon sat on his usual chair to collect himself, when Clancy approached him, dangling an envelope in his hand.

"Here, this arrived today when you were on break." Jon hesitated for a moment and then took the envelope from Clancy with his hand shaking.

"What's the matter lad? Had too much to drink last night?"

Jon smiled feebly and then began to tear open the envelope seal. There was sweat growing on his brow and his hands were still shaking as he read the opening line:

> "My dearest Jon,
>
> It was so wonderful to receive your long awaited letter. You can't imagine how much I have missed you, especially on the evening of my birthday. When everyone was partying, I slipped away and visited our secret place at the mountain ledge. The visit was both devastating and exhilarating. It was a beautiful clear night and stars were everywhere, sparkling like jewels in the dark sky. God, how I wished you were there to hold me and kiss me, and God forgive me, but I wished you were there to touch me. Jon, I need to be with you soon, so please, hurry. Now, I have bad news—." She told him about the arrest and imprisonment of his father. She said further that his brother would have them released because of lack of evidence. Her letter ended with loving words and more pleading with him to hurry and send for her.

CHAPTER 6

The villagers gathered at the square in front of St. John the Baptist Roman Catholic Church, whose gothic architecture was another reminder of a past conqueror. "Father Marin, Father Marin," a voice shouted from the midst of the crowd. "What do you intend to do about freeing Andrew Valen and his friends? Is it true that they have been removed from Sabvinov and transferred to a prison in Presov?" Before Father could respond, he continued his heated questioning. "Did you know that the Magyars burned his barn to the ground along with his prize bulls? Did you?" he repeated vehemently.

Father Marin stood silent for a moment pondering an answer that might pacify him. Finally he spoke. "My dear friends, there is nothing to be alarmed about. They were moved to Presov where there are more adequate facilities."

"What you mean to say is that there are more adequate instruments to torture them and make them confess to a crime they did not commit. Where have you been Father?" he shouted, losing his temper to the naiveté that Father Marin displayed. "It has been going on for centuries."

"But that was long ago and things have changed."

"How long ago was it when Peter Ondreas was hanged and burned alive in this very square?" Father stayed silent. "And what about the burning of the barn and the bulls? How long ago was that, Father?"

"Yesterday," he spat sarcastically. "They were drunken soldiers and they were punished severely for their violent act."

The spokesman continued his argument, "Through the years we have been asked to abide by the Magyars' demands, no matter how demeaning or detrimental, and we silently obeyed. But again they have gone too far. They want to eradicate our language, and that in time will obliterate the Slovak race. Father, is that what Cyril and Methodius had in mind when they brought us the word of Christ? I think not . . . so, no Father, enough is enough. I am one of the teachers that have been threatened with dismissal if I do not abide by the ultimatum. You can tell the Magyars that if they don't release Andrew and his friends, this village will not stand still and tolerate any more injustices. Make it clear to them that if they are harmed, it will set a fire in the heart of Slovakia that will spread from the lower Carpathians to the high Tatras."

The crowd roared with approval and began to chant, "Free them! Free them!"

Father Marin turned abruptly, entered the church, fled to the altar and fell to his knees and prayed. One at a time the villagers stooped to shake the hand of the young firebrand, Mikhail Yancovic, and assured him they would fight to the death if need be.

"Fight to the death!" a voice arose from the edge of the crowd. "Have you all gone mad?" The people in the center parted as Mikhail made his way and met the challenger face to face. "Well, well. Stefan Nagy. I should've suspected, half Hungarian and half Slovakian, and fortunately the half that gives you privilege is your paternal name, Nagy."

Stefan's calm belied the glare in his eyes that he directed at Mikhail. He thought better of his first impulse to strike Mikhail with his fist, and turned to the people and said, "I am not here to take sides, as Mikhail has so clearly pointed out the nature of my neutrality. I am only asking you to be realistic. What weapons will you fight with?"

"The truth!" someone shouted.

"And what is that?" Stefan asked.

"That we are created equal by God," Mikhail answered. "The Magyars profess to be followers of Christ who preached 'Do unto others as you would have them do unto you' and that God is the only one to answer to." Mikhail paused for a moment and then said, "Stefan, you are right. We have no weapons, except the truth, as someone already has aptly put it. We will march to Presov and on the way; other villagers will join us. When we arrive in Presov, we will demand proof that Andrew and the others were planning some insurrection. I will ask them if they found any weapons in the barn. Is that why you set fire to it? If their answers are no to these questions, we will demand their release."

"Demand their release?" Stefan Nagy said laughing sarcastically. "You have lost your minds, all of you!" he shouted, turning to the crowd, and then shook his head in disgust and left.

"We will all meet here tomorrow. Not in secret but in the open air at the square that is sanctified by the presence of our church and then we will begin our march to Presov. The woman and children will join Father Marin in the church and pray for our safety and the release of Andrew Valen and his friends."

CHAPTER 7

Jon was reading Stasha's letter over and over in his room when there was a knock on the door. "Jon," a voice shouted, "are you there?"

"Yes Lucas," Jon answered, recognizing his gruffy voice. "Where have you been, old friend? I haven't heard from you in a long time," Jon said, as he opened the door and let him in.

"Hell, Jon, since the fire, the hotel management has been cleaning up all the damage and is now in the process of rebuilding the half that was destroyed. There wasn't as much damage as we thought. Actually, the north side, where the lobby was, got the most damage. The rest of the building down to Forty-first Street was mostly smoke damage and broken, shattered windows from the panic of the people and the intense pressure of the heat. Twenty people died and fifty more were critically injured. They asked me to stay on the job and help with the clean up. When it is reconstructed, I will have my old job back with a big raise. I heard them talking about installing telephones that will be direct connections with both the firehouses and hospitals and probably the police stations. Hell, they are also hiring plumbers to install some kind of system that will sprinkle water from pipes placed in the ceilings in the event of a fire. Fireproof walls will be installed made of a new substance called asbestos. I'm telling you Jon, this city is going to be sprawling with new fangled gadgets in no time. Well Jon, what's up with you? You don't look happy."

"Trouble, as usual, back home." After Jon told him of his father's dilemma, Lucas suggested that they go out on the town and try to forget his problems for awhile. "I know where there is a Slavic club not far from here where we can have a few drinks and maybe if we get lucky, get the attention of some willing young ladies," Lucas said, winking a wicked eye at Jon.

It was early Sunday evening and twilight was slipping into the last day of summer as Jon and Lucas made their way down Pearl Street, heading up Fulton to Broadway where the club was located. A small dull burning light bulb hung over the entrance three steps below street level. Lucas opened the door and Jon followed him down a long hallway that eventually led to what appeared to be a huge warehouse. The floor was concrete, and above steel girders crisscrossed one another, forming long squares, supported the ceiling. A polka band was blaring in full swing as dancers twirled frantically to the music. Cafeteria-style tables with long benches hugged the outer wall of the room. The orchestra was located at the far end of the building, leaving more than ample space for dancing. In contrast to the enormity of the room, the tiny dance floor was so jam packed that you could not see from one side to the other. There were some shelves hammered to the side of the wall where patrons stood drinking beer.

They ordered a pitcher of beer from a wooden bar that was anchored to the cement floor in the shape of a horseshoe. They filled their glasses, clinked them together, and drank to one another's success and good health. Lucas noticed that Jon's thoughts were still back home.

"Listen to me," Lucas said, shaking him by his shoulders, "there is nothing you can do now. You are here. Your hands are tied. You must trust your brother to work things out. Be realistic. What could you do if you went back? You would lose all that you have worked so hard for. How much money have you saved? The passage fare back is a hell of a lot more than when you came here. Am I making sense Jon? Am I?" Lucas persisted.

Jon stayed silent for a moment and begrudgingly said, "Yes" and then he looked into Lucas's eye and said, "I will wait." Then he added, "For now."

Three hours and four pitchers of beer later, Lucas and Jon were staggering down Fulton Street. It was about ten thirty, the evening was young, and there was still a lot of activity in the streets. The immigrants made Sunday the day of rest, a euphemism for party time. The five-day working week was still a long way off, so they slept late on Sunday and then partied late. This was Jon's first venture into that lifestyle.

After a fifteen-minute walk they were within a block of Clancy's when a scream rang out from an alley that was squeezed between two tenement buildings, the noise caused them to focus their attention towards the end of the dark alley.

"Leave me alone," a feminine voice shouted in a language they understood. They raced to the end of the alley where they found two men standing over a young, terrified girl. One man was down on one knee with the sharp edge of a knife at her throat.

"Please help me," she pleaded when she saw Jon and Lucas. It was a language not of their dialect, but it was close enough to be understood.

Without hesitation, Jon grabbed the man with the knife by the collar and yanked him away from the girl, while Lucas slammed the standing man viciously against the brick building, knocking him unconscious.

The young girl was cowering in the corner when Jon approached her gently and said in Slovak, "Come with us. We will not hurt you." Blood was trickling down her neck from where the point of the blade had pressed menacingly to frighten her into surrendering her body. Her blouse was torn open on her right side, exposing her breast that was bleeding from the slash of the knife. As they were preparing to leave, one of the men stirred. As he looked up, Jon kicked him square in the face that brought a rush of blood from his nose and mouth. He went on kicking him relentlessly until Lucas drug him away, shouting, "Enough."

Ten minutes later, they had her lying on Jon's bed. Lucas attended to stopping the bleeding while Jon ran down to the bar for whiskey that he was going to use to pour on the open wound that ran under her breast forming a crescent. He warned her first that it would hurt, but added that it was necessary to keep it from getting infected until they could get her to a doctor. She looked up into Jon's eyes and said that she was ready. Lucas drenched the cut with the burning alcohol. She winced, but did not give out the slightest cry. They were impressed by her bravery.

They dressed her wounds with strips of cloth and then brewed some strong Irish coffee and urged her to drink it. Mercifully, it put her right to sleep, away from the pain that she experienced that evening both mentally and physically.

Jon turned to Lucas and asked, "Why would anyone want to do this to an innocent young girl like her?"

"Hell, Jon. This has been going on with the immigrants for a long time. When they came into Castle Garden before Ellis Island was built, they were constantly abused by the con-men with very little protection from the police. It's slowed down some since they were sent to Ellis Island for their entrance exams. It still goes on but now the federal government has stepped in, so it should get better."

"How did they get their hands on her?"

"They probably said they had a job waiting for her."

Before Lucas could continue, Jon interjected, "For Christ sake Lucas! She's only a child, maybe fifteen at most. Where the hell are her parents?"

"Who knows?" Lucas answered, shrugging his shoulders. "Her parents could have been delayed at customs for one reason or another. I don't know. But what I do know is that this is common. They more than likely told her parents, who were desperate at the time, that they had work for their daughter. They probably said they would take her to get signed up and given living quarters, and that they would get back to them about placing them somewhere. It happens all the time."

"Then why were they going to rape her?" Jon asked, raising his eyebrows.

"Because they wanted to degrade her and make her feel unworthy as a woman. She would lose her virginity and then what decent man would want her for a wife? Just like your Stasha, she's probably promised to some young man."

"Are you saying that their sexual pleasure has nothing to do with it?"

"Well, somewhat, but mostly for business reasons."

"Business reasons!" Jon repeated, looking puzzled.

"Yes, the business of prostitution after the rape. She would feel she is no longer worthy and goes along with them with no further resistance."

"Where the hell are the police?"

"They know what's going on and they are doing all they can do to solve the problem, but it's not that easy with all the corruption going on. Policemen and even custom officials are being paid off by the con-men."

As she slept, they pondered what they would do from here. Jon suggested taking her to the nearest hospital. Lucas didn't think that was a good idea.

"Why?" Jon wanted to know.

"Well, for one, we would have to pay for the cost of treating her. And two, her wounds are not deep and won't require stitches. Tomorrow, I'll take her back to customs and let them handle the problem. Don't worry, Jon, you go to work tomorrow and I will take care of things. Anyhow, from the looks of her dark skin, she's probably a low life Gypsy. She's only going to grow up to be a thief and a liar. Come to think of it," Lucas said, pinching his chin with his thumb and index finger, "we would have been better off not saving her."

Jon stood dumbfounded. Lucas noticed his discomfort and asked, "What's the matter, you don't know about Gypsies? Why, they have been a plague to mankind for centuries. The way I was told, they got booted out of India hundreds of years ago and made their way across Asia and Europe, stealing everything they could get their hands on. That's why they had to keep moving on. Hell, they were always running from the police. We finally Christianized some of them, but they went on stealing anyhow and cavorting with the devil, saying they could tell a man's future by looking at playing cards and into crystal balls. I guess, you being raised in the country, you never came across the Gypsies. They're all over the cities where there's more to steal and more people to fool with their fortune telling."

"I don't know about those things. I only know that this young girl was being forced to do something she didn't want to. Isn't that why we left our country? We wanted to escape from the Magyar-Hungarian bastards who were always forcing us to do what we didn't want to do. Did you ever think that her people had the same things happen to them when they were driven from their homeland? Now, you must promise me, Lucas, that tomorrow you will take her to customs and see that she is safe. If you feel that she won't be, then you will bring her right back here."

Lucas took a deep breath and said, "Yes, I promise."

CHAPTER 8

The orange harvest moon was silver plated by the early morning sun as the villagers assembled in the square for their freedom march to Presov. The people were milling about impatiently waiting for Mikhail to speak from the top of the stone steps at the church entrance. Mikhail called for their attention and began to speak. The crowd hushed, stopped moving, and some momentarily ceased breathing.

"Today, my fellow countrymen, might well be our last chance to save our race. They want to take our language from us, want us to learn to be Magyars. Believe me, my friends, countless races have vanished from the face of the earth by conquerors that slaughtered the populace, raped the women, and killed all the female newborns, so that they could not bear children of their race. Many of the raped women bore half-breeds, and as generations went by, the half-breeds became quarter breeds, and then one day no one remembered or knew that they ever existed. The Austrians, the Czechs, and the Hungarian Magyars all have a say in the political agendas of the empire. But not us Slovaks," he said, pointing to himself.

"Do you remember what that makes us?" he asked, lowering his voice to a rasp. "Do you? Do you?" he repeated, raising his voice, and then continued with venom. "I will tell you loud and clear . . . that makes us slaves." He paused for a moment and then said with a tone of disbelief, "Is that what you want to be?"

There was silence for a moment and then a lone voice shouted from amongst the crowd, "No!"

Soon voices from all directions began chanting, "No, no, no." Two hundred able-bodied men were hand-picked by Mikhail, leaving the children, women, and elderly behind under the spiritual supervision of Father Marin. The men were lined up in twenty rows of ten, armed only with their strong will to be free of centuries of servitude and to free Andrew and his friends from an unjust incarceration. The fiery speech of Mikhail galvanized their courage for the difficult task that awaited them in Presov.

As Mikhail was giving last minute instructions, Stasha approached him, out of breath from racing from her house at the edge of the village. Before she spoke, she took a moment to catch her breath. During the pause, Mikhail asked, with concern, noticing the frightened look in her tear-filled eyes. "What is it child? Are you hurt? Is someone chasing you? Tell me please, what's wrong?" he asked again, shaking her by the shoulders.

"Please don't do this," she finally gasped. "They will kill all of you."

"Either way we will die," Mikhail answered stoically. "Look Stasha," he said, directing her attention towards the men who were moving about nervously, waiting for orders to move on, "do you see any guns, any swords, or any form of weapons brandished by any of the men? Are the Magyars so cowardly that they would fire at a handful of unarmed peasants?"

"Yes," Stasha sobbed, "they will."

"Why are you so positive that they will?" Mikhail snapped back, irritated by her relentless insistence.

"Stefan Nagy told me so," she said, obviously reluctant to reveal the source of information.

"Stefan!" Mikhail shouted, exploding in a rage, "that lying half-breed."

"I believe him, Mikhail. Why would he tell me this if he wanted us to die?"

"Because he is afraid that our efforts might succeed, that arrogant bastard."

"But his mother is Slovak."

"Yes, and under the protection of his father, Mr. Nagy," he spat. "Why would he give a damn one way or another, Stasha? Tell me, will you please, so that we can get on our way."

"His concern is for Andrew."

"For Andrew? But why? To my knowledge they are not related, or friends. Not even acquaintances."

"Because I asked him to," she answered emphatically, knowing that she was treading on dangerous ground.

"Oh," Mikhail responded, somewhat puzzled by her statement. He paused for a moment, grasping the back of his neck with the cup of his right hand and then suddenly it hit him.

"No . . . no, please tell me it is not true!"

"The only truth is that you are all going to die if you go on with this and that Stefan is in love with me, but I swear to you in the name of God that it is not mutual. God forgive me because I am taking advantage of the feelings he has for me, and asking him to help free my fiancé's father. He said that he would do all that he could do. Let Stefan and Andrew's son Jozef handle the problem, please. Mikhail, you are an educated man and a teacher. Ask yourself; is this decision worth dying for?"

Mikhail turned to face the men who were stirring about impatiently, waiting for him to give the command to march. He told them of Stasha's warning from Stefan that they would be killed.

"Are you still willing to take our peaceful trek to Presov in the name of freedom for our countrymen? These men were imprisoned because they spoke against the ultimatum, which would surely obliterate the Slovak race. Are you still willing to plead for representation in the political agenda of the empire? Are you willing to put your lives on the line for our God-given rights to be our own people?"

They responded, chanting, "Yes, yes, yes!"

With that settled Mikhail turned his back on Stasha and gave the command to march. Through the cobblestone streets and through the harvest time fields they plodded until they reached the road to Sabvinov, where they expected to recruit more people, and then without further delay they continued on their last leg to Presov. The cheering was overwhelming as they passed through the streets of Sabvinov. Their rows of twenty were soon doubled to forty, and by the time they reached the dusty country road, farmers working in their fields greeted them. Some wished them well and others joined, increasing the rows to over fifty. They were flanked on the east by the Carpathian ranges that trickled south to Presov and by the endless fields of grain and vegetables on the west. Herds of cattle crossed the road from time to time, slowing their progress. The autumn sky was clear and azure with puffs of cotton-colored clouds scattered carelessly across the horizon. The sun shot its rays like a beacon, leading the marchers to their destination.

A lone horseman could be seen riding towards them in the distance. Ten minutes later, the rider arrived, pulling his horse up on his hind legs. The horse danced nervously in different directions while the horseman tried to calm him.

"You must turn around and go back to your village," he said after saluting Mikhail from the brim of his hat.

"And if we don't?" Mikhail asked defiantly.

"I am not at liberty to tell you sir, but I will say this; you are putting yourselves in grave danger. I have a message from Jozef Valen. He told me that he is negotiating for his father's release and urges you to have patience."

Mikhail pondered for a moment and then responded, "We will wait here in the shade of the trees until sundown. If we do not hear any word of his release by that time, we will continue to Presov."

The soldier saluted, kicked his horse, and galloped south, disappearing into the dust and glaring midday sun.

CHAPTER 9

The lunch rush dwindled to a few patrons sitting at the bar drinking when Lucas entered the tavern with the Gypsy girl at his side. The cut on her throat was freshly bandaged and she was wearing a different blouse. Jon rushed to meet them, raising his eyebrows and turning up the palms of his hands and asking, "What's up?"

Lucas pursed his lips and shrugged his shoulders and said, "Her parents were nowhere to be found. They might be out on the streets, they could have been sent back because of medical problems, or more likely, because of a criminal background." Jon motioned for them to sit down at a table that he had just cleaned up.

"All I can tell you," he said, while pulling up a chair to sit down, "is that her name is Helen Sivac, and wait 'til you hear this; she is from Kosice."

Jon's eyes strayed over to Helen while Lucas talked. She looked so vulnerable with her small, sad, dark eyes. Her complexion was the color of powdered cocoa. Her mouth too, was small with thin lips that were just a shade or two lighter than her overall complexion. Her oval face was interrupted by a shallow dimple in her chin and framed with coal black hair that reached to her lower back.

"Well, what now?" Jon asked.

"I don't know. I only brought her here because you seemed overly concerned about her. I had only two choices; I could have left her back at customs where they said they were free of responsibility because she had been officially released last night. That left her back on the streets again where she would probably fall into the same situation we found her in. Or I could bring her back here and try to work something out."

"But what?" Jon asked.

"I have enough trouble trying to fend for myself."

"Hey Lucas," Clancy shouted from behind the bar, "where the hell have you been? Haven't seen you for a long time."

"Been busy cleaning up the mess the fire made so that we can start rebuilding. We should be getting on it next week when the building material is expected to arrive."

Clancy walked over to the table carrying a bottle of wine and three glasses. Before he set them on the table, he glanced at Helen who was sitting in her chair with a combination of shyness and fear in her eyes. She had no idea what her fate was going to be. Jon made a pact with Lucas that they would speak only English when they were together in order to facilitate Jon's grasp of the language; hence, Helen was at a loss during their discussion as to what they would do with her.

"And who is this young lady?" he asked in his natural brogue.

Jon and Lucas took turns relating the events and how a fortuitous meeting on the way back from the club led them to her rescue. Lucas pointed to her bandaged neck and told Clancy how she had also been slashed under her breast. Clancy shook his head in disgust and then asked where she was from. Lucas explained that she had arrived early yesterday morning with her parents from Europe and soon got separated from them when con-men on the streets told them they had work for her and a place to stay and then told her parents that they would contact them later in the day. "It's an old con game that's been going on since immigrants started arriving here. Where have you been, Clancy?" Lucas asked incredulously. "You've been here ten, fifteen years or so."

"Oh, I heard about it. But she's so young. How could her parents take such a chance?"

"Because most of the immigrants come here without a penny in their pockets. They scrape up just enough money for the fare and then when they leave the ship, they are without money. How much money did you have when you arrived, Jon?"

"I had twenty-five dollars, which I was told I was required to have when I went through customs or I would be deported. What about you, Lucas?"

"Well, I didn't have any money except what the ship's captain gave to those who didn't have it."

"That was required by law," Clancy said.

"I was getting to that, Clancy. Well, before we left the ship, the captain would ask who didn't have the money. The hands would go up and everyone was given twenty-five dollars. You should have seen the smiles but they were soon wiped off. When we cleared customs they would have some of their people waiting at the end of the line demanding the money back with the threat of having you deported. I was one of the fortunate ones because I had relatives that were already settled here waiting for me. Not everyone had that arrangement. Many found themselves in desperate situations. Luckily for some, they found their way to places that looked out for their welfare.

Religious and government organizations were springing up all over Lower Manhattan, making food and shelter available until they could find jobs for them. We can always take her to one of those shelters." Lucas said, turning to Jon.

"Where did you say she was from?" Clancy interrupted.

Lucas smiled, shaking his head and said, "Would you believe it, she is from my home town of Kosice, not that far from where Jon comes from."

"Boy, she sure fooled me. Why, with that dark skin and all, I thought she might've come from North Africa, one of those dark-skinned Arabs."

"No, Clancy, she's a Gypsy. From what I was told, they worked their way into Europe over several centuries of nomadic living. They got kicked out of one country after another because of their stealing and cavorting with the devil, saying they could tell your future by looking at playing cards and looking into crystal balls."

"Yeah, I heard about them. We got them in Ireland, too. Not many, but I heard they were there. She looks harmless enough."

"She's only a child. Customs said she is fifteen years old."

Clancy glanced at her full breast pushing against her loose blouse and said, shaking his head in amazement, "She is a little girl in a woman's body."

"Yeah," Lucas said.

"That's why she was so appealing to the con-men. Men would pay a lot of money to have sex with a girl of her tender age."

"Yeah, perverts," Jon said angrily.

"They are everywhere, especially in a large place like New York City. They breed all kinds of weirdoes."

Through all this conversation, Helen sat silently. She wondered what they were saying. Her eyes finally got their attention. They were saying, "Please, what are you going to do with me?"

Jon, realizing her frustration, looked straight into her bewildered eyes and said in Slovak, "Don't worry, Helen, I will take care of you until I can find a safe home for you to live." Jon paused for a moment and then turned to Clancy and said, "Look, I have an idea. This weekend I'm going to Jersey City and I'll see if my friends will care for her temporarily. Meanwhile, I'll have to keep her here with me."

Clancy grabbed his chin with his thumb and index finger and said, "Look Jon, I have a room upstairs next to yours that is full of junk. Clean it out and she can sleep there for the remainder of the week. I have a couple of old army cots lying around here somewhere. I think they are in the room with all the other junk. She can do dishes and help do odds and ends to earn her keep."

"Thanks," Jon said, rising from his chair, reaching out to shake Clancy's hand. "You're a good man, Clancy"

Embarrassed by Jon's compliment, Clancy barked, "Get the hell upstairs and take care of the room and then get your ass back here before it gets busy and earn your damn keep."

CHAPTER 10

The sun sank into the distant west beyond the fields bringing cool crisp air into the encampment. Mikhail waited until the last flash of light was absorbed by the darkness before he called for the men to form their ranks and move on to Presov. Two hours had passed when the damp air filled their nostrils with the aroma of salt that emanated from the salt mines of Solivar, a tiny village on the southern outskirts of Presov. Mikhail called for the men to halt and then sent messengers back to the end of the long line that had accumulated to tell them that they would rest here until he contacted the authorities in Presov. The men quickly disassembled, welcoming the respite. The moon set the Salanka mountaintops south of Presov ablaze with eerie orange-red hues. The scene by the mountains entranced Mikhail, shuddering with the possibility that it was an ominous metaphor for disaster. Farmers and residents of Presov were arriving in droves with food and warm blankets, wanting to contribute to the quest for justice.

Mikhail's rational intellect was battling with his heart and soul over his do-or-die decision to risk leading men to their death in the name of freedom. What if he was wrong? Was Stefan telling the truth? As he was pondering and weighing his decision in his mind, that same horse soldier that intercepted them earlier that afternoon dismounted and walked his horse to the tree where Mikhail was so deep in thought that he was startled by the soldier's address.

"I'm very sorry to disturb you sir, but I have been sent again to ask you to give Chief Valen until daybreak to secure his father's release. They are waiting for the emperor's advisors to arrive early this morning to arrange some fair compromise."

"Compromise! What possible compromise could they devise?" Mikhail shouted angrily.

The soldier ignored his outburst and handed him a sealed letter with his name inscribed below the emperor's seal. He tore the seal open and removed an official handwritten paper that read:

"Mikhail, please wait until I contact you. I promise that the matter will be solved sometime this morning. Thank you, Jozef."

Mikhail turned to the men closest to him and asked them to pass the word to everyone that they would be delayed further until after daybreak at the request of Chief Valen, who promised to have the issue solved by that time. Some of the men were relieved by the delay, and others grew angry. Mikhail could see the fire he had set in the men subsiding with every postponement.

Jozef Valen appeared taller than his five-foot-nine-inch frame. His build was slender but sinewy. He brought many a criminal to his knees with just the grip of his hands. His dark brown wavy hair was parted in the middle and shaved close on the sides, military fashion. His long, straight nose accommodated his narrow shaped face and pointed jaw. His dark brown eyes were penetrating and set in deep sockets with bushy eyebrows, rendering a sinister look.

The commandant of the occupying forces of Saris County arrived at Caraffa Prison, which was an important site during the war against the Ottoman Turks and the anti-Hapsburg struggles in 1687, and engendered the Presov slaughter of twenty-four noblemen by General Caraffa as a counter revolutionary measure. Jozef was well acquainted with the history of Caraffa Prison, and he was determined not to have a repeat performance, and have his father released at any cost. Jozef was sitting in the prison's visitor's waiting room when the commandant entered the room with the Emperor's consultants. The commandant introduced the parties to one another as he directed them to his office where he had a conference table and seats prearranged. After they were seated, the meeting began.

"These officials have been sent by both sides."

"But what is there to negotiate?" spoke Jozef. "No crime has been committed by the men in question. The only crime committed has been against the men that have been imprisoned. The Emperor's soldiers burned Mr. Valens's farm to the ground, and in the process killed his prize bulls that he depends on for part of his livelihood."

"According to information that we received from a witness, they met in secret to discuss what they could do to thwart the emperor's ultimatum."

"Yes," Jozef answered, "that is true . . . to discuss what they could do," he emphasized, "but there was no talk of forming an army and going to war with the Empire. Please sir," Jozef asked as politely as possible, fighting to keep the sarcasm out of his tone. "Do you really believe a handful of peasants or even a multitude of them could raise an army and obtain the weapons required to supply such an army, and how long do you think it would take to train such an army? With all due respect, I don't think the Empire is in any danger."

"With all due respect, Chief Valen, there is a great deal for us to fear. Rebellions start small and then germinate, spreading like a plague from village to village, city to city. You must remember also that there are many Slovak soldiers among our ranks. They could do a great deal of harm. Do you understand now, from our point of view?"

"Well," Jozef replied begrudgingly, "yes, I see your point." He paused for a moment and then said, "By God, gentlemen, you are right. The way to solve the problem is to release the prisoners. That in turn will satisfy the Slovaks and send them a message at the same time that the Emperor is a fair and just man, a man who is willing to sit down with a representative of the Slovak people to discuss the ultimatum." The advisors conferred with one another and then informed Jozef that they would give him their final decision on the matter in the next two hours. Jozef nodded in agreement and then reminded them of Mikhail's ultimatum to enter Presov at daybreak.

CHAPTER 11

By mid-afternoon, Helen's room was cleared out and made reasonably livable for the short duration that she would be sleeping there. It would probably be the most comfortable abode that Helen had ever experienced. Gypsies usually traveled in covered wagons and slept on their hard wooden floors over the bumpy back roads of Europe, or on the hard ground under makeshift tents not only in the fair season, but also during the cruel European winters.

Jon and Helen came downstairs at about 3:00 PM when business was still slow. Jon suggested to Clancy that he would instruct Helen of her duties, and then he would catch up on repairing the roof that had been leaking for the past two weeks, and replace the broken window next to the front door that was shattered by two rowdy drunks.

"If you need me I will be close by. Helen shouldn't have any problems waiting on tables. She speaks Slovak, and you know enough words now that I taught you when I relay the orders to you. If you don't understand something, I have instructed her to point to things."

Clancy shook his head, doubting that they could communicate, but he told Jon to get going on the repairs and get done with it quickly.

"Don't worry, Clancy. I'll be close by up on the roof. Just step outside and give me a yell."

"Okay," Clancy agreed as Jon hustled out the door.

Jon finished the job on the roof in less than an hour, and then climbed down the ladder and measured the window after removing the cardboard he nailed to the frame to keep the cold autumn air and rain from entering the confines of the tavern. He re-nailed the cardboard onto the frame temporarily until he could run down to the hardware store to purchase the proper window size. He opened the door to check on how business was going. He was relieved to see that business was slow. It took the pressure off of Helen as she learned how to go about her duties.

"Hey Clancy," Jon shouted, "I'll be right back. I'm going down Pearl Street to the hardware store to get a replacement for the window."

"Okay, but hurry. Business should be picking up soon." Twenty minutes later, Jon walked through the door with a broad smile on his face. "What the hell are you grinning at?" Clancy asked quizzically.

"Look outside. It's raining."

"So what?"

"I finished the roof just in time," Jon said proudly, and then turned in the direction of the broken window. On the way, a drop of water splashed on the floor in front of him. He looked up and watched the rain water seep through a crack in the ceiling. Jon looked at Clancy with a sheepish grin on his face. "What are you waiting for? Go get a bucket." By the time Jon replaced the window, the heavy downpour had subsided, bringing the leak in the ceiling to a halt. Jon removed the bucket that Clancy had placed strategically under the drops of the water that fell from the ceiling and then called to Helen, who was busy wiping the bar down, to get the mop out of the closet. While Helen was mopping, Jon tapped her on the back with the tip of his fingers and asked how things were going. She turned abruptly, somewhat startled by the intrusion, and said after recognizing Jon, "Oh, It's you." Suddenly she burst into a smile, showing her white even teeth that had just the slightest over-bite, causing her to have a slight lisp when she spoke. Jon stood frozen for a second, not knowing how to react to this new attitude. Before he could respond, she threw her arms around him and hugged him exuberantly. Jon's arms hung at his sides like a rag doll and then he slowly raised them to embrace her.

"Okay, you two," Clancy shouted, "get your asses to work. Here comes the after work crowd, and put the bucket back under the leaking roof you didn't fix.

They looked at one another for a moment, laughing at Clancy's sarcastic remark and then Jon said, "Go back to work; we'll talk later."

The business was hectic allowing little time to escape unnoticed. The tables were all empty about an hour before closing time, and several men were sitting at the bar. Jon took care of the dining area. Helen washed the dishes and cleaned the bar while Clancy called for the last round of drinks just about the time Helen and Jon finished their chores. Jon motioned for Helen to come sit with him at one of the tables. She removed her baggy kitchen apron and directed herself to the table where he was sitting. Two old men with scraggily beards standing at the bar couldn't help but notice Helen as her braless breasts bobbled with every stride she took across the floor. A couple of younger men, noticing the old geezers ogling, laughed and joked about how they couldn't handle that. Helen heard them speaking, but couldn't understand what they were saying, but Jon could. He flew off his chair and ran to the bar and grabbed the closet man to him by his beard and pulled him viciously to his knees and said, "Look you Hungarian son of a bitch. You say one more word about this young girl and I'll break every bone in your body."

Suddenly the other bearded man leaped and pulled at Jon, trying to make him give up his grip on his companion.

"That's enough!" Clancy screamed from the other side of the bar. "You all get the hell out of here!"

Jon kept on looking at the bearded man and said, "Not until you apologize to Helen." He had him by the throat and squeezed until his eyes bulged. Finally, the old man nodded yes. Jon released his grip and helped him to his feet and said with his teeth clenched together in his best Hungarian, "Now you tell her that you are sorry."

He started to talk, but nothing would come out. He was still trying to catch his breath from the strangle hold Jon had had on him. Finally it came out. "I'm sorry."

"No, look at her and say that you're sorry."

He turned to Helen, who was standing next to Jon staring in complete bewilderment and said again, "I'm sorry," and added, "If I offended you."

Jon translated what he said to Helen, even though she had no clue as to why there was an apology. The two younger men watched in wonderment, recognizing that Helen was a Gypsy. When it was all over and the old men were gone, one of the young men asked Jon what the big deal was over a Gypsy girl.

"No disrespect," he quickly added, watching Jon's eyes flash with anger.

"My God, what the hell is the difference what she is? Isn't she a human being, flesh and blood? Do you think we Slovaks are human beings? Have you forgotten how the Hungarians treated us? We have been fighting; it seems, forever to prove that we are equal to them. Right now back in Slovakia, the Hungarians have my father and some of his friends in jail because they spoke against the ultimatum that would surely destroy us as a people. I'm tired of all of this shit that some the people are better than others. She breathes and bleeds and wants the same things that we all need, but because she is a Gypsy, she is treated like a dog. Look at her! She is a frail, shy young girl that was born to Gypsy parents. She did not ask to be a Gypsy anymore than we asked to be Slovaks. We all came to America, I thought, to get equality. Or are we going to exclude certain people that we think aren't as good as we are?"

Clancy stood by Jon waiting to finish his tirade, not understanding a word that was said, but by the expressions on the young men's faces and Helen's, it looked like he got his point across in a positive way.

"What was that all about, Jon?" Clancy asked as the young men were leaving the tavern without a word of rebuttal. Helen rushed to Jon and not only hugged, but kissed him. Jon, of course, blushed and pushed her gently away and said, "At the end of the week, I will be taking you to friends of mine from my village and see if they will care for you until we can find work for you, and maybe even send you to school to learn English. Meanwhile, Lucas and I will make an effort to find your parents." Helen smiled, and for the first time was not afraid.

CHAPTER 12

The morning light struck, suddenly arousing the men from their restless slumber. Mikhail summoned some of the men from the front lines and asked them to pass the word that they would be leaving as soon as their ranks were restored.

"Who would like to turn back?" Mikhail asked with no rancor in his voice. "No one will think the lesser of you if you do. I know most of you have families who rely on you for their welfare. I have parents, but no wife or children. I don't know what my decision would be if I had. You must ask yourselves if you want to risk your life so that your children and future generations can be in charge of their own destinies and not slaves to any emperor and to be only ruled by officials elected by the people, be they peasants or aristocrats. Take five minutes to pray and weigh your decision and then those who choose to go, fall into your ranks. Those who choose to leave, go with our good will."

Fifteen minutes later they completed the forming of the rows and without the loss of even one man, they headed for Presov. Dark clouds were gathering over the mountains and soon a fine drizzle fell on them, but they pushed on; nothing would stop them now. They had made their final decision. Once again, the horse soldier appeared, galloping towards them, pulling a chestnut stallion by his side. Mikhail signaled for the men to halt. The soldier dismounted, pulling the chestnut towards Mikhail and handed him the reins.

"A gift from the Emperor?" Mikhail joked.

"No, I don't think so," the soldier answered, ignoring the smirk on Mikhail's face. "Jozef would like you to join him in the negotiations."

"Why me?"

"Jozef said that you proved yourself a leader and are the obvious choice to speak in behalf of the men you have led here. Since you are a teacher, Jozef felt that you are more capable than he to debate the Slovak opposition to the ultimatum and the release of the prisoners."

Mikhail turned to the men and shouted, "Matthew Sokolosky, where are you?"

When Matt arrived at the front, Mikhail explained, "Matt, I want you to take command until I return from Presov. Jozef sent for me to help in the negotiations."

"But Mikhail," Matt stuttered, "I know nothing about commanding. I'm just a simple blacksmith."

"I know, and that is why I have chosen you. You are and honest, humble man and I know your decision will be made in a straightforward manner. Now Matt, trust me. If I'm not back in . . . let's say three hours, continue to Caraffa Prison and inquire of my whereabouts."

Mikhail grasped Matt's shoulder and said, "Don't worry, you will be fine." And then he mounted the chestnut stallion and followed the soldier into the misty rain-soaked streets of Presov.

The villagers spent the most of the dark hours praying in the privacy of their homes and some entered the sanctity of the church, importuning with the Almighty for the safety of their loved ones. The women and children lined up before the Statue of Mary the Mother of God, lighting candles while asking her to intercede with her son of heaven and earth to protect them from the evil Magyars.

The cock crowed, bringing dawn followed by dark clouds and a cold rain. The parishioners began entering the church for the early morning Sunday mass about the time that Father Marin was entering the confessional box preparing those who wished to receive the body and blood of Christ who died for their sins. They finished by reciting the Act of Contrition, which absolved them of all their past sins and only then receive the ultimate sacrament of Holy Communion.

"Bless me Father, for I have sinned," a feminine voice whispered through the transparent frail screen that separated the sinner form the forgiver. This was the moment that Stasha both dreaded and welcomed. She felt the wooden kneeler press harder against her knees as she continued, "My last confession was about three months ago. I was late for mass one time, and I missed mass two times. I lied to my mother and deceived her." Then with her voice barely audible, she said in a shaky whisper, "I had impure thoughts and I took pleasure in impure acts," then added quickly, "but Father, it was only for a moment or so. It didn't go any further than that."

For an excruciating moment there was silence. Then Father Marin asked her what impure thoughts she had, and what was the nature of the impure acts. She told him what happened on the night of her birthday party, how she slipped away to be alone, where she and Jon used to meet. She then told him of Stefan's arrival that later led to the sexual encounter that in turn led her to lie to her mother. Stasha broke down and began to cry and asked, "Father, what can I do? I not only sinned against God, but I have betrayed my fiancée, who is now in America working hard to make it possible to send for me to be his wife."

"Look young lady, you are still a virgin, are you not?"

"Yes." She nodded.

"Well then, only you and I and the Almighty know of your moment of weakness. Sins of the flesh are the most difficult to resist. You are obviously sorry for you sins and that is all that God asks. So for your penance, say ten Our Fathers, ten Hail Mary's, and recite the rosary for seven consecutive days. Go in peace and remember that God has forgiven you."

Stasha prayed the Act of Contrition and then left the confessional and went straight to the altar. She knelt before the Virgin Mary and began her penance. "Dear Mother of God, I am sorry," she said as she wept. She put her head down and silently recited the Rosary, squeezing her fingertips tightly around every bead. Father Marin entered the altar just as she finished her prayers that would forgive all her past transgressions. The mass went swift, interrupted only for a few moments for Father Marin to report to the people that a message came informing him that the men were at the outskirts of Presov. There they were waiting for Jozef and Mikhail to negotiate the release of Andrew Valen and his compatriots.

Before the mass ended, Holy Communion was served. Stasha knelt at the altar, waiting nervously for her turn to receive the host of unleavened bread. Her knees began to grow weak as Father Marin lifted the host from the golden receptacle that harbored the Body of Christ, and before he could place it on her tongue, Stasha grew nauseous. She cupped her hands together and placed hem under her mouth and fled out of the side entrance that led to the rectory and vomited

CHAPTER 13

Jon was in his room taking his afternoon break when there was a knock on the door. "Yes, who is it?" Jon asked grumpily.

"It's me, Helen," a meek voice answered.

"Oh," Jon responded apologetically as he opened the door to let her in.

"I'm sorry to bother you but it is Thursday already, and you still haven't told me what you are going to do with me."

"Helen," he said, motioning her to sit down on the edge of the bed with him, "Tuesday morning I spoke with my friends while they were shopping at the Fulton Fish Market. I told them of your predicament and the Maliks agreed to keep you until we can find a permanent place for you to live and work."

Helen pushed herself up from the bed and said, standing with her back turned, "Do they know that I am a Gypsy?"

"Yes, and you must not worry, Helen. Mr. Malik was a schoolteacher in Slovakia. He is an educated man and knows about their history and the injustices that have been done to them. He compares it to the Slovak plight with the Magyars. He said it would be a betrayal to his intelligence if he too were prejudiced just because their skin is dark and their culture is different. He said he judges people by their behavior and I assured him that you were very sweet and shy and well behaved."

"Oh Jon," she said, turning around and showing a happy smile with tears streaming down her cheeks, "you are so good to me. In all my life I have never felt so at ease, so safe. I have been running from place to place with my parents. My father worked at smithing and metal working until the Gadzo chased us out of their towns."

"Gadzo!" Jon interrupted.

"Yes, Gadzo. They are the people who are not Gypsies. My mother had a tent at the outskirts of town where she made money fortune telling from the same Gadzo that treat us like dirt. My parents converted to Christianity, thinking that it would make our lives better, but still they are treating us like we are beneath their feet. I don't understand Jon, do you?"

"No, but I never really thought about it until now. I never ran across Gypsies when I was back home in Dubovica. I was always busy in the fields on our farm or caring for my father's bulls. I was up at dawn and finished when the sun went down. There was only my brother, my father, and me. My mother died when I was ten, my brother was thirteen. When my brother was eighteen he became a policeman in Presov and later at twenty-two, he was promoted to chief of police in Sabvinov. That's when I decided to come to America. The farm was too much to handle and there was little in return. The Hungarians were becoming more demanding. So you see, I never really had a chance to learn or see what was going on around me. The only time I left the farm was to see my brother graduate from the police academy in Presov and again when he was made chief of police. The only people I was aware of were the Hungarian Magyars who treated us too, like dirt. They refuse to give us independence or have a say in the government. Now I am here in America where everyone has the right to be his own man, no matter what their race or nationality. So Helen, don't be afraid anymore. My friends will see that you are treated well and I will do everything I can to find your parents."

"Oh Jon," she said returning to sit at the edge of the bed, gazing adoringly into his eyes and said, "What can I ever do to repay you?" Then she reached out and embraced him, pushing him back onto the bed and kissed him warmly on his unsuspecting lips. He felt the back of his neck grow hot as the kiss lingered. Until this moment, he always thought of Helen as a young innocent child, but now he slowly began to realize that she was only a year younger than Stasha. It had been so long since he felt the softness of a woman. Suddenly, he pushed her away awkwardly, feeling a mixture of embarrassment and guilt.

"What is it, Jon?" she asked, not realizing in her innocence the compromising position she had put him in.

"Nothing," he stammered, "I guess I'm just tired."

"Oh yes Jon, I know how hard you work."

"No it's not that. I'm tired of waiting . . . waiting to succeed, waiting to hear about the release of my father from Caraffa Prison in Presov."

"In Presov? That's where I lived before my parents were forced to leave Kosice."

"Yes I know, Lucas told me."

"What did your father do wrong?"

"Nothing really, except question an ultimatum that the emperor decreed . . . that would deprive Slovaks of their language and their way of life."

"You sound like my father. I remember him saying the same things about the Gypsies and how America was our last chance. Converting to Christianity didn't lessen our pain and now here we are in America. Look already what has happened to me, and God only knows what happened to my parents. Do you really think America will give us peace and allow us to be ourselves?"

"Yes, I think so, but it will not be easy. We will all have to work hard, make sacrifices, and save our money so that we can invest it in our futures. Back home, we worked hard just to put a roof over our heads and food on the table. That was all we got in return for our labor. Now, anything will be an improvement, so we must take the gamble and hope for the best. Helen, about your parents, I talked to a couple of people that work at Ellis Island and they told me that the chances of your parents being sent back are very improbable. They would have to be proven hardened criminals or have a highly contagious disease. The captains of the ships that brought them here would also be liable for their expenses to return them to Europe. Don't worry. What I've heard about the Gypsies so far is that they are survivors so I wouldn't be too concerned. Somehow, someway, we will find them. Now, let's get back to work before Clancy comes looking for us. And by the way, remember, without Clancy, you or I would not be here. The streets are filled with homeless people off the boat with no one to turn to."

"Yes, I know, and if I could speak English, I would thank him. Will you thank him for me please?"

"Yes, now let's go downstairs and get to work."

When they entered the tavern, Clancy was at the bar having a conversation with two men. Helen disappeared into the kitchen behind the bar to catch up on washing the dishes while Jon went to the dining area to clean up some of the tables and wait on customers.

"Jon!" Clancy yelled.

"Yes Clancy?" Jon answered, turning while he was wiping off a table with a damp rag.

"These guys want to know if I have hired a Gypsy girl. The two Hunkies that you tossed out of here early this week are spreading it around that you made a big deal out of them making a pass at a Gypsy girl."

"Yeah, so what's it to you?" Jon spat, glaring at the two men.

"Because we are making it our bloody business," the man said, leaning on the bar with a glass of ale gripped in his right hand. His accent was thick British, probably Cockney dialect that was indigenous to a district in East London. Jon glanced over at Clancy looking for him to interpret for him.

He hadn't a clue that what the man spoke was English. Clancy paraphrased what he said. The translation was close enough to get Jon boiling. The man was about Jon's height with piercing blue eyes, wavy reddish-blonde hair, and an angular face so he had no problem looking him square in the face when addressing him.

"Just how is it your business?" Jon snapped.

The man looked over to Clancy; apparently having a problem with Jon's broken English. Clancy translated, and then the man said to look at his friend standing aside of him. His face was pummeled, and his right arm was broken.

"Yeah, so what does that have to do with the Gypsy girl," Jon answered, speaking slow enough and using hand gestures that he understood without the aid of Clancy.

"Because Gypsies beat him up and killed his friend."

"Why would they do that?"

"Because they are cheats and thieves."

"How so?"

"Because we made a deal with them and gave them money for the girl."

"For what purpose?"

"To find her work. We are like an employment agency. For a price, we find immigrants off the ferry from Ellis Island and get them jobs."

"What kind of jobs?"

"Usually, we get the women domestic jobs, house cleaning, or maids for the wealthy people uptown."

"Is that all you do with them?"

"Yeah."

"Tell me, what happened after they paid the Gypsies the money."

"Well, they headed down Water Street on their way to the shelter where they were going to place her until they found a job for her. All of a sudden five or six Gypsies attacked them from behind and pushed them into the back of the dark alley."

Jon looked over at the man with the smashed in face. "Is that the way it was?"

He nodded his head yes.

"What's the matter with him, can't he talk for himself?"

"Nah, his jaw is broken."

"Well, let's go over this. You said that you and the other guy were attacked from the back and pushed into a dark alley, right?"

The man with the broken jaw nodded his head yes.

"If that's so, how did you know how many men attacked you and how did you know that they were Gypsies? I guess you figured that they had to be because you couldn't see them in the dark. Another thing, if it was Gypsies, then why would she be here and not with them?"

"Yes, we gave that some thought."

"Jon, Jon," Helen called, coming out of the kitchen.

"Yes, what is it?"

"There's a pipe leaking under the sink."

The two men caught sight of her as she leaned over the bar. The slash across her throat was still very visible and her dark hair and skin shouted Gypsy loud and clear. They looked at one another, perplexed at the sight of her. Confused, they headed for the door.

"We'll be back, Hunky," the man who did all the talking shouted as he slammed the door shut and disappeared into the milling crowd on their way to the Fulton Fish Market.

CHAPTER 14

Three hours and twenty minutes had passed when Matt gave the order to move on to Caraffa Prison. The church bells were ringing, reminding the populace that mass was about to begin just as the men crossed the Torysa River Bridge that led to the main street of Presov. There was a sea of umbrellas floating down the pavements and crisscrossing the streets on the way to their respective places of worship. A strong wind sailed up the street, sending umbrellas skyward and turning some inside out. The blowing rain and the urgency to arrive at church on time distracted their attention from the army of peasants that was invading their city. Quickly, the streets were clear of people and the gusty wind had blown the rain out of the city into the countryside, bringing the pungent odor of salt from Salivar. When they arrived at Caraffa Prison two lone guards stood at the main entrance. Matt halted the men and then approached the guards, asking them if they knew the whereabouts of Jozef Valen. Both shook their heads no, but did not speak.

"Mikhail Yancovic, have you seen him? Where is he?"

Again, they nodded that they didn't know.

"Well then, can you please find someone of authority who can tell me where they are?" Before they could nod no again, some of the men stepped forward, displaying impatience and anger.

Thinking the better of it, the one guard said to give him a minute. He opened the door and then closed it behind him. Not more than a minute passed when the door opened and the guard appeared accompanied by a short balding man with a waxed handle bar mustache and bulging eyes. He was dressed neatly in a dark blue policeman uniform with gold stripes running down his sleeves and pants.

"What can I do for you gentlemen?" he said, as if completely oblivious to why they were there. "My name is Peter Zombrela. I am the Chief of Police here in Presov."

"My name is Matthew Sokolosky," he said, bowing slightly at the waist. "We are looking for Mikhail Yancovic who came here at the request of Jozef Valen, the Chief of Police of Sabinov."

"Yes, of course. They have been here and left about two hours ago."

"But, where did they go? What happened to Andrew Valen and his friends?"

"They have been released and have been allowed to return to their village."

"Impossible!" Matt shouted, scratching his head. "We would have met them on the road back to Sabinov."

"No, I don't think so," he replied. "They were moved to Kapusany as a precaution when the commandant got word that the village of Dubovica was gathering men to use force to free the prisoners.

Without listening any more, Matt turned the men around and started back to Sabinov. When they arrived, Jozef greeted them and thanked them for their concern for his father and then told all the men to head back to Dubovica where the women were preparing hot meals, and he added slyly, warm beds.

"Where are your father and his friends?" Matt asked inquisitively.

"By now, they should be home with their families."

"And Mikhail?" Matt asked, his eyes searching the crowd for his presence.

"Mikhail?" Jozef said, looking bewildered. "Isn't he the one who organized the march?"

"Yes, but a soldier on horseback met us at the outskirts of Presov with a handwritten message stating that Mikhail joined you in the negotiations. He rode off on a horse that the soldier brought, and that was the last we saw of him."

"I really don't know what to make of this," Jozef answered. "The commandant and I made a plea to the emperor's advisors and then they left and told us that they would have a decision by daybreak. Keeping to their word, we were informed early this morning that they had been released at Kapusany, and that we were to meet them here in Sabinov."

CHAPTER 15

When Jon and Helen arrived at the Maliks residence, Jon was waiting anxiously for Paul to give him the good news of his father's release. They embraced vigorously as Jon and Helen were admitted into the living room. Jon introduced Helen and then Mrs. Malik invited Helen to join her in the kitchen for a cup of tea while the men talked.

"Sit down Jon." Paul said, pointing to the sofa. "I received a letter yesterday from my brother informing me that your father and his friends were set free through the efforts of your brother and just about every able-bodied man in the village. Do you remember Mikhail Yancovic?"

"Yes, of course," Jon answered. "I had him for a teacher in elementary school. He was a man I admired very much. I only wish that I would have taken his advice and studied more. He was always telling me how I was wasting my ability and how I was not living up to my potential. Hell, I was too busy on the farm to spend my energy on schoolwork. If it hadn't been the law, my father would never have allowed me to go to school. I was needed on the farm, especially with my mother passing away."

"Well, it seems Mikhail had enough of the Magyars, so he gathered all the men in the village that he could and directed them on a march to Presov to put pressure on the authorities, and to release your father and his friends and also to discuss the flagrant ultimatum. When they arrived at the outskirts of the city, they were halted by a soldier who supposedly had a message for Mikhail from Jozef to have him come to Caraffa Prison and help him in the negotiations. He put Matt Sokolosky, the blacksmith, in charge and went off with the soldier. After a few hours there was no word from Mikhail, so Matt marched the men into the city to Caraffa. They were told that the prisoners were released and set free in Kapusany. Matt turned the men around and when they arrived in Sabinov he found Jozef who verified that the men had been released. When they asked of Mikhail's whereabouts, Jozef had no knowledge that he was summoned to assist him. Presently, Mikhail is nowhere to be found and some of the men in the village are determined to find him and this time there will be no compromise."

"What do they think happened to him?" Jon asked, shaking his head in disgust.

"The letter didn't say, but don't you think it is obvious what happened?"

"Yeah, it looks like they were more afraid of Mikhail than my father. He's educated and motivates a whole village to put their lives on the line for my father and promote a resistance to the ultimatum. What the hell did they expect my father, an uneducated peasant, to do? They were just trying to make an example out of him like they did Stasha's father, and now they found a bigger fish to fry."

"Yes, that's true Jon. But what can a handful of peasants do to force his release? That is, if he's still alive. Maybe your brother can find out."

"I don't think so, because if he wasn't aware of Mikhail being called into the negotiations in the first place, why should they let him in on what happened?"

"Well. I guess we will just have to wait and see, Jon."

"It looks like someone traded him for my father."

"But who?"

"I don't know."

"Do you think it was Jozef? After all, it is his father."

"No, no. My brother would not do that and my father wouldn't allow it."

"Maybe he didn't know. Well, there is nothing either of us can do about it so let us take solace in the fact that your father is free and hope for the best for Mikhail. Now, let's get down to the business of Helen. What would you like me to do to help?"

"I would like her to live here until she can find work, or better yet, get enrolled in school. I want her away from New York City where she will be safe and not have to be looking over her shoulder, wondering if those filthy men will find her again. Get in touch with my cousins in Pennsylvania. Maybe they can find work for her."

"Yes, I'll do that for you," Paul assured him, then they got up and entered the kitchen where Ana and Helen were having what looked like a serious conversation over a cup of hot tea. Ana and Helen stood up respectfully when the men came into the kitchen.

"Oh, Paul!" Ana said, almost with tears in her eyes. "Helen told me about her horrible experience. We must take her in and protect her. We will, won't we Paul?"

"Of course, Ana. Jon and I have discussed it and I have told him that she could stay here as long as it takes to get her settled in a job."

"Oh, and by the way, Paul, I will give you compensation, say two dollars a week until she can fend for herself. Will that cover her expenses?"

"Yes, that will more than cover it. Ana will give her duties to perform. She can help clean the dishes. And all the things she did at Clancy's. Ana will teach her to cook so that some day she will be a good wife for some young man, and since Helen's only clothes are the ones on her back, Ana will help her to make her own dresses, and I'm sure you will provide her with shoes temporarily until she can get another pair."

"Don't worry Paul. On my next trip here, I will bring shoes for her."

"Well then, now that everything is settled, let's see if we can put all our troubles aside and enjoy the rest of the day."

Ana prepared a breakfast of sausage and eggs and served it with thick slices of rye bread smothered with homemade butter. The women sipped tea while the men indulged themselves with hot black coffee sweetened with sugar. After the dishes were cleaned, Paul announced that they would all be going to church just two blocks down the street. Jon balked for a moment, getting the attention of Paul.

"What is it Jon?"

"Well, I haven't been to church since I landed in America. I had a problem with church for quite awhile now. With all the things that happened to us at the hands of those bastard Magyars, you wonder whose side God is on. Father Marin's constant harping on being good to your fellow man. He says that's what Jesus preached. Goodness to everyone. The damn Magyars must be deaf, dumb, and blind to the teachings of Christ. No, Paul, I have a hard time believing anymore. If there is a God, He sure as hell doesn't have any use for the Slovaks and," he added, glancing over at Helen, "and he sure doesn't care for the Gypsies. Paul, there's something wrong with this religion crap."

"Oh Jon, please don't talk like that," Ana interjected. "God will strike you dead for talking such blasphemy."

"I'm sorry, Ana, but that's the way I feel."

Paul put his arm around Jon and said, "I understand where you are coming from. The more educated I got the more I questioned. It got to the point where I had to make a decision. So for Ana's sake, I continued to go to church and pray for God to show me the light. So far, I haven't seen any light. But Ana is happy and that makes me happy."

"Well Paul, in that case let's be off to church. I don't want to make Ana unhappy either, especially after that great breakfast she cooked up for us this morning."

All eyes were glued on Helen as they entered the church. It made Jon nervous.

"What the hell are they staring at?"

"She's a beautiful girl," Paul said, hoping that it would calm him down.

"Yes she is, isn't she?" Ironically, the sermon was about "Do unto others as you would have them do unto you." Ana received communion and then the mass ended with the priest reminding everyone that this coming Thursday, November 1 was "All Saints Day" and he reminded the congregation that it was a holy day of obligation and that he expected to see them present.

The Maliks greeted friends and acquaintances and introduced Jon and Helen telling them that they were from their village in Slovakia and that they would be sponsoring Helen until she was able to go on her own. No mention was made of Helen's plight or that she was a Gypsy. One of the women took Helen's hand and squeezed it, saying that she was looking forward to seeing her again in the near future. Helen wasn't used to being treated so courteously. Her only reaction was complete paralysis. Her tongue was stuck. She wanted to speak but couldn't. Ana could see that she was in a state of shock just by the look in her eyes, and came to her rescue.

"Helen, Thursday I will bring you to mass and you can get more acquainted with my friend Mary," Ana said, pointing to the woman who had just held her hand in welcome. "She has a daughter that is your age and through her you will meet other young people. Oh Mary, I think after the Christmas holiday I would like to have Helen enrolled in the Parish school. Could you arrange that for her?"

"Yes, Ana. I will talk to Mother Superior first thing tomorrow."

"Until Thursday," Ana said, and then took Helen by the hand and began walking in the direction of their house with Jon and Paul following close behind them.

CHAPTER 16

When Matt and the men arrived back at the village they could hear the sound of music as they walked through the fields. By the time they reached the square, the women were running towards them in search of their husbands and loved ones. After a frenzy of kisses and embraces, the women served the men hot meals that they finished preparing only minutes before their arrival. The rain clouds disappeared along with the sun leaving the night sky crystal clear between infinite constellations. It was time to go to home where there would be soft lovemaking on soft beds and a few hours of escaping reality until the morning light woke them from their short-lived freedom in the Land of Nod.

The next two days, the village went about their business as if nothing had happened. No one made an attempt to contact Andrew or any of his friends, and then "All Saints Day" made itself known with the ringing of the early morning church bells reminding them of their holy obligation to all the saints whose Herculean efforts saved the Holy Roman Catholic Church from destruction so the future souls could earn their way into heaven by the goodness of God's grace.

Father Marin entered the pulpit with his moment of silence, as if to collect his thoughts, and then he began as usual with, "My dear friends, in Christ today we celebrate the men and women who dedicated their lives and sometimes gave up their lives to defend the honor of God and to show the world that this life was only the beginning and that suffering would even bring you closer to the Almighty and assure you everlasting happiness in the next world. This day comes at an opportune time, a time when our lives are at odds with injustices and suffering. How small our sufferings are when we think of our Savior being nailed to the cross and our first Pope Peter and disciple of Christ who was nailed upside down on the cross. They were just the beginning of a long line of holy men and women who died excruciating deaths for our sake. Let us dedicate this day for all those who make supreme sacrifices, not only for God, but for those who do it for the good of their family, friends, and their countrymen. Maybe, Mikhail Yancovic is one of those courageous individuals that has decided to make a sacrifice for the good of, not one, but five of his fellow countrymen. Let us all rise and hold hands and hope with that chain of human brotherhood that our prayers become powerful enough to persuade God to free him from whatever adversity he is facing. Let us have a moment of silent prayer and plead with God for the safety of Mikhail. The silence was broken by a voice that rang out from the last pew.

"Where is Mikhail, Father?" an elderly woman asked with anger in her voice and sorrow in her eyes.

"Mrs. Yancovic, I do not know. I only know what Jozef Valen said through one of his messengers. He never sent for Mikhail, and he never saw him, and that he would do all he could do to locate him. I will keep you informed of what progress is being made. Now let us receive communion and go in peace."

The parishioners left, but not in peace. Everyone was concerned for Mikhail. Many approached Mrs. Yancovic, a widow, whose son was either dead or in grave danger, and gave their condolences. Mikhail's three married sisters and their families gathered around Mrs. Yancovic and did all they could to calm her.

"Don't worry Mrs. Yancovic, I will see to finding Mikhail," a determined voice said from behind them.

"But how, Matt?" she asked, recognizing the blacksmith.

"I can't tell you how, but trust me I will. Mikhail left me in charge and I will continue to be until he is found. Now if you will please excuse me, I have business to take care of." Matt searched through the crowd for Andrew and finally found him standing at the entrance of the church conversing with Father Marin and Stasha Ondreas. Matt approached them asking Father Marin and Stasha politely if he could have a private word with Andrew. They both bowed their heads and said of course. Matt led Andrew out of earshot of any informer.

When Matt was sure they wouldn't be heard he said, "Andrew, you must tell me all that happened to you."

"My friends and I got together at my barn to discuss the ultimatum and what we could do about it. We never really concluded what we would do. I suggested talking to my son Jozef and see how he could help and the next thing I know my barn is on fire and the soldiers came in and dragged us off to Sabinov, but not before they made me watch the barn burn to the ground along with my prize bulls. Later that night we were transported to Sabinov in a horse-drawn prisoner wagon where we were stripped of our clothing and given prison garb to wear. From there we were delivered to a cell in Caraffa Prison at Presov."

"When you arrived in Sabinov, what did your son have to say about the arrest?"

"He wasn't there. They said he had been sent on an assignment to Kapusany and that he would be informed of the arrest when he returned the next day."

"Then what?"

"They took us out of our cell one by one and interrogated us."

"Did they torture any of you?"

"No, they just threatened. They said they would give us time to think about it and then if we didn't divulge what plans we made at what they called our secret meeting, they would have to take stronger measures with us. We found ourselves back on the prisoner wagon in the middle of the night where they took us to the old dilapidated castle dungeon in Kapusany."

"Did they tell you why?"

"Yes, they said it was for our own protection. 'From whom?' we asked. They said that they were not at liberty to tell us. The next morning they unshackled us and said that we were free to go. The guard told me I was to meet my son in Sabinov."

"How did you get there?"

"They provided us with a prison wagon and then told us to deliver it to Jozef.

"All that time you didn't hear anything about Jozef or Mikhail?"

"No, we did not."

"Didn't you think that was strange?"

"No, they told me Jozef was on a case in Kapusany. That's his job, so I didn't think any more of it. I figured sooner or later he would be informed. I only found out later when we arrived at Sabinov from Kapusany that Jozef had been involved for a few days negotiating for our release. He told me about the village men marching to Presov to ask for our release, but he didn't know that Mikhail had organized it."

"Well damn it, someone knew! Look Andrew," Matt said, moving closer so that he could whisper to him, "I'm going to do everything in my power to find out what happened to Mikhail. I want you to stay out of it. You did enough already, but I will ask you one favor. I want you to ask Jozef if he will help us find out what happened to Mikhail. Tell him it has to be done in the utmost secrecy."

"Of course, Matt. This Sunday coming I have already made plans with him to have dinner with us at the Ondreas'. I will expect you to be there, say about 2:00 PM?"

CHAPTER 17

Jon spent the rest of the day preparing a makeshift bedroom in the attic for Helen. After supper and wine, he took the last ferry to Manhattan. Clancy was sitting at one of the tables drinking hot coffee when Jon arrived at the tavern.

"What are you doing here?" Jon asked, surprised at his presence. "I thought you were going to visit your brother in Brooklyn."

"I was until Lucas showed up early this morning all banged up."

"What do you mean banged up?"

"Those men that were in here last week inquiring about Helen caught up with Lucas and knocked the crap out of him. The only reason he is still alive is because they want you to take this as a warning."

"How bad is he hurt?"

"Plenty bad, he can barely walk. They cut his face up and sliced one of his ears off. They busted a couple of his ribs, when a bunch of them took turns kicking him after he was knocked down."

"Where is he now?"

"He's up in Helen's room. He dragged himself to the firehouse where he was recognized by some of the men that you lads helped out at that hotel fire. He didn't want to go to the hospital so they patched him up the best they could, then at his request, they transported him down here in the fire chief's wagon."

Jon made a move to go upstairs to see Lucas, but Clancy's arm intercepted him and said gently, "No, I just checked on him and he is sound asleep. He was in terrible pain all day. He couldn't sleep, so finally I gave him some strong Irish coffee and that knocked him out. You can move your mattress and blankets into his room and keep watch over him until he wakes. I'm not sure he'll sleep 'til morning."

Lucas woke up the next morning with a splitting headache and throbbing pain on the right side of his head where his ear was severed. Jon was standing over him just shaking his head.

"My God Lucas, what have they done to you? This is my fault."

"No Jon, I would have done it under any condition. She was a young girl about to be raped by the con men that are enemies to all the immigrants. It had nothing to do with her being a Gypsy. Since then you have convinced me of how stupid I've been. I found Helen sweet and not anything like I was told a Gypsy girl was like, and the next time I see her I will apologize. Clancy told me you took her to Jersey City to your friend's house for her safety. Did they agree to help her?"

"Yes, as a matter of fact, they are going to enroll her in school for the next semester. Paul is going to teach her as much English as he can in the next two months. It is a Slovak Parish School and the nuns speak both languages. But Paul said it would be difficult for Helen because Gypsies were not allowed to go to school. It has been against the law for hundreds of years to educate them."

Jon could see how much pain Lucas was in and suggested taking him to the hospital where the doctors at the hotel fire had attended to them. He begrudgingly agreed while Jon helped him up and guided him slowly down the outside steps onto the pavement. Jon opened the door to the tavern and hollered to Clancy that he was taking Lucas to the hospital and that he would be back as soon as possible. Clancy nodded his head that it was okay and then they went to the corner and waited for the trolley car to go uptown to the hospital.

A half hour later they arrived at the hospital that was a few blocks north of the Hotel Royal; it was still in the process of being rebuilt. Lucas signed in at the desk and then was told to sit and wait in the emergency room. The waiting room was filled with immigrants coughing, bleeding, and moaning from injuries probably sustained on their manual labor jobs. Lucas looked at Jon and said, "You better get back to the tavern. It looks like I'm going to be here awhile."

Jon looked around and asked Lucas if he would be all right. Lucas shook his head yes and just as Jon was ready to leave, a voice shouted outside the entrance to the waiting room.

"Well, look who it is! My two heroes from the fire."

"Doc, are we glad to see you," Jon said, relieved to see him.

"What the hell happened to you Lucas? Not another fire?" he asked incredulously, as he began examining him. "I don't see any burns."

"No Doc, there wasn't another fire," Jon went on to tell the whole story as the doctor led them into the examination room. The doctor checked Lucas thoroughly while Jon told the story. "How long has it been since he had that ear severed?"

About, maybe close to forty eight hours." He removed the bandages that were already stiff with dried blood and then proceeded to cleanse the wound with medicinal alcohol.

"Who applied the bandages? They look professional."

"Well, after the beating they left him lying in the alley unconscious. When he came to, he somehow managed to get to the firehouse a couple of blocks away from the hotel. The firemen recognized him from the hotel fire. Lucas was stubborn about going to the hospital so they patched him up the best they knew how. They bandaged the areas where his ear used to be and then taped up his ribs that were bashed in pretty good. Well, Doc, what do you think?"

"It looks like the wound is not infected."

"Yeah, probably from the whiskey they poured on his cut ear."

"Yes, sometimes that will work in a pinch and they did a good job taping the ribs. The ear will heal quickly but it will leave a nasty scar. It's too late to stitch because it has already begun to close. As far as the ribs go, they will take a little longer to heal."

"What about working?" Lucas asked.

"Well, you'll be able to do some light work, but no heavy lifting. Don't worry, Lucas; I'll talk to the hotel management on your behalf. I'll remind them of how much money you saved them with your quick thinking and courage. I'm sure they will cooperate and give you ample time to recuperate. Look now, Lucas, you must follow my instructions about taking it easy for awhile, and if you see any signs of infection or your ribs give you more pain than you can bear, please come back to the hospital and ask for me, Doctor Ginsberg."

"Ginsberg! Don't tell me, you're a Jew?"

"Yes I am. Is that not okay with you Lucas?"

"Hell yes, Doc, that's okay," Jon said emphatically. "Why wouldn't it be? Knowing that makes me more confident about making it in America. Hell, if a Jew can become a doctor here in Christian America, a Slovak should have a good chance of succeeding. Don't you think so, Doc?"

"Well, it might be tougher because you are Roman Catholic. This is Protestant territory, my friend." With that said, the doctor started smiling.

"What's so funny, Doc?" Jon asked.

"I was just thinking about how you two got into all this trouble."

"What do you mean?"

"Well, two Slovak peasants rescue a Gypsy girl and now here a Jew gets in on the Act. Now that's irony."

"Whatever you say, Doc. Look, we have to catch the next trolley back downtown. We'll keep in touch."

When they arrived at Clancy's, two policemen that they recognized from the fire were sitting at a table waiting for them.

"Well, Lucas, you don't look so good," the policeman sitting on the chair that was facing them said. Lucas started to tell them what happened when the one with his back to them turned around in his chair and said, "We know what happened and that's why we're here. Clancy told us the whole story. We got wind of it from one of our informants. That's just a warning for worse things to come. Jon, Lucas, you have to get out of town. These guys will kill you if they get the chance. Take it from us, we know."

"If you know, why the hell can't you do something about it?" Jon asked angrily. "You're the police for crissake."

"The problem is that this island is growing faster than we can get personnel to cover every district. These hoodlums are backed up with a lot of money from uptown big shots. Hell, some of our policemen are on the take. Look, we came down here on our own time. We gained a lot of respect for you two at the fire and we think you deserve to get a good life for yourselves. You won't get that here. Go away for awhile until it blows over."

"How long?"

"A couple of years or so."

"I haven't got that kind of time," Jon said, shaking his head.

"Look, we have to get back to the precinct. All we are asking you to do is to give it some hard thinking. Look at all of your options and take it from there. Good bye and good luck."

Jon and Lucas looked at one another, wondering what options they had, if any, as the policemen hurried out of the tavern.

CHAPTER 18

After dinner, Mrs. Ondreas and Stasha cleaned the table and brought out a bottle of homemade wine for the men to drink while they had their discussion about what they could do to resolve the problem of Mikhail. Stasha set glasses in front of the five men that were present and began pouring the wine. When all the glasses were filled, Andrew lifted his and said, "To the freeing of Mikhail, where ever he may be and whatever it takes." They clinked the glasses together in agreement. Andrew began to speak by saying that he noticed that Stefan Nagy was resentful.

"I understand why you feel that way, but you must remember Stefan had no control over the fact that he is part Magyar. My future daughter-in-law convinced me that Stefan is on our side on this issue and will do everything he can to help us find Mikhail. Of course, we all know why Matt is here." He then looked across the table where Father Marin was sitting looking overly concerned as usual. "Father, you were invited to this meeting so that the Magyars, should they find out again about this meeting, they will be assured by your presence that there is nothing going on that would meet their disapproval."

Father Marin just shook his head with his eyes looking up to heaven and thinking, "Forgive them Father, for they know not what they do."

Andrew turned his attention to a gentleman that was sitting on his right side.

"Before dinner I introduced you to Mr. Roman Polsky. Mr. Polsky is from Poland and is an expert in acquiring guns and ammunition for causes like ours. It will cost us money. Where will we get this money, you are probably wondering? Roman tells me that there are organizations in the United States of Polish and Slovak decent that will raise the money we will need to acquire weapons. There is a Slovak organization called Jednota that was organized some years back in Slovakia and those who immigrated to the United States continued it. Yesterday, I wrote a letter to my son Jon. As you all know, he is now living there. I asked him to look into it for us. Meanwhile, we will see what we can do to settle this peacefully. That's where Stefan will come in. He will not be under suspicion and will be able to investigate as to the circumstances of Mikhail's disappearance. If worse comes to worst, Roman will smuggle the guns through the remote narrow mountain passes of the Tatras. It will be dangerous, but he promises that it will be done. He will teach every man how to use the weapons. Now, let's all have another glass of wine and then go home and go about our business as usual. I will not contact any of you until we have no other choice but to use our second plan. Matt, this is between us for now. Don't inform any of the men until we know for sure. This meeting must be kept a secret; and Stefan, you above all must swear on your mother's Slovak soul that you will not reveal anything that was discussed here today.

"You have my solemn word. But out of respect for my Hungarian father, I will not participate in any of the killings of the Magyars."

"That's fair enough, Stefan," Andrew said, and they then shook hands to seal the gentlemen's agreement.

Josef turned his attention to Matt and assured him that he would do all he could, but that he would also have to be careful not to tip the Magyars off. They trusted him and that was good because he could find out more than if he was under suspicion. He pleaded with Matt to be patient. Matt then turned to Roman Polsky and exchanged information about one another. Roman was elated when he found out that Matt was a blacksmith as well as a metal worker. With that skill he could manufacture bullets for the guns if it became necessary. While the dinner guests filed out of the house, Andrew approached Roman and said that as soon as he got word from his son in America, he would contact him.

Mrs. Ondreas came into the dining room after she thought everyone had left and found Stefan still sitting at one of the table chairs.

"Yes Stefan, what is it?" she asked. "Is there anything wrong?"

"No, no, I was just wondering if I could have your permission to talk to Stasha. I would like to assure her that I will keep what was said here a secret."

"Of course, Stefan. Let me get her for you."

"Stasha, Stasha," Mrs. Ondreas called out in the direction of the kitchen where she was putting the finishing touches on cleaning the dishes.

"Coming Momma," she answered, seemingly out of breath as she entered the combination dining and living room.

"Oh," she said, surprised to see Stefan. She turned to her mother and said, "What did you want?"

"Stefan would like to have a word with you before he leaves."

"Please, would you walk me to the barn while I prepare my horse for riding? That is, if it's alright with your mother."

"Go ahead Stasha, but put a coat on."

"The nights are getting cold," she said, faking a shiver.

"There's already snow in the mountains. Think about it, Christmas day is only seven weeks away!"

"I don't want to think about that now, Momma," she said as she closed the door behind her while buttoning her coat.

The night was pitch black and the moon was full, shining enough light to reveal the late autumn snow peaks that enhanced the natural beauty of the Carpathian bow. Stefan grasped her right hand with his left and walked at a fast pace towards the barn, forcing Stasha to run because her feminine legs could not keep up with the long strides of the Magyar soldier. She was out of breath when they arrived inside of the barn where Stefan's horse was tied to a gate inside of the first stall. Stefan ignored his horse and moved onto the next stall that was empty except for the thick bed of straw that was spread out evenly on the floor. He opened the latch and pushed the gate open and set Stasha gently down on the straw floor until her whole body lay flat from the back of her head to the edges of her heels. Stasha hurriedly began to undo her coat buttons and then her blouse, as Stefan unbuckled his belt and unbuttoned his pants and dropped them to the floor with his manhood protruding from his underwear. She pulled up her skirt and Stefan tore her underpants from her quivering body. Stasha reached out to his hardness, grasped it and pulled him down and pushed it into herself with her two soft hands and embraced him until he could plunge no more and fell limp as both their body liquids ran down between her soft, white inner thighs.

The horse whinnied, waking them from their sexual slumber. Stefan struggled to his feet, pulled his pants up, buckled up and reached his hand out and helped Stasha to her feet. She buttoned her blouse and brushed the straw from her skirt. Once more they embraced, but void of the passion and fire. Stefan mounted his horse and galloped off into the cold autumn night as Stasha's last words lingered in his ears.

"Remember, I still love Jon."

CHAPTER 19

Two weeks had passed since Jon and Lucas had been given an ultimatum by the con men to leave New York City or pay the consequences that could ultimately lead to their demise. Jon was caught between realities and loyalties. His job with Clancy was lucrative and at the same time he grew fond of him. Clancy had become like an older brother to him and further, since he started working at the tavern, business had picked up considerably, because of Jon's ability to speak the Slavic languages. Clancy was on the verge of giving him a pay raise, but balked at offering it because he thought under the circumstances that faced Jon it might engender a decision that could endanger his life. He pleaded with Jon to go on to Pennsylvania where his cousins were residing, at least for a time, like the policemen advised him, until things blew over. Jon realized that Clancy was right, but then he pulled the other way when he thought of his friend Lucas and all that he would lose. He had a promising future with the hotel. When it was obvious to Clancy that Jon wasn't able to make the decision alone, he asked Lucas to visit the tavern on Sunday and they would try to resolve the problem.

On Sunday, November 11 at twelve noon, Lucas entered the tavern where Jon and Clancy were sitting at the bar drinking beer.

"Well," Clancy said, while setting his foaming glass of beer down on the bar counter, "you're looking a lot better than the last time I saw you."

"Yeah, and I feel a hell of a lot better. My ribs are still a little tender and my ear, or should I say where my ear was, has healed with no infection. By the way," Lucas said, turning to Jon, "I went back to see Doc Ginsberg for a check up a couple of days ago and he gave me the good news about my health, but he also gave me some bad news that our health could end if we don't get out of town. Doc said that earlier this week some thug stopped at the hospital and told him to tell us that the next time Doc sees us it will be in a body bag."

"What did Doc say about it?" Clancy asked.

"He went straight to the police about it."

"Yeah, and what did they do about it?"

"Advised us to get out of town as soon as possible."

"What did the Doc say to that?"

"He agreed with them when they told him that they couldn't guarantee us proper protection."

Jon finally interjected and said, "But what about your job at the hotel?"

"Well, like Doc promised, he fixed it up with the hotel management that I could only do light work for now and they whole heartedly agreed with it."

"See, Clancy," Jon shouted, "Lucas has worked hard at his job and gained even more favor with his bosses since the fire and now you want me to ask him to walk away from all his good fortune. No, I don't think so. Who will take my place? I just can't walk out on you. You have been so fair with me. I could never have made the income anywhere else."

"Jon, that's true, but I must tell you this. When you first came here you were just another dumb Hunky peasant off the boat who couldn't speak a word of English and while I was thinking that, I got the idea about you not speaking a word of English and realized that more and more people were coming to the tavern who spoke Slavic languages and then you told me you were a trained carpenter. I hired you based on your skills that would help the business and keep my building maintained. My reasons for hiring you were strictly for making me more money. Then as time went by and I watched how hard you worked, never complaining, and how skillful you were in your trade and the firefighters and policemen coming in here and telling how courageous you and Lucas were. You went back to save the boy when probably no firefighter might have gone under the most extreme dangerous circumstances, then Helen, and how you two saved another life. To tell you the truth, you made me feel ashamed of myself. You have to understand, when I lived in Ireland, I was dirt poor. I wasn't raised in the fresh country air where you could at least grow your own food. Shit, I never knew where my next meal was coming from. That's how it was being raised in a big city like Belfast. On top of it, I was a Catholic living in Northern Ireland that is mostly Protestant. We weren't given a pot to piss in. All I can remember growing up was hunger and beatings by the Protestant bullies. I had enough, but what could I do? I had no money, so I quit school and took a job cleaning the streets. But I couldn't save money fast enough. So one night, I waited outside their fancy club where all the rich Irish Protestant bastards spent their leisure hours drinking and gambling money away that they stole from the poor working man. Yeah, I remember that night well because it was cold and raining. I waited outside until one of them walked out onto the street. I followed him until he reached the far end of the building where there was a dark alley. I caught up to him until I knocked him unconscious and to my good fortune, he obviously had been one of the big winners at the poker table. I took all his money and I stripped him of all his jewelry and do you know what?" Clancy said softly, "I never regretted doing that. Later I counted what added up to at least a hundred in American money, not counting the value of the jewelry that I pawned for a fair sum here in New York City on the black market. I guess it was sold to some rich Anglo bastard. I was sixteen years old when I arrived here, but I had a better start than most of the immigrants. I had a lot of money, close to two hundred dollars after my ship fare. I had cousins living in Brooklyn. They took me in and I got a labor job in construction and they let me live rent-free until I got on my feet. I never told them about the two hundred I had stashed away in my room under a floorboard. I never felt guilty about doing that either because I said to myself if I ever became successful, I would pay them back one way or another. Ten years later I bought this tavern for a song and a dance. It happened that the old owner's wife ran off with some customer and he was so upset about it, he took my offer, which was his first, and went back to Ireland. A couple of years later, my cousin's wife needed an expensive operation that would save her life. I provided the money. That was my first and last good deed. Since then, all I cared about was making money and the hell with everyone else."

"Clancy, I hope you don't mind me asking, but what about a woman in your life?"

"Women," Clancy said laughing, "I get all the bloody women I want. All you need is to show them some money."

"No Clancy, I mean a special woman. Didn't you ever meet one that you wanted to marry?"

Clancy hesitated for a minute and said, "Yes, there was a girl in Ireland that I was very much in love with, and her with me. But she was a Protestant and I a Catholic. Her parents found out and sent her to a convent on a remote island in the Irish Sea. She wasn't even Catholic for chrissake. I heard that she was seen walking into the sea where she was swallowed up by the waves. Days later, her body washed up on the shore and they buried her without blessings of the church, because they said she died by suicide."

"How could they be sure of that?" Jon asked.

"They went through her belongings in her room and found a letter that she wrote for me. She wrote things like 'I don't want to live my life without you.'" Tears came to Clancy's eyes and his voice began to quiver and then he said, "There never will be another woman for me."

"I'm sorry that I had to open an old wound."

"Hell," Clancy responded, "it's been about twenty-four years or so. Don't you think it's about time that I at least learn to live with it?"

"Maybe if you started to see another woman, it might help you forget. I noticed a lot of older women that come in here give you the once over. You aren't a bad looking man for a Mick. You better get on with it. Hell, you're only forty. You have plenty of time left to pick up the pieces."

"Talking about picking up the pieces, if you two don't get the hell out of the city, I'll be picking up your pieces. Look Jon, I have an idea that will make it easy for both of us."

"Yeah, and what's that?"

"Before you leave town get a letter off to your village and see if there is anyone willing to come to the United States to work here doing the same job that you did. I will be the sponsor and I will provide the passage money and the required twenty-five dollars. At arrival, you can arrange to have your friend Paul in Jersey City meet him and bring him here."

"That's fine for me, but how does that help Lucas?"

"Trust me and I will take care of that too. Lucas, just go back to the hotel like nothing has happened."

CHAPTER 20

Stasha closed the stall gate behind her and as she turned came face to face with her mother. She grew pale as her mother turned crimson with rage.

"How could you?" She rasped as she struck Stasha across her face with a stinging blow from her right open hand and then she lurched forward and grasped her straw covered hair and pulled viciously until it brought Stasha to her knees. "How could you?" Mrs. Ondreas repeated over and over until she too sank to her knees, her hysteria now subsiding to a quiet rage.

"I don't know what to say," Stasha finally answered, her head bent, her long dark hair covering her face, draping itself on the cold dirt floor.

"Why would you jeopardize your chance to go to America to be with Jon and have a better life? Tell me why," she asked, pulling her hair again.

"I did this for Jon," Stasha said, rising to her feet.

"You did this for Jon?" her mother repeated incredulously as she stood up. "Yes, I did!"

"Explain to me child, how you could have sex with Stefan and say you did it for Jon."

"Please, let's go into the house and I will tell you how I got into this mess."

Mrs. Ondreas put fresh wood into the fireplace to fight off the chill in the room and then sat down and listened to what Stasha had to say. When it was all said and done, Mrs. Ondreas told her daughter that if her father were still alive, he would probably kill Stefan and put you in a convent.

"No one must know of your affair. Do you understand? Jon must never know."

"But Mother, won't he discover that I'm not a virgin?"

"I think that you can fool him. I don't think men know the difference. I fooled your father into believing that I liked sex, when in fact, I hated it."

"But why?"

"My mother was very religious and told me sex was only necessary to have children and that to take pleasure in it was a sin."

"Do you still believe that?"

"No, but I do believe that having sex outside of marriage is a sin."

"Even if it means saving a life?"

"I don't know, child. You will have to ask Father Marin that question."

"I already have."

"You have!"

"Yes, when I went to confession."

"What did he say?"

"He said that sins of the flesh are difficult to overcome and are forgivable."

"Is that the Sunday you vomited before receiving Holy Communion?"

"Yes."

"You threw up because you were nervous about telling Father Marin about your sin?"

"No! I did that because I was afraid God would strike me dead when the host touched my tongue."

"Why in God's name did you think that?"

"Because I lied to Father Marin in confession. I told him that I did not go all the way with Stefan and that I was still a virgin, so I would have received the body and blood of Christ in the state of mortal sin. I don't know what got into me. I wanted to have Mr. Valen freed, but at the same time I found out that even though my conscience told me it was wrong, my body wouldn't cooperate. I love Jon in spite of what I have done. I have no answer for why I did what I did, but now that Mr. Valen is free, I don't feel that it was all in vain. Do you understand? And now Stefan has promised to help us find Mikhail. Just think how terrible it must be for Stefan. He says that he truly loves me after I told him emphatically that I love Jon and that I would eventually go to him in America. He said that he could give a good life here if I married him. He would take me to live in Budapest where the wives of Magyar soldiers are treated like royalty. I told him that no man, no matter how much he offered me, could tempt me to betray my people. He said that his mother did it and never regretted it. I had no answer for that, except that her love for his father was stronger than the love for her country, as my love for Jon is."

"If Stefan is telling the truth about his love for you, he may go to any means to have you."

"In what way?"

"Well, Mikhail's strange disappearance for one. It looks like someone arranged to have Andrew and his friends freed in exchange for Mikhail."

"Do you think that Stefan was responsible for that?"

"Could be."

"Well, Mr. Valen is free."

"Maybe Stefan had no other choice."

"Maybe."

CHAPTER 21

Matt Sokolosky was a handsome young man in his early thirties. He was exceptionally tall for a Slovak and something even more peculiar about his characteristics was the deep, dark complexion of his skin tone. He was the subject of ridicule by his classmates since he could remember.

"Hey Matty," they shouted, "where's your momma? We saw her last week when we were in Presov with our parents. She was telling fortunes in a tent at the outskirts of the city." Then they would run off singing, "Matty is a Gypsy, Matty is a Cigan."

In the beginning when Matt was not yet in his teens he took it all heartedly, but as he grew into manhood he began to be curious about his dark skin. He examined himself in the mirror from time to time and noticed that his hair and eyes were dark, so why should his skin not be dark? He began to observe his neighbors and saw that most of them had dark hair and eyes, but he could not find even one with his complexion. It drove him to approach his father, whose complexion was nothing like his, nor was his mother's or his sister Mariska. He asked him why he was different from the rest of them in skin color. He also noticed that his nose was long and straight, where the rest of his family's noses were short and pugged. His father was in the barn shoeing a horse when he accosted him. For a moment, Mr. Sokolosky stood motionless with the horse's right rear foot in his left hand, as he was ready to drive a nail into the hoof. Slowly, he put his tools on the wooden chest beside him and led Matt to a bench and asked him to sit. He waited for a moment, wondering what he should say and then he decided that the truth was the right thing and then he began:

"Matt, when I was eighteen years old, I was drafted into the Hungarian army and for a time I was stationed in Budapest. One night, on a weekend pass, I was having a good time drinking at a dance hall that was frequented by soldiers. Well, that night I unknowingly danced with some officer's girlfriend. After an evening of partying together she asked me to escort her home. Of course, being the gentleman that I was, I took her by the arm and led her out of the dance hall and started to walk to her house that she said was only a few blocks away. I dropped her off and I bid her good night, but not before I asked if I could see her again. She politely said that it would be better if we wouldn't. I asked her why.

"'Well, you're a Slovak and I'm Hungarian. My parents would kill me.'

"'We won't tell them,'" I said. 'Where are they now?' She said that they were visiting some relatives in the country. 'All the better,' I replied.

"'No, you don't understand, Charles. I am promised to someone.'

"'Where is he now?'

"'He is a captain in the army and you are a private and a Slovak.'

"'Do you love him?' I asked.

"'It doesn't matter,' she said, 'I am promised.'

"Then she asked me to leave before someone saw me. With that said, she turned, and went into her house. Still intoxicated from her and the whiskey I drank that night I headed back to the dance hall.

"When I arrived a soldier stepped in front of me and snapped, 'Where is she?'

"'Who?' I asked.

"'Eva, the girl you left with.' I told him I took her home and then I asked what business it was of his. 'She is my fiancée. If you have laid a hand on her, you slimy Slovak, I will tear your balls off.' He turned to a crowd of men that was standing nearby and said to teach this Slovak scum a lesson.

"The next thing I remember is waking up and looking up at the ceiling of a tent. I tried to move but I couldn't without feeling extreme pain. Every bone and muscle in my body was sore. A voice whispered for me not to move, and then a moist, warm cloth was set on my forehead. I opened my eyes and looked into the darkest eyes I have ever seen.

"'Don't move,' a voice said again, until I clean the blood and dirt from your wounds.'

"A long flow of hair brushed across my face. It was then that I realized it was a woman. Her eyes were roaming all over my body, searching for cuts and bruises. 'I think your nose is broken,' she finally said, 'and your lip is cut' and on and on it went.

"For three days, she treated my wounds with healing herbs from the forest and chanted prayers over me in a language I never heard. When I recovered my senses, I watched her move and began to realize how beautiful she was with her long dark hair, her dark skin was smooth as silk, and her dark, sad eyes were like a doe that looks up just before the hunter pulls the trigger. All the time I spent in the tent she was all I saw. I could hear voices outside, but I had no idea who they were or where I was. On the third night in the midst of a summer thunderstorm, she led me back through the muddy outskirts of Budapest. We both stared at one another for a long time and she wished me good luck, and I answered, 'What can I do to thank you?'

"'Pray for me and my people,' she answered.

"Puzzled at her request and wanting to do whatever she wanted, I answered, 'Yes, I will.'

"Those sad eyes of hers captured all of my being and without any resistance from her, I embraced and kissed her long and soft.

"The thunder, lightning, and rain grew furious as I turned to get one more glimpse of her. I knew then that someday I would have to come back and find her.

"When I got back to my regiment, I was put under military arrest for not reporting back on time. I did three month's hard labor."

"Wasn't that severe punishment?" Matt asked.

"Sure, but I was a Slovak in the Hungarian Army. I still think that it was the young Hungarian lady's fiancé that was responsible for my harsh sentence."

"Didn't you tell them what happened?"

"Yes, but they said that was no excuse. A year later after doing my required army time I went back to Budapest to see if I could find the girl. I went back to the same dance hall and tried to retrace my steps, but I had no clue as to where I spent those days in the tent until one night I ran into an old army buddy and told him the story.

"He said, 'Hell, from what you told me, about the time you left the tent in the rain, wading through the mud, before you reached the city streets, and the description of the girl, you must have been in a Gypsy enclave where the dark-skinned devils live.'

"'Some devil,' I said. 'If she was such a devil, then why did she help me?'

"'I don't know. Did you check your money or any of the valuables before you left?'

"'Yes, and everything was accounted for.'

"It wasn't the first time that I heard bad things about them, but I really never had an encounter with any of them; so I never suspected for a moment that I was in the hands of a Gypsy."

"A Gypsy," Matt shouted, suddenly remembering being called that in his early childhood. "Well, what did you do next?"

"I took his advice and the next day I went to the spot where she left me and with the help of people on the street I found my way back to the Gypsy camp along the riverfront.

"I arrived there about mid-morning. They set up business along the edge of the city street that bordered their campsite. They had tables set up with handmade jewelry and beautifully carved jewelry boxes. There were dresses laying on tables with artistic needlework designs. Another table had leather belts with silver metal designs; it was really impressive. At that moment I found it hard to believe that this was all the work of the devil, until I came upon a tent that said,

"'Come in and I will tell you your fortune.'"

"Well, what did you do?" Matt asked.

"I went in hoping to find out if anyone could tell me who the mysterious Gypsy girl was that helped me that night. When I entered the tent, a woman of about forty years asked me to sit on the ground and she would tell me my fortune for a small price. She was speaking Hungarian, which of course I understood. But for some reason I answered her in Slovak. Before I got a response, I said that I came here in search of a Gypsy girl that found me laying in an a alley in Budapest about one year ago when I was a soldier stationed here. She hesitated for a moment, and then asked me to wait and then she left me alone. A few minutes passed when the flap of the tent unfolded and there she stood with the morning sun sparkling on her black hair. She was just like I remembered. She sat down beside me and we talked. I had so many things to ask her. Why did she help me? After all, I was a Gadzo, the non-Gypsies, the ones who make their lives a living hell. She explained that she and a group of Gypsies were on their way back from working the streets in Pest selling their ware when she saw me crawling out of an alley, dazed and beaten from head to toe. She said they were going to ignore me until she heard me plead in Slovak for help. So the men that were with her helped carry me back to her tent. I still didn't understand.

"She said, 'Slovaks are in the same boat with the Gypsies. We know that you hate the Magyars as much as we do, and that they treat Slovaks almost as bad as they do us.'

"I couldn't keep my eyes off of her as she talked. She was beautiful. In the next few days I met the rest of the clan and they invited me to stay as long as I wanted. It was there I learned about metalworking and blacksmithing. It was there that I fell madly in love with your mother, Mariska."

"Mariska," Matt said dumbfounded.

"Yes, your sister, that is, your half-sister, is named after her."

"But I don't understand."

"A year after the first meeting, your mother had become pregnant with you."

"Were you married then?"

"No."

"But why not?"

"Because Gypsies have iron clad rules about marrying Gadzo. As much as they had respect for me, she would lose her parents and friends if she did. It was a difficult decision for her to make. You were born the following August. With you here, I had to start thinking about our future. I told your mother that I would be leaving for a month or so to find work as a blacksmith. A week later, I went back to the Gypsy camp only to find it under military control. I bribed one of the guards to let me into the prison compound they had set up behind barbed wires. I found Mariska and you all bundled up in a corner, cold and hungry. All night she begged me to take you where it would be safe and then come back for her later. Against my better judgment, I left and took you back to Lupany to stay with your grandparents and then headed back to Budapest. When I arrived at the camp, it had been burned to the ground and all the Gypsies had been taken away. The men were taken to work in the salt mines in Salivar and some worked in the coal and copper mines. The women were sent to work in the fields or forced to work as maids in wealthy Hungarian homes."

"What about the children?"

"They were put in homes and given to families that raised them to be Magyars."

"What happened to Mariska?"

"I was told she was caught trying to escape and was given a hundred lashes, which she died from and then . . ."

"Yes, and then?" Matt said.

He looked up at Matt, tears flowing freely from his eyes and said, "They hung her by the neck and burned her beautiful body until only her bones dangled from the rope."

"How do you know it was her?"

"I saw the ring lying on the ground under her. When we were denied our marriage, Mariska had rings made by her brother, Emile. One night we vowed to love one another and be faithful to one another for as long as there was a breath in our bodies. Then Emile pricked both our thumbs with a dagger and placed them together and let our blood mix, never to be parted again. When that was done, we placed the rings on our fingers as a symbol of our everlasting love."

Matt embraced his father while he cried and then said, "What about Mother, does she know about me?"

CHAPTER 22

Jon and Lucas went about their business as usual just like Clancy had asked them to do. Clancy approached Jon before opening up Monday morning and told him that he would like to have him spend the weekend in Jersey City with the Maliks. He said he had some important business to attend to in reference to negotiating with the hoodlums who wanted Jon and Lucas run out of town. Jon asked what he would do to prevent it from happening. He said that he was in touch with some Irish hooligans from Brooklyn that might be able to cut a deal with them.

"Saturday night after closing, we're going to meet here and see what I can do to help persuade them to come to some kind of compromise," Clancy said. "Trust me Jon; I will work something out with the help of my friends."

Jon agreed and then went about his daily routine at the tavern.

Early Friday morning he received a long overdue letter from Stasha:

> "Dear Jon,
>
> I'm sorry that it has been so long since I have written to you, but as you know there has been so much going on here in the village, your Father's imprisonment, and then the march by the villagers to Presov to have him freed. Now, Mikhail Yancovic, who organized the march, disappeared after he was supposedly called to Caraffa Prison by your brother Jozef to help in the negotiations."

She told him of the dinner meeting they had at her house to see what they could do about finding Mikhail. She was in the kitchen cleaning up when they were discussing what they would do, so that's all she knew to tell him. She did mention that Stefan Nagy would help in finding out what happened to Mikhail. This puzzled Jon because he knew that Stefan was an officer in the Hungarian Army, and even though his mother was Slovak, when she married Stefan's father, she gave her allegiance to the Magyars. The rest of the letter told him how much she missed and loved him and how she was finding it difficult to wait to be with him. She suggested coming to America now and that she would be willing to work until he reached his goal. Jon gave some thought about bringing her here. He would have to send her passage money, which would cut into his savings a great deal. He talked to Clancy about it and he said that he would keep his promise and sponsor her and pay her passage fare and that she could work for him until he went on his own. Clancy told Jon they would talk about this after he solved his problem.

Jon left the tavern about an hour after closing time and took the last ferry to Jersey City. When Jon arrived at the Maliks, they were in bed. Jon expected to see them earlier in the week when they did shopping at the Fulton Fish Market, but they never showed, so they weren't expecting him. After several gentle knocks, a sleepy-eyed Paul opened the front door. His first reaction was panic. "What is it Jon? Is something wrong? Come in and sit down and tell me what's the matter."

After Jon told him about the ultimatum he and Lucas were given by the con men, Paul said, "Wait here a minute. I have a letter for you from your father along with a letter from my brother. It is sealed so I didn't read it. I'll be right back. I have it on the desk in my study."

A moment later, Paul came back into the living room holding the letter in his hand and handed it to Jon. The letter read:

"Dear Jon,

By now you know that I had been arrested and later freed by the efforts of the many villagers that marched to Caraffa Prison in Presov to plead for my release. While your brother Jozef was negotiating I was transferred to the old broken-down castle in Kapusany and then shortly released. Meanwhile, Mikhail Yancovic, your former schoolteacher who organized the march, was called to Caraffa Prison to help Jozef. A soldier came to Mikhail where they were camped outside the city and told him that Jozef needed his help. Mikhail had put Matt Sokolosky, the blacksmith's son in charge and told him if he wasn't back by dawn, he should come looking for him. When he didn't return, Matt went to the prison looking for Mikhail and us. They told Matt we were transferred earlier that morning to Kapusany, where we were to meet Jozef and be freed. Later, when Matt arrived in Sabinov where he was told Jozef was, he learned that Andrew and his friends were back at the village already. Matt looked about for Mikhail but couldn't find him anywhere and then asked Jozef of his whereabouts. Jozef didn't know and Matt said, 'You called for him.' and Jozef said, 'I never did.' Mikhail is still missing and we are determined to find him even if it means using force, which brings me to tell you why I wrote this letter. I had a meeting recently with Roman Polsky, a Polish patriot who is an expert in acquiring weapons for people who are fighting for their freedom from injustices. The problem is that we need money to buy these weapons and Mr. Polsky told us that there is an organization called Jednota that was organized here in Slovakia a long time ago and they continued it in America."

Jon slowly laid the letter down on his lap and then picked it up and gave it to Paul to read. Paul finished the letter and asked Jon to go into the study and get some sleep and tomorrow he would speak to some of his co-workers after mass that know about Jednota, and see what could be done.

Jon was awakened by the excited voice of Helen saying, "Good morning. It's so nice to see you again. Have you found any information about my parents, and how is Lucas?" she blurted out in one long breath.

"Give me a minute to wake up," Jon said, "then I'll fill you in on everything. Would you hand me my trousers please? They are over there on the chair."

Helen picked up his pants and tossed them to him as he turned from under the covers and placed his bare feet on the floor and then she left the room to give him time to dress. As he dressed, he observed that more shelves had been constructed and filled with more books. The study was starting to look like a library, Jon thought to himself. At that moment, Paul opened the door and poked his head in.

"Good morning Jon. Are you feeling better this morning?"

"I don't know yet. Give me a chance to wake up."

"Here, Jon," Helen said, entering the room with a hot cup of coffee. He took a sip and then he set the cup down on the desk in front of him.

"That hit the spot," he said, and then told Paul that he noticed that the walls of the study were filled with more books. "How soon will it be when you teach?"

"I've been looking into that now. I'll be starting night school at a local high school that has college prep courses. Meanwhile, I can practice teaching Helen. I've been working with her, trying to prepare her for starting school after the holidays. It won't take her long. She really is bright. What a waste it has been denying Gypsies an education. They could be contributing so much to the world. Ana was going to teach her to make dresses. She ended up showing Ana a few things about designing clothes. Her needlework is unbelievably artistic. Helen said that is how the Gypsies made their living and that it is a skill that was handed down through the ages. Every Gypsy girl was taught needle work from the day they could hold one."

Paul turned to Helen and said, "Is breakfast ready?"

She nodded her head yes and then they walked to the kitchen where Ana had ham, fried eggs, and potatoes on the table ready to eat. After breakfast, Jon took Helen aside and told her of his problem with the con men and that he just couldn't find the time to look for her parents. But he did talk to a few customs officials from Ellis Island that frequented the tavern, and they were pretty sure they were somewhere in Manhattan. They said that work was plentiful and that they were probably working somewhere. They said that there were immigration organizations run by the churches to find missing people. It wasn't uncommon for people just off the boat to get separated. Sometimes people were kept for medical reasons before they were released, or they just got lost in the shuffle. Jon assured her that he would make an effort to find them as soon as he resolved his problem.

The sky was clear and filled with hues of pink and sea blue with scattered puffs of cotton clouds that belied the cold wind that licked at their cheeks like tongues of fire as they walked down the avenue to the house of God where everyone went in search of salvation

CHAPTER 23

"Yes, I know," a feminine voice spoke softly.

"Mother, how long have you been here?"

"Long enough to know that your father finally told the truth about your real mother."

"But you are my mother too and you always will be. Now my birth mother will be a beautiful memory. After all, she died so that I could live a better life and you helped fulfill her wish. Tell me, does Mariska know?"

"No, and I don't think she should."

"Why not? I find it hard to believe that she didn't notice how different I look from her. Her skin is so white and her hair is red like yours. I noticed how different I looked from you, too. You always stood out from the other women in the village. Can you explain that to me?"

"Charles?" she said, her eyes asking for permission to tell all. He nodded yes.

"Here, sit on the bench with me, Mother, and you too, Papa," Matt said, patting the bench with both palms of his hands. "I want to know everything. First, how did you meet?"

"I already told you," Charles interjected.

"You did?" Matt responded, puzzled.

"Do you remember the night I was on the weekend pass and went to the dance hall where I met that Hungarian girl whose fiancé was an officer?"

"That was the woman who got you in trouble that night."

"Yes. She is that woman!"

"Charles," Mrs. Sokolasky interrupted, "let me tell the rest."

"Are you sure you want to?" Charles asked, raising his eyebrows.

"Yes, I am sure. This is something I've been living with for a long time" She looked directly at Matt and said, "That Hungarian girl your father walked home that night from the dance hall was me, Eva Horvath, daughter of a wealthy copper mine owner that got rich with the slave labor of Gypsies and Slovaks that were arrested on false charges and then forced to work in my father's mine. He saw that the police officials were paid handsomely for their dirty work. The night I met your father, I told him my parents were in the country visiting relatives, but what I didn't know was that they had arrived home a short time before your father and I did. When I entered the house, they asked where I had spent the evening. They called the servants and reprimanded them for allowing me to leave. They hadn't known because I slipped out the front door when they were in the kitchen relaxing, having tea. That was something they didn't have time for when my mother was around. She was about to have them whipped when I finally convinced her that I had snuck out. They thought I was in my bedroom. I still wouldn't tell her where I was, so she sent me to bed and said she would deal with me tomorrow. When I woke up the next morning, the maids were scurrying around in my bedroom. I asked them what was going on, and they said they were getting my clothes together to pack in suitcases. I asked, 'For what?'

"They said I was going to my Aunt Agnes to live with for a while. I jumped out of my bed and asked why.

"'I'll tell you why you slut, because you spent last night with some low ranked Slovak soldier,' my mother shouted as she entered the bedroom.

"'Mother, all he did was escort me home from the dance hall. He was a perfect gentleman,' I told her.

"'That's not what your fiancé Andre told me. He came here this morning in a rage. He said you wouldn't have to worry about your Slovak soldier anymore. He had his men settle with him.'

"'What do you mean Mother?' I asked. 'Did they hurt him?'

"'I don't know, and I don't care,' she answered, obviously annoyed that I cared what happened to your father. That afternoon I was taken to my aunt's house in the country where I would be away from the temptations of the city. They set my wedding day for June, which was three months away. Andre came to visit me but I wouldn't see him. My mother visited me later and said that if I refused to see him again I would be whipped like a common servant. The following weekend Andre visited me and asked me to take a walk in the surrounding woods with him where we could be alone and talk, and maybe work things out. I asked him why he was still intent on marrying me after all the things he accused me of the night I was at the dance hall. After all, Andre implied that I had sex with your father. He said that it didn't matter and that he forgave me. I told him that he made me sick and that I didn't want to marry him in the first place because I never liked him, let alone loved him. Then I asked him what he had done to the Slovak soldier. He answered that he only had him beat up by his men. I told him again that he made me sick and then I told him I would rather marry a Gypsy than marry him. He slapped me in the face, and then threw me to the ground with my lips cut and bleeding. He tore my skirt off and raped me.

"When it was over, he helped me up and said, 'We will be married now that you are mine. No other man will want you now.'

"'Why would you want a woman that doesn't love you?' I asked him.

"'Because you are not just any woman, you are Miss Horvath, the daughter of one of the richest men in the Empire.'

"When we arrived back at the house he told my aunt that I ran into a broken tree branch and that it cut my mouth."

"Did you tell her what really happened?" Matt asked.

"No."

"But, why?"

"Because I just couldn't let them know that I lost my virginity. I needed to think further about what I would do. Andre told me he would be away in Austria on duty for the next month, and when he returned he would start making arrangements with my parents for the wedding. Before the month passed, I knew that I couldn't marry Andre under any conditions, and when my mother visited me I told her so. When I said that Andre raped me she called me a liar and had one of my aunt's farm hands whip me."

Eva turned her back to Matt and asked him to unbutton the back of her dress. After opening the three top buttons, Matt uncovered some of the lash scars that she endured the day her mother ordered punishment for her supposed lie.

"My God, Mother! What did you do?"

"The night before Andre was to visit me. I packed a suitcase with enough clothes to get by on and walked all night through a path in the woods that led to the outskirts of Budapest. My aunt's farm was only about ten miles from the Pest bank on the Danube River. I stopped and rested several times. The weight of the suitcase tired me, and my back was still bleeding and painful. Fortunately, it was April and the night was cool, which helped soothe my wounds. I arrived in Pest just as the sun came up. There was no activity on the streets."

"Where were you going?" Matt asked, anxiously.

"I had a friend who lived in Buda and I was hoping to take a boat across the river and contact her. We had been close friends at school. The problem was that I didn't have any money to pay the toll."

"Well, what did you do, Mother?"

"I headed for the river hoping that my father's name would give me credit for the toll. A short time later I arrived at the pier where the boats were docked waiting to ferry paying customers across the river to Buda. I tried several times to convince some of the boatmen who I was, but no one seemed to know who my father was or they just didn't believe me. Finally, one of the men noticed a gold locket that I had clasped around my neck and asked me if it was gold. I removed it and let them examine it. He decided that it was and said that he would take it as a payment to transport me. Around noontime, I was knocking on the front door of my friend Rose. A servant answered the door and led me to her bedroom where he said she was taking her noon rest.

"Of course, she was surprised to see me. I told her the whole story and then she asked me what I was going to do. I told her I didn't know and then asked her if I could stay until I decided. She said that it was all right with her but didn't know if her parents would approve because I had run away from home and that might be a big responsibility for them. Not to mention, they were close friends of my parents. It wasn't until I showed her my back that Rose decided she would tell her parents that I was there to visit for a few days. That gave enough time to make up my mind what I would do."

"What did you do?" Matt asked, mesmerized by the turn of events in her story.

"Let me take it from here," Charles said before Eva could continue. He paused for a moment and then continued the story.

"At the time I was just finishing up my three months hard labor for being late for duty, and six months or so later I did all my required military time. I was stationed in Austria, so I never did get back to Budapest until I finished my tour of duty. The day I was discharged I went to visit my parents in Lupany for a couple of weeks and then went to Budapest in hope of finding Mariska. A day hadn't gone by that I didn't think about her.

"I also thought about what happened to the young Hungarian girl I escorted home. I suspected that she brought some trouble to herself. It wasn't too often that you find a young lady, of her breeding, in a rowdy dance hall filled with common soldiers. When I approached her the first time and asked her to dance she refused me, so I backed off and said, 'Perhaps later.' She just nodded her head yes.

"About fifteen minutes later a drunken soldier asked her to dance and would not take no for an answer. I went to her rescue and told the soldier that she was my girlfriend and to get the hell away from her. We went out on the floor and finished the dance and then she asked me to please take her home. Of course, I asked her what a young lady of her stature was doing in a bawdy dance hall. She answered that her parents were away and that she got bored.

She was curious to see how common people entertained themselves. Later, after Mariska and her friends cared for me, I went over what happened that night. I figured that the soldier who I told to keep away from Eva exaggerated what happened when her fiancé came looking for her. After Mariska died, I took you back to Lupany and left you with your grandparents. I told them that I was going to look for work, and then I headed back to Budapest to spend some time with the Gypsies.

"The time I spent with them was both productive and spiritually healing. It was through the skills of the Gypsies that I learned smithing, how to work with metal, and how to handle and train horses. Unfortunately, I also learned how to drink wine. Every night I would sit down with a bottle of wine and drown my sorrows. I couldn't get over the loss of your mother, but in doing so, I neglected you for the first year. Then one night I decided to go out on the town at the advice of Mariska's brother, Emile who was lucky enough to escape down the Danube by boat the night of the massacre. He said it was time for me to get on with my life and that I must look for another woman. I decided to go back to that same dance hall where I had met Eva. I spent most of the night drinking at the bar. I searched the dance floor, but I could find no woman that caught my eye. At about closing time, someone tapped me on the shoulder and asked me if I was finished with my glass. I looked up and said yes to a lady I assumed was one of the barmaids. She took the glass from my hand and then looked at me for a moment and then turned and walked away.

"She suddenly spun around and said, 'You are him, aren't you?'

"'Who?' I asked, not knowing who she was referring to.

"'You are the soldier who took me home from this very place a couple of years ago.'

"I knew I had plenty of wine to drink that night, but I'll be damned if I recognized that lady claiming to know me. She came closer and then something about her light skin and green eyes reminded me of someone . . . but whom? The only girl I ever walked out of this place with was a redhead and this young lady's hair was a chestnut brown color. We stood and looked at one another for a long moment and then she said,

"'Yes, you are that Slovak gentleman who escorted me home that night.'

"I looked back at her, obviously perplexed and then she said,

"'Yes, I am Eva.'

"'Your hair is different. I remembered it being red.'

"'Yes, it was,' she answered, but that's another story. 'Would you wait for me?' she asked, 'until I finish my work here and then you can walk me home once again?'

"I must have had a cautious look on my face because she threw her head back laughing and said, 'Don't worry. I can assure you that you won't be hurt by anyone this time. I have no parents, no husband, and no gentleman friend.'

"'How in God's name did you end up being a barmaid?'

"'Only two days after I arrived at my friend Rose's house, one of the servants knocked on her bedroom door and told me that someone was at the kitchen door asking for me and that I should be careful not to let Rose's mother see me. When I entered the kitchen, to my surprise, it was my aunt's handyman who was forced to whip me. This big strong man put his arms around me, crying and begged for my forgiveness. I told him I knew he had no choice. He took a moment to compose himself and then told me that Rose's mother sent word to the Horvath's that Rose was hiding me at their residence, and that they were on their way to pick me up. I thanked him and then pleaded with him to leave before my parents arrived. He wished me luck and left abruptly, leaving me in quandary.'

"'Do you want to go home with them?' Rose asked.

"I hesitated for a moment and said emphatically that I didn't want to return with my parents.

"'Where will you go?' she asked. 'Do you have any money?'

"I told her I didn't know and that I had no money.

"'Don't worry. I will lend you some.'

"She took a ring off her finger and said that I should take that too. I told her no, that I couldn't take it because it looked expensive.

"She said, 'That's why I'm giving it to you. One day it might be of service like your locket was. Let's hope you never have to use it.'

"Then she reached into her vanity drawer and handed me a bag of money. She hugged and kissed me and then told me to hurry and to leave Budapest or my parents would surely find me."

"Where did you go then?" Matt asked.

"I went to the train station and went to Kosice where I thought I would be safe from anyone recognizing me. It was early evening when I arrived in Kosice. I got off the train and stood around for a while thinking about what I would do next. All my life I had been raised to depend on my parents. I'd wake up in the morning and someone dressed me and fed me. Wherever I went I had an escort. The only time I was away from my mother was at the academy where I took singing and piano lessons. I was terrified and I must have looked it because a young woman stopped and asked me if I was lost.

"'Sort of,' I answered.

"'Do you have a place to stay?'

"'No,' I answered.

"'Would you like to come home with me?' she asked.

"'Why would you take a perfect stranger home with you?'

"'Because I have a friend that I'm sure would like you to work for him.'

"'Doing what?' I asked.

"'Come with me," she said, 'and we'll talk about it later.'

"I said, 'No thank you' and started to walk away from her.

"'Here,' she said, handing me a paper with her name and address written on it. 'Stop by if you ever need a job and a place to stay.'

"After two weeks of sleeping at the train station and in the back alleys and spending the last money that Rose gave me, I was glad I saved the address that the woman gave me that day when I arrived in Kosice. When I knocked on her door, she wasn't at all surprised to see me. She invited me in and said that she was expecting me.

"'Let me show you where your room is,' she said, 'and then after you take a much needed bath, we'll talk.'

"An hour later I was dressed in clean clothes that she brought me and then asked me if I would like to sit for an artist friend of hers. He pays his models well and meanwhile I could live there free until I made enough income, and then I would start paying her rent. I had no money and no place to live, so I said yes.

"The next day my new friend Joanna introduced me to an artist friend Martin, who was enthralled with my emerald eyes, flaming red hair, and creamy white skin, as he described me. The first thing he asked me to do was to take all my clothes off. I just stood there, not moving.

"He looked at Joanna and said, 'Well!'

"'How much?' Joanna asked.

"He quoted her a sum of money. She grabbed me by the arm and said that I had nothing to worry about. He was only interested in painting me nude, for art's sake only, and besides, she said, if you don't do this I would be back on the streets again. All that time I didn't receive any money from Joanna and when I asked her why, she said, 'You have a roof over your head and you eat every day. You will have to do a lot more for me to put cash in your pockets.'

"A week later she came into my bedroom and told me I would have an opportunity to make some real money."

"'Great! But how?' I asked.

"'Well,' she said, 'Martin was showing one of his paintings of you to an art collector who is also one of the wealthiest men in Europe.'

"'What does that have to do with making money? Is Martin going to give me a percentage of the sale price?' I asked.

"'No,' Joanna said.

"'But what then?' I asked.

"'He wants you to spend the weekend with him at his estate in Vienna.'

"'To do what?' I asked.

"'Don't be so naïve, Eva. You know what. He wants to sample some of that creamy skin of yours that he saw on Martin's canvas,' she said, laughing.

"'Never!' I shouted.

"'Yes you will, or I'll see that your parents know where to find you. Eva, you should never have told me why you were on the run. Your first lesson: Never trust anyone.'

"'But I can't go to Vienna, Joanna,' I told her.

"'Why?'

"'Because that's where my fiancé is stationed with the army.'

"'Alright, I will arrange for you to stay at another location,' she said."

"Did you go, mother?" Matt asked.

"No, I still had the ring that Rose gave me, so the day before I was to leave, I went out on the streets and made a deal with some Gypsies. I knew that I didn't get what it was worth, but I got enough to buy a train ticket back to Budapest and still have some left over to get a cheap room to rent. I had no trouble getting a barmaid job, especially when I told them that I could play the piano and sing in between tending bar. My only problem was my red hair was too conspicuous, so I had it dyed brown. Everything was going fine for me. I made a decent living, and was becoming popular with the patrons. But that's what the problem was. I was always worried about getting recognized. I was on the verge of moving on when I found your father that night at the same dance hall where I first met him. Was it fate? I don't know, but I thank God every day of my life for finding your father again. That night I left with him and went to the Gypsy camp, and look," she said, showing her ring finger to Matt, "I got Rose's ring back from the Gypsy I made the deal with. Your father offered to pay him, but he wouldn't take anything for it. I learned a lot about Gypsies the few weeks we spent with them. The Cigans, as we called them, were nothing like we were led to believe growing up."

"Whatever happened to your friend Rose?" Matt asked.

"She married a man of means and went to America."

"One more question, Mother. What happened to your parents? Did they stop looking for you? It seems with all the money your father had he could have paid someone to track you down."

"He did, and then one day a woman was found drowned in the Danube with red hair. She had been there for a long time before they found her body. The police, who were already informed by my father about my running away, contacted him and asked him to identify the body. But the corpse was beyond recognition. He told them he couldn't be sure and then they showed him a locket, the same one that I gave to the boat man for passage money the day I went to see Rose. I was declared dead."

"What happened to your mother?"

"I was told years later by Rose that she became mentally ill and my father had her locked in our attic until she finally committed suicide and then I later heard that my father married some countess from Romania. I never tried to contact him because I was afraid he would try to hurt your father. And I never regretted that."

PART 2

HARD COAL

CHAPTER 24

Jon mingled with the newly arrived immigrants that were recently processed at Ellis Island and transferred to the Pennsylvania Railroad Station. They prepared to take an overnight train to the anthracite coal regions in north-central Pennsylvania. Slovaks, Czechs, Poles, Russians, Lithuanians, and Italians were confined to their railroad cars. Lunchroom and laundries were provided for them. These amenities were created as a precaution to protect the unsuspecting Greenhorns to be swindled by the con men that lurked in the dark streets, like leaches waiting to draw the last contents of money from their near depleted pockets.

Jon's cousins in Pennsylvania were in a quandary as to why he was so intent on coming to work in the coal mines where the pay was meager and the work dangerous and backbreaking. Men died every day in mine explosions or cave-ins, and many were buried alive with no hope of reaching them. The shacks where the miners and their families lived held funerals several times a month where death came swiftly by mine mishaps, or excruciatingly slow from black lung disease, or poisonous gas. The miners had had enough and went on strike, looking for safety measures and medical compensation and pensions for the widows. The newly formed union, the American Federation of Labor, which was spearheaded by Samuel Gomphers, backed them up.

"Jon!" a feminine voice shouted from the main entrance to the train station. He turned and recognized Helen as she ran towards him. "Oh Jon," she said, gasping, out of breath from running, "I thought that I would miss you." He looked up at the immense clock that was centered in the Romanesque arches that spanned the entrance where the trains entered, sending the engine smoke up through a slot in the sky-lit roof.

"It's only ten thirty Helen. We're scheduled to leave at midnight," he said, smiling as they embraced, and then he asked where the Maliks were.

"They're coming," she answered, pointing to the entrance where she saw them searching for Jon and walking at a fast pace. "Over here," Helen shouted. The Maliks were out of breath too, and at the same time relieved to see that they had arrived in time to see Jon off.

"We won't be leaving for another hour and a half," Jon told them happily, and then asked everyone to sit with him in the waiting room that was just a couple feet away.

After they were seated, Jon asked Paul if he had any word from home. Paul responded, "Nothing new. They are waiting to see if your brother and Stefan can find out where they hid Mikhail, and until they have the weapons that they need that's all they can do. I'm still inquiring about where I can find the money through the Slovak organizations. I've talked to some people at the Parish and at the docks. As soon as I know something Jon, I'll let you know. I don't think they should do anything even if they get the guns, until they find out if Mikhail's alive. My bet is that he has already been murdered by the Magyars."

"Hell, Paul, then why are they keeping it a secret?"

"Because they don't want to make him a martyr. There's nothing like a martyr to start a revolution."

"You know Paul," Jon said, lowering his head in exasperation, "I'm also worried about Stasha. It's been about six months since I've heard from her. It was sometime after Christmas. Her birthday is coming up this month. I already wrote to her last month and wished her a happy birthday. I have this terrible feeling that something is wrong. It's not like her to wait so long to write to me. In her last letter, she pleaded with me to bring her here now. I told her it all depends on how well I do working in the coal mines. My cousins haven't done anything to encourage me, but I have no choice."

"Look Jon, why don't you just stay and live with us and work on the docks?"

"It's too close to New York, and Clancy made a deal and gave his word. I must honor that. Just find out what's going on with Stasha. Paul, do me one more favor."

"Sure, Jon, anything you want."

"Take good care of Helen. See that she gets a good education and a decent job, and see if you can find her parents. Maybe you can find them through one of those religious organizations in Manhattan."

"Whatever you want. I'll do my best."

Jon reached into his pocket and pulled out a roll of money and said, "This is to help with her expenses. Later, I'll send you more money."

"Okay Jon, if that's what you want."

"That's what I want."

After bidding them goodbye with warm hugs and kisses, Jon boarded the train at midnight with his brand new suitcase that was a gift from Clancy, and his old cloth bag letting him know that he wasn't there yet. The steam engine chugged out of the station blowing smoke up through the slot in the sky roof with its steel wheels spinning on the steel tracks and soon picked up speed and disappeared into the dark humid summer night. Several hours had passed when the train raced across the southern tier of New York State, stopping from time to time at wooden tower tanks to satisfy the steam engine's insatiable need for water. Jon's mind was swimming with a mixture of doubt and anxiety as the train slipped across the New York State border into the mountain regions of north central Pennsylvania.

Six months had passed since the con men had given Jon their ultimatum. He spent Christmas with the Maliks and New Years with Clancy. He had worked four more months for Clancy, and with the substantial raise that Clancy bestowed upon him, he was able to save a lot of extra money. In April, Jon had been visited by the con men, telling him his time was up. He had packed up his belongings and went to stay with the Maliks, and soon contacted his cousins in Pennsylvania. His cousins, not realizing the danger he was in, never ceased to be baffled by a decision to come to work in the coal mines where every day was a living hell, and where death was always lurking somewhere just around the corner.

CHAPTER 25

There was no party for Stasha on her seventeenth birthday and there were no shining stars or luminous moon to guide her way to the ledge that she now fled to in despair. She walked slowly through the fields and struggled up the mountain path until she reached the secret haven where she and Jon consummated their love, not physically, but spiritually. Although the night was hot and sticky, Stasha shivered as she stroked her soft hands gently over her swollen belly. She was two months pregnant with Stefan's child, but was able to conceal her predicament. She fell to her knees and looked up into the ominous night sky and prayed to God to solve her dilemma. She reached into her skirt pocket and retrieved a string of rosary beads and began to pray to Mary the Mother of God who conceived her child Jesus without giving up her virginity and self-respect. "What can I do, dear Mary?" she importuned. Bead after bead she repeated over and over. "Holy Mary, Mother of God, pray for us sinners now at the hour of our death, amen."

The black night exploded with flashes of lightning followed by thunder echoing through the valley below. Large raindrops began splashing on the rocks, forcing her to retreat into the recess of the ledge. The lights of the village vanished behind a wall of torrential rainfall and gusting winds.

She sat back and fell into a trance as she waited for the storm to subside. Her mind drifted back to the days when she and Jon swam naked in the cool mountain lake. They were very young and still innocent, not yet aware of the warm surges that ran through their bodies as their flesh touched by accident.

The rain stopped as quickly as it came, bringing a cold wind that absorbed the humidity. Stasha slowly escaped from her reverie. She stood up and walked to the edge, looking out over the valley. Thunder and lightning faded behind the mountain tops that were faintly coming into view as the dark clouds were melting away from the blinding light of the new moon. She gazed down at the sharp rocks below that were waiting like executioners to tear the fetus from her sin ridden body and then cast her wanton flesh into the everlasting fire of hell.

"Oh my God, I am so heartily sorry for having offended thee, for I dread the loss of heaven and the pains of hell," she whispered as she stepped forward with her right foot dangling in the air.

Suddenly, a hand grasped her left shoulder and yanked her back on the hard stone floor and said, "No Stasha, you can't do this. You have no right. The child is mine too."

She looked into Stefan's pleading eyes and said, "But what will I tell Jon?"

"You will tell him the truth. If you can't, I will."

"Who will tell my mother?"

"I will. When everything is settled here, I will take you to Budapest."

"But why to Budapest?" Stasha asked, puzzled.

"Because in Budapest, my mother will arrange a lavish wedding as quickly as possible while your pregnancy can still be hidden by your gown. We will take a short honeymoon at my father's mountain resort and then we will go back to Vienna where I will serve the rest of my army time. After my discharge in two years, we will celebrate our child's second birthday. No one will be the wiser." And then he said with his usual smirk on his face and sarcasm in his tone, "We can live happily ever after."

"There's one thing that you are forgetting; I still love Jon."

"Well, that's too damn bad. You should have thought of that before you got sexually involved with me. I didn't put a gun to your head, and don't tell me that you did it to get Jon's father out of jail. If you remember correctly, we had sex before that incident came up."

"Yes, I know that, but I don't understand what came over me the first time."

"Because you are human."

"Yes, Father Marin said the same thing when I confessed it to him."

"You confessed it to him!"

"Yes, but I lied and said that we didn't go all the way. In my mind, I was only confessing what we did when you escorted me home on the night of my birthday party. I just couldn't face how weak I was, so I pretended that it never happened."

"Well, it did, and the baby in your womb is the final result. There is no way you can deny it. If you want to take your own life, that's one thing, but you have no right to take the life of your child . . . Do you?"

"No," she finally answered. "Do what you have to do. And you won't have to tell my mother, I will."

CHAPTER 26

The early morning sun that was darting in and out of the peaks and valleys of the surrounding coal beds aroused the passengers one by one, sending intermittent flashes of sunlight and shadows through the car windows. Jon, not quite awake, was startled by a strong hand shaking his shoulder, commanding him to wake up. "What is it?" Jon asked a man sitting next to him.

"I guess we are arriving at our destination," he answered, yawning. "Look out the window," he said, pointing to a mountain slope that was dotted with wooden shacks and what appeared to be women and children moving about. It was too far away and the train was moving too fast to see exactly what they were doing. The man that awakened them was back in the car again telling everyone to gather their belongings and be prepared to get off in the next fifteen minutes.

The steam engine slowed to a crawl as it neared the train depot at Wilkes-Barre, where coal was king and miners were its subservient. Throngs of miners crowded the platform waiting to seek out and greet their countrymen, and out on the street that bordered the train station was a mob of angry men, women, and children brandishing wooden clubs and displaying placards printed with threatening words such as, "Go home you dirty scab Slavs and greasy dagos." One by one, car by car, the immigrants debarked, aided by one of their countrymen who were handpicked by the mine owners to supervise their departure in their native languages. They were led out onto the streets in the face of the maddening crowd that was fortunately being controlled by the iron and coal police that were under the auspices of the mining corporations. Different modes of transportation were waiting to carry them to their assigned mine sites. Trolley cars were filled to their capacity and mule drawn wagons rumbled down the bumpy dirt streets while a hail of stones were being hurled at them by children as they ran alongside of the open windows, shouting, "Scabs, Scabs!"

Jon became enraged by the sight, but was powerless to intervene. He slipped away from the line that was being formed outside of his car and went in search of his cousins. Soon he heard his name being called as he approached the steps that led to the street.

"Down here, Jon," his cousins shouted in unison. "Here, give me your suitcase," one of them said while the other snatched his cloth bag and threw it into the rear of the wagon along with his suitcase and then whipped the horse into a gallop and fled the city at full speed until the mob disappeared behind them in a cloud of coal dust. It was close to midday and the sun was high and extremely hot, causing the horse to froth at the mouth. They stopped in fear that the horse would collapse and die before they reached their destination.

"What the hell is going on?" Jon asked in English. His cousins looked at one another and smiled, surprised at how well he spoke English.

"Where did you learn to speak English?" they asked anxiously.

"From my boss Clancy, an Irishman whom I worked for in New York," he answered in Slovak.

"An Irishman!" they both responded loudly.

"Yes, an Irishman, and he was like a father to me."

"You must be joking," they replied, obviously flabbergasted,

"So what's the big deal with the people back at the station," Jon asked, changing the subject.

"Yeah, what about them?"

"Well, probably more than half of them were Irish and Welsh so what's their problem."

"They're pissed off because you scab Slavs came here to work the mines."

"Scab?" Jon asked, scratching his head. "What the hell is that?"

Jon's younger cousin Stan described the word scab to him in Slovak. Jon still didn't get it, so his older cousin Francis explained to him that scabs are workers that work in the mines when the men are striking.

"What's a strike?" he asked, confused.

"Do you remember the things I wrote to you trying to discourage you from coming here because the coal mines were a dangerous place to work? Well, the men had enough and refused to go to work until the demands they made were given to them."

"What demands?" Jon asked inquisitively.

"Pensions for the miners, compensation for widows of workers who got killed in mine accidents, more safety methods, and medical compensation."

"No one told that to the people on the train."

"Of course not, Jon. Every day that the miners aren't working, the owners are losing money. So they bring in immigrants off the boat who are desperate for jobs and who can't speak English and who don't have any idea what a strike is."

There was a moment of silence and then Stan said, "Well, Jon, do you still want to stay and work in the mines?"

"I have no choice for now."

"Well, okay Jon, then that's settled. We did all we could to stop you. We've made arrangements for you to stay at a boarding house run by a Slovak widow. It will cost you two dollars a month. For that, she will do your wash, cook for you, and provide a space on the floor for you to sleep on. The house is located only a block from the mine site that you will be working in." Stan pulled a heavy towel out of the back of the wagon and wiped the sweat off the horse and gave him some water to drink, and then they set off for the village of Ashley that was just a mile outside the city of Wilkes-Barre.

The sun smiled down on them like a tyrant who watches his slaves' labor under his lashing whip. The sweltering humidity drove them to strip their shirts from their sweating torsos. The horse too faltered, enervated by the intense heat and suffocating humidity. The men stepped down off the wagon to relieve the horse from some of the burden, gave him the last of the water, and then began walking at a slow pace towards the coal mining patch of Ashley where men were invited to work to live, and more often to die.

CHAPTER 27

Andrew Valen had just finished washing his hands and face after a blistering workday in the fields. He was about to sit down at the dining room table when he heard an urgent knock at the front door.

"Yes, yes, I'm coming," he said as the knocks continued at a rapid pace. "What's the problem?" Andrew shouted angrily as he flung the door open.

"I'm sorry, Mr. Valen, please excuse me for my impatience."

"Matt? What is it? Is there something wrong?"

"Yes, there is a problem. How long has it been since Mikhail has been missing? When are we going to do something about it, and where the hell is the help that bastard Magyar Stefan Nagy was supposed to give us? You can't tell me that by now he couldn't find the whereabouts of Mikhail. My God, Mr. Valen, nine months have passed and still no word. What about your son Jozef? Surely being chief of police he should have found out something by now." Matt got this all out in one long breath.

This prompted Andrew to say, "Slow down Matt, take it easy," and then he pointed to a chair and asked him to sit down and listen. When Matt was seated and calmed down, he told him that Jozef did find out where Mikhail might be. The information was passed on to Stefan and at this very moment he was looking into it.

"Where is he?" Matt asked pleadingly.

"At Kapusany, in the old dilapidated castle dungeon where we were taken after our release. Jozef was waiting for us when we arrived, so we never entered the castle. He was probably there the whole time."

What do we do now?" Matt asked impatiently.

"We wait until Stefan investigates and make sure he's there and then we will act on that."

"With what?" Matt asked, then adding sarcastically, "Oh, with our bare hands? We need guns, dynamite, and ammunition. Where will we get them without money? Have you heard from Jon yet about the money?"

"No, but I received a letter yesterday from Jon's boss Clancy and enclosed was a stack of American money. I have the letter here in the cupboard." He retrieved it from the shelf and handed it to him.

He looked at it and began to laugh. "It is written in English."

"No problem, Matt. Do you remember Cyril Lesko?"

"Yes, he went to America about six years ago."

"Well, he just came back to marry and take his bride back to America. He translated it for me. It said:

"Jon went to work in the coal mines but before he left he told me about the problem you were having in Slovakia and about the money you needed for weapons. When I was cleaning out Jon's room, I found an old letter that he received from you with the address on it. Please accept this as a favor for Jon, who I think of as a kid brother. I know he will repay me one way or another. Lots of luck. I understand your predicament. We have the same bullshit going on in Ireland. Sometimes talking is not enough to get your freedom."

"How about that," Matt said, shaking his head in disbelief. "Maybe there is a God after all!"

"Well, what do we do now, Matt? We have the money, but no place to buy the weapons."

"Don't worry," Matt responded, as he stood up and turned in the direction of the door. I will get us the weapons that we need. Let me have the money." Andrew hesitated for a moment and then handed Matt the money. "Trust me," he said as he closed the door behind him, leaving Andrew perplexed.

Just as Matt mounted his horse, Mrs. Ondreas came out of the barn, walking as if she were in a trance and right behind her was Stasha, pleading with her to wait.

"Please, Mother, you must listen to what I have to say."

"We have nothing more to say," she spat with rancor and then entered Mr. Valen's house and slammed the door behind her, leaving Stasha alone with Matt.

"What is it?" Matt asked anxiously.

She hesitated for a moment and then said, "Nothing important. Just a mother and daughter argument. What are you doing here?"

"I came here to talk with Andrew about our progress with finding Mikhail. I need to get in touch with Stefan," he added. "Do you know where he is?"

"Why should I know?" she asked defensively.

"No offense, Stasha, but everyone knows that he is infatuated with you. I need to talk to him. By now he must have some information that will help lead us to freeing Mikhail. It's amazing that Jozef found out where they have him incarcerated before Stefan did! If you see Stefan, tell him nothing about what I just told you. I don't trust that son of a bitch."

The late afternoon sun showed no mercy on Matt's eyes as he galloped home to the western edge of Dubovica where he found his father gathering his tools for storage after a hard day's work: shoeing a couple dozen horses that were contracted to him by the army.

"Where have you been, son?" Mr. Sokolasky asked as Matt dismounted from his chestnut mare. "I could have used your help today."

"I'm sorry Papa, but I had to talk to Mr. Valen about when we were going to take action to find Mikhail. I feel guilty," Matt said, lowering his head.

"Guilty of what?" Mr.Sokolasky asked, puzzled.

"Mikhail put me in charge before he went to Caraffa Prison and I failed him. I should have gone sooner, before they took him away."

"Nonsense, son, there was nothing you could do. You had no weapons. All of you would have been slaughtered. Your wooden clubs and hammers would have been no match for their guns."

"Maybe so, but now that we have the money we can buy what we need."

"What money?" Mr. Sokolasky asked, wrinkling his forehead. Matt told him about how the money was acquired and then told him that he was leaving Presov to visit his Uncle Emile, where he hoped to purchase guns through the help of the Gypsies that were serving in the army.

"I know that Uncle Emile can do this for me. He always told me that Gadzos could all be bought for a price."

"I don't know if I should permit you to do this, Matt. It will be dangerous."

"Charles, let him go." a voice rang out from the open barn door. "He is a man now; a man very much like you. Go now, Matthew, and do what you have to do

"Thank you, Mother. I promise I will be careful."

An hour later, Matt hitched his horse to a wagon loaded with supplies that he would need to facilitate his journey to Presov, and hopefully it would be overloaded with weapons on his return to Dubovica.

CHAPTER 28

When the first semblance of a shelter appeared, Jon and his cousins were exhausted and famished. Children were rolling down the coal banks that flanked them, laughing as they crashed into each other at the bottom.

"The heat doesn't seem to be bothering them none," Jon said, shaking his head.

"That's kids for you," Francis said, smiling, and then continued with a frown. "But they won't be children for long. By the time they are twelve, the mines will have aged them considerably, and by the time they are twenty, more than half of them will be dead from mine mishaps."

Francis was about to continue when he was interrupted by a loud noise coming from a crowd of men that were crammed into a circle shouting in different dialects of Slavic: "Beat the scabs' brains in" and other obscenities that were of Slavic origin and others that were unfamiliar.

This puzzled Jon. He turned and asked Francis why one Slav would call another Slav a scab. "I thought it was the Irish and Welsh that were pissed off at us for working during the strike."

"Yeah, that's true, but you see, there are many Slavic people here that can't afford to stop working at the risk of their families starving."

"Why can't they help one another until this strike is over?"

"You don't understand. This could go on for many more months. Everyone would go down then."

"Well, then, why don't they look for jobs somewhere else?"

"Many have left for jobs down river in iron smelting plants in the Lehigh Valley, and some went as far as Philadelphia. There are some jobs for the women doing housework for the rich mine owners' families, but there are only so many openings. That's why a lot of them headed for the large city of Philadelphia, were there are endless domestic jobs for both men and women. Mostly the young people leave with the hope that they can send part of their earnings home to their parents. Some of them have joined the National Guard and the Coal and Iron Police, but that puts them in sticky situations when they are called here to keep order when the strikers start getting violent."

Jon shook his head in dismay while he grasped the reins of the horse and urged him on past the maddening crowd. Fifteen minutes later, he was tying the horse up at the hitching post in front of Maria Novak's boarding house. His cousins excused themselves and said that they were going to the general store to buy some food and beer for lunch. Jon started to reach in his pocket to give them some money, but they told him to hold on to it, they would take care of it.

Jon was lifting his luggage from the back of the wagon when a feminine voice shouted, "Jon Valen? Are you Jon Valen?"

"Yes I am," he answered, looking up as he set the luggage down on the black dusty ground.

"I am Maria Novak," she said, extending her hand and smiling. Her rough hands belied the smooth, soft texture of her skin that adorned her face like the angels that were painted on the ceiling of the village church in Dubovica. Her green eyes struggled desperately to hide the pain and sorrow that life had dealt so cruelly to her since she arrived in the Land of the Free, and the Home of the Brave.

"Here, let me help you," she said in a Slavic dialect that resembled his friend Lucas's. While Jon balked, Mrs. Novak picked his suitcase up from the ground and carried it into the ramshackled pine wood dwelling. He followed behind her with his cloth bag slung over his shoulder. Before he sat his bag down, he gazed around the room which measured about twenty-feet by twelve-feet, and in the center sat a coal stove where all the cooking was done and the water boiled for washing the miners' clothes. Next to the stove was a small table where three heavy irons were sitting, waiting to be put on the hot stove to prepare them for pressing the men's clothing after they were washed. Mrs. Novak did all of this with the help of her two young daughters and a nephew that were under the ages of ten. When the boy reached twelve, he would be sent to work as a breaker boy, where he would spend twelve hours a day in the colliery, separating the slate and slag from the coal that was crushed and being made sellable for the open market. The daughters would continue to work with their mother at the boarding house until they reached marriageable age. At the far end of the room was a door that led to a room that measured nine-foot by twelve-foot. This was where Mrs. Novak and her children slept. Thirty miners occupied the larger room, leaving little space for breathing, let alone sleeping comfortably. This was the situation in most of the boarding houses, but fortunately the men in this house were able to arrange different work shifts, allowing less-crowded sleeping quarters. Mrs. Novak's husband created the idea. After laboring in the mines for seven or eight years and proving himself to be a diligent and loyal worker, his easy grasp of the English language won him the job of supervisor. This provided a higher income and more privileges. With the extra income, he saved enough to buy the cheap pine wood to build the boarding house with his own hands and the help of some of his relatives. Unfortunately, like many of the miners, he died from being buried alive in a mine explosion, leaving his family in sole charge of their lives. Mrs. Novak was surely up for the task after years of washing, cooking, and childbearing, along with four miscarriages. Now that her husband was gone, she was going to pursue her own dream and take her children out of this hellhole one way or another.

She assigned Jon space at the far right corner of the room that was just a few feet from her bedroom door. Wooden clothes hangers were nailed all along the four walls, providing the men with a place to put their clothes giving them more sleeping and walking space.

When Jon was finally settled in, Mrs. Novak informed him that after he paid his two dollars monthly rent, she would provide him with a mattress and covers, and if he wanted her to cook his meals and pack his lunch, it would be fifty cents more. Jon reached into his back pocket and retrieved a brand new wallet that was a going away gift from Paul Malik, and he removed a crisp twenty dollar bill and handed it to her.

"But . . . but," she stammered, "I can't change this for you."

"You don't have to. This is for my meals and my rent in advance. Is that enough?" Jon asked seriously.

"Yes, yes, of course," she answered, still in shock. No one had ever paid her in advance before; to the contrary, she often had to wait two or three pays or more before they caught up to the rent and meal expenses. "Excuse me," she said, still trying to gain her composure. "I have to put this in the strong box for safe keeping." She turned and disappeared into the back room.

While Jon waited for her return, he walked around the room avoiding stepping on the mattresses and other personal items that the boarders had carelessly left lying around. He examined the ceiling, the windows, walls, and the floor. "What a mess," he thought to himself.

"Jon," Mrs. Novak called, startling him. "Have you had anything to eat?"

"No, not since I left New York around midnight."

"You must be starved. I can cook something up for you. I have some left over pirogues with cheese."

"No, no. My cousins went to the general store for something to eat for me. They should be here any moment, but thank you for your concern."

"Well, okay, I'll see you later," she said, removing her kerchief from her head, allowing a long flow of blonde hair to fall softly down to the middle of her back.

"Where are you off to?" he asked, suddenly noticing how beautiful she was.

"I'm going out to play with the children. It's God's day, Sunday. A day of rest, finally." With that said she ran out and slammed the door behind her.

CHAPTER 29

The sun was digging into the western mountains when Matt arrived in Sabinov at the police station where he hoped to find Jozef and tell him about the money and his plan to acquire the weapons that they would need to free Mikhail. Jozef was sitting behind his desk busy with paper work when Matt entered his office.

"Matt Sokolsky to see you sir," the desk sergeant snapped.

Jozef looked up, seemingly a little annoyed by the sudden intrusion, but after recognizing Matt, he smiled.

"So good to see you, Matt," he said, extending his hand. "Pleases, have a seat." He thanked the sergeant and then excused him. Jozef waited until the sergeant was out of earshot and then asked why he was here. "Good news, I hope!"

"Yes," Matt answered, and then told him about the money Andrew had received from Clancy and what he intended to do with it. It didn't surprise Jozef when he heard that the Gypsies were going to help. Jozef's family was one of the select few that knew about his Gypsy bloodline.

"What can I do to help?" Jozef asked.

"First, find out how many soldiers are on guard and where we can hide after we free him."

"I will see to it. What else can I do?"

"Well, I could use a little sleep. I would like to time it so that I arrive early in the morning when there is a lot of activity going on. That way I will be less conspicuous among all the other wagons on the streets."

"No problem. You can use one of the bunk beds in one of the empty cells. When would you like to be awakened?"

He paused for a moment to give it some thought and then said, "Around 3:00 AM. That should get me into the Gypsy camp around daybreak."

Jozef came from behind his desk and embraced Matt. "Be careful, and may God be with you. Sergeant," Jozef shouted, "please see that my friend has an empty cell bunk bed to sleep on and also inform the night clerk on duty to awaken him at 3:00 AM. And sergeant, see that his horse is fed."

"Yes sir, I will see to it."

"Oh, and one more thing," Matt said before he turned to leave, "have your father contact Roman Polasky. We will need him to teach us how to work the weapons and what tactics we will have to use to make the plan work. If things go well for me in Presov, I will see you on my way back."

The sun squeezed out of the eastern horizon with an explosion of a myriad of red colors, sending its rays across the deep blue morning sky. The city was coming to life with people moving in different directions on their way to their respective jobs as Matt crossed the Torysa River Bridge. The Gypsies camp too were alive, setting up their tents along the riverbank, preparing to sell their wares as Matt rolled into the compound with his horse-drawn wagon.

"Matt! Matt!" a feminine voice called out.

Matt turned and saw his cousin Magda, Emile's daughter, running toward him full speed, holding her skirt high above her ankles. "Where have you been? It's been so long," she said as Matt jumped down off the wagon into her waiting arms.

When they finally parted, Matt stepped back to look at her. "My God, Magda, what happened to you? You're not a little girl anymore."

"Well. I am sixteen, and I'm soon to be married."

"How beautiful," Matt thought. Uncle Emile always said that Magda was the spitting image of his mother, Mariska.

"Hitch the horse up and come with me," Magda said anxiously. "My papa will be so happy to see you."

A few minutes later, they entered Emile's tent where they found him shaving his face.

"Papa," Magda shouted, startling Emile as he was stroking the razor across his chin, causing him to cut himself.

"For God's sake, look what you made me do!" he yelled, as he reached for the towel to wipe the blood off that was trickling down his chin.

"Look Papa, look who's here," Magda said, ignoring her father's outburst.

Emile looked up, the towel in his right hand, pressed against his chin to stop the bleeding. "Where have you been," he said, as if he had seen a ghost. "It's been a couple of years."

"I know, Uncle Emile, but with my father's business and all the bullshit that the Magyars are giving us lately, I just couldn't find the time."

"How did you finally find the time now?" Emile asked, raising his eyebrows in a mocking gesture, and then laughed as he hugged Matt. "Well, you are here now so let's make the best of it."

"Uncle Emile, I'm a little ashamed to tell you this, but this isn't just a social visit. I came here because I need your help with something. Magda," Matt said, turning to her, "would you please excuse us? I have to discuss something with your father."

"Of course," she answered respectfully, and left closing the tent flap behind her.

"What is it Matt?" Emile asked with deep concern in his tone. They both sat down on Emile's straw bed and then Matt related the turn of events that happened in the past year. He told him of the ultimatum, the imprisoning of Mr. Valen and his friends, the march to free them, and then the disappearance of Mikhail.

"What can I do to help you?" Emile asked.

"We need weapons. Can you get them for us?"

"I could, but it will cost you."

"No problem," he said, pulling the envelope out of his pocket that contained the money. "Here," he said, opening the envelope and dropping the money down onto the bed. Emile fingered through the bills, realizing that there was probably more than enough to get what he needed.

"What exactly do you want?"

"We want guns, ammunition, and dynamite."

"How long can you stay here, Matt?"

"As long as it takes to fill my wagon with the weapons."

"In that case, let me find you sleeping quarters. I will have one of the men set up a tent for you to live in while you are here, and I'm sure that Magda will be glad to hear that you are staying so that you can see her get married next week."

"Married," Matt said, shaking his head, pretending that he didn't know. "Why, she's still a little girl."

"I think that you better take a closer look the next time you see her."

"I already have."

Emile stood up and said, "Now get out of here and ask Magda to prepare some breakfast for you while I make the arrangement to have your tent set up. Tomorrow I will look into the other matter."

Matt spent the rest of the day visiting friends with his cousin Tomas, Magda's brother, who was born the year that his mother was murdered.

CHAPTER 30

Daylight was sucked into another dimension as the massive steel sheave wheels drove the miners' elevator cage down the thick greasy cables relentlessly into the abyss. The decent was slow at first and then picked up speed as they plunged to a thousand feet below ground level. The depth gauge indicated that the cage had reached the gangway that would lead Jon and his helper to the location where they would be picking away for the next twelve hours at a coal seam.

The engineer above pulled the lever, bringing the cage to a jolting stop. Jon was immediately led by his helper, who was an experienced miner, onto the black dusty floor. The air was filled with the smell of rotten lumber, carbon gas, and sulfuric acid. Jon's breathing began to labor as they worked their way through the mine tunnel, or gangway, as the miners called it. They walked a mile, their high rubber boots crunching on the soft ground and squishing in ankle deep water. The silence was broken occasionally by the sound of coal cars rumbling in the distance. They walked another mile with the roof of the mine tunnel just inches above their heads. Jon tried not to think about all the weight that was bearing down on the flimsy wooden structure. Finally, they arrived at a large wooden door which regulated the flow of air. After knocking, a young boy no older than fourteen opened it and allowed them to pass. A half mile later they arrived at a small shed where they were checked in by the fire boss whose job was to examine the working area. He would inspect the roof and check for gas and see that the ventilating shafts were working properly. When he was finished they were directed to their working area.

The next twelve hours were spent chipping away at the face of a coal wall where their only company was the skin-crawling sound of creaking timber and loose dirt falling from the slime-ridden moss roof of the gangway. Jon wore heavy, coarse overhauls held up by suspenders to protect his body from the cold damp air, and also to shield it from injuries he could sustain from falling or from the sharp edges of the timberline walls. On his head he wore a steel helmet that was mounted with a carbonated gas lamp that flickered orange, red on the black coal seam like a comet soaring through space on a dark cloudless night.

Three weeks passed before Jon's body stood up to the rigors of the mine work. Although he was in fine physical condition when he arrived at Ellis Island, that soon waned after the less strenuous job of waiting tables and doing rudimentary carpentry. He spent his first two weeks sleeping and resting and having an occasional chat with Mrs. Novak. Being the perfectionist that he was, the ramshackled condition of the boarding house annoyed the hell out of him. There were holes in the roof and cracked windows, doors falling off the hinges.

"Jesus, Mary, Joseph," he said out loud in exasperation. When he told Mrs. Novak that he was going to start making repairs as soon as he felt up to it, she smiled sheepishly.

"But when will you find the time?" she asked wide-eyed.

"On Sunday," he replied.

"But the Lord said that was to be our day of rest."

"Easy for Him to say," Jon said with a frown on his face. "When was the last time He worked all week in a coal mine?"

"Jon, that's blasphemy," she snapped, seemingly appalled by his comment, and then she laughed and said, "Come with me. It's about time you go to mass. It will give you a chance to meet some of the other families."

After passing the general store and the local saloon, they walked about a quarter of a mile before they sighted the simple wooden church that looked like it was hastily constructed by the miners.

"This is it?" Jon asked incredulously. "I've seen better built outhouses back home."

"You just can't help yourself," Mrs. Novak said, shaking her head, trying not to laugh.

"Help what?" Jon asked, squinting his eyes.

"Blaspheming!"

"That is blasphemy, Mrs. Novak," Jon replied, pointing to the church.

She just grinned and said, "By the way, my name is Maria."

She took his hand and led him into the vestibule that was jam-packed with miners and their families.

"No wonder," Jon thought to himself, "that the street was quiet." Now he knew where all the people were. It was standing room only. "Is it always crowded like this Mrs.—Maria.?" Jon asked.

"Yes. Then after mass they will all be at the saloon getting drunk."

The people hushed as the priest and two altar boys entered. They turned and genuflected before a large wooden crucifix and then without delay, the mass began in a language that only ancient Romans would understand, then the magic began. The consecration, the part of the mass where the priest turns bread and wine into the body and blood of Christ who died for our sins, was starting. Father Karnovsky stepped down off the crudely constructed altar and walked onto a creaky pine wooden floor until he reached the wobbly communion rail. He gripped the rail with both hands for a moment and then suddenly he released them and began to speak.

"Good morning and God bless you all. It is heartwarming to see the vast majority of the mining families in attendance." Again, he leaned forward and grasped the rail, bowing his head. After a moment's pause, he looked up and shouted the word "solidarity," and then paused again, his eyes moving, searching to see the reaction of the parishioners. "It is the key that will open the door to uniting all the mine workers, regardless of their nationality or religion. The Irish, Welsh, and Germans have decided to join in with us. Hard to believe? After all, we were the dumb Hunkies who couldn't speak a word of English, and who were willing to work like slaves, no matter how high the cost. Or should I say no matter how small the wage? After this strike is over, many good things will come. We will learn to be friends with non-Slavics, who after all, are the same faith as us. The Pope is our leader on earth. As for the Lutherans, well," he continued with a smile breaking out on his face. "We both have the same boss up there," he said while pointing his finger upward.

This brought a chuckle or two from the miners. "I understand also that there are some families that cannot be without work or their children will starve. Please, do not punish your fellow Slovaks for ignoring the rules of the strike. Everyone must lift a hand to help these people, including the church. Now let us pray that God will ease some of our sufferings and enlighten the mine owners to give us what we deserve, no more no less. One more reminder before we end the mass. Please, no violence and no excessive drinking. Remember, solidarity is the key to the success of the strike."

CHAPTER 31

The Gypsy camp was in frenzy: dancing, singing, musicians fiddling and strumming, weaving all the ancient Gypsy songs for the wedding feast. Both the daughter-in-law and the father-in-law would be toasted several times with strong old brandy. The groom was hand picked from a tribe of Gypsies that lived along the Danube in Budapest from where they had fled when the Magyars whipped Mariska to near death, and then burned the rest of her life from her bloody, flesh torn body. Although he was pursued by many of the young village girls, he kept a shy distance from their advances. Revenge and hatred were deep-seated in his blood when he remembered the violent death of his mother, the same blood that Magda would display to her in-laws after the consummation of her marriage. The blood-soiled sheet of her wedding bed would be proof of her virginity.

The early morning quiet was broken by the Gypsy wagons jerking into motion, hobbling over the rough ground and then onto the cobblestone streets of Presov. The last wagon dissolved into the eastern sunrise as it crossed the Torysa Bridge and then headed south to the land of the Magyars.

"Hello, are you there, Emile?" Matt shouted, standing outside his tent.

"Yes, yes I am," Emile answered, yawning. "Come in." Matt pulled the tent flap aside and entered. Emile was slipping on his boots. "I know why you're here," Emile said, looking up as he pulled his right boot on.

"Well?" Matt asked anxiously.

"Well," Emile answered, as he pulled his left boot on and then he smiled and said, "It's done. All we have to do now is find a way to sneak the weapons into camp and then build a false floor in the wagon with bales of hay. If you get stopped for any reason you can tell them who your father is and that the army contracts their horses to him for shoeing. That will explain the bales of hay. The horses have to be fed while they are waiting their turn. Even an idiot Magyar would surmise that."

"Yes Uncle Emile, that ought to work fine," Matt replied, smiling.

"What the hell are you snickering about?" Emile snapped.

"I was just thinking about how deceptive the Gypsy mind is." Emile just shook his head in mock disgust. "How many rifles are there?" Matt asked inquisitively.

"There are fifteen rifles and a hundred rounds of ammunition for each rifle . . . all automatic. They are an obsolete rifle made in the United States, but effective enough to do what has to be done to free your friend. I'm sure that Polasky fellow will explain the ins and outs of them. There is also a box of dynamite sticks, enough to blow the prison wall out and then some."

"Well, how does it feel to be a father-in-law?" Matt asked, changing the subject.

"Not yet I'm not."

"What do you mean?" Matt replied, raising his eyebrows. "I saw the bloody sheet from the marriage bed."

"In our world the marriage is only made final when the first child is born," Emile answered.

Matt scratched his head and said, "Do you know what would happen to a woman in our village if she said she had a child before a priest blessed their marriage?" Before Emile could answer, he finished saying, "They would be run out of the village in shame, never to return."

"Emile," a voice spoke from outside the tent. "Is Matt with you?"

"Yes, I'm in here," Matt answered while he opened the tent flap. "What is it, Tomas?"

"There is someone here to see you."

"Who is it?"

"It's me Matt," a voice shouted as he approached the tent."

"Jesus, Mary, Joseph," Matt whispered under his breath. "It's Roman Polasky." And then dread filled his body. "What is it, Roman . . . nothing bad, I hope."

He got right to the point; reaching out and holding Matt by his shoulders, he said bluntly that Stefan Nagy had been found shot to death.

"What!" Matt half whispered, shocked by the news, but not surprised. "Who did it?" he finally asked after he regained his composure. "I understand that he had a lot of enemies, being half Magyar. I was one of them, but he was an important part of our plan. We needed his inside connections. He was a trusted officer in the Hungarian Army, but he gave his word on his Mother's Slovakian soul that he would help us free Mikhail. And I believed that even he could not break that vow. If he did betray us, who found out? Or did the Magyars find out that he was helping us?"

"I don't know," Roman answered with a sigh, and then continued, "but what I do know is that we must act quickly. Have you acquired any weapons?"

"Yes," Emile answered for Matt, who was in deep thought. "Later today we will be sending Matt's wagon out to the country to be loaded with hay and then this evening we will meet some of our Gypsy soldier friends at a designated location where the guns will be concealed under the false wagon floor and then covered with the bales of hay."

Saris County began to appear as the early morning sunlight pushed its way through the darkness. Roman, sitting high on his dappled gray horse, looked down at Matt.

"Sabinov is just ahead." Without answering, Matt whipped the horses and sent them running as fast as they could gallop until they reached the police station in Sabinov. He jumped off the wagon and turned to Roman and asked him to feed and water the horses and to keep an eye on things while he went inside to speak to Jozef.

The sergeant recognized Matt as he approached his desk and said, "Jozef is expecting you. Go right in."

Before Jozef could greet him, Matt shouted, "What the hell is going on?"

Jozef put his index finger to his lips for Matt to quiet down.

"What happened to Stefan? Did he betray us? Do you know who killed him?"

"You better sit down and calm yourself and I'll tell you all that I know, and what I don't know. The authorities including myself are still investigating the murder of Stefan. My superiors haven't given me any indication that they knew of Stefan's plan to help us."

"Well then, who the hell killed him?"

"You're not going to believe this, but we have only one suspect."

"Who?"

"Mrs. Ondreas."

"Stasha's mother!" Matt blurted incredulously.

"Yes, I'm afraid so," Jozef answered, as if he too found it hard to believe.

"What in God's name brought you to suspect her?"

"Two things: we found the gun in her kitchen cabinet, and blood on her clothing."

"What is the other thing?"

Jozef hesitated for a moment and then said, "Stasha is missing. The last time someone saw her was the afternoon before Stefan's body was found."

Matt lowered his head in disbelief, and then he looked up and asked Jozef what he thought of the whole mess.

Jozef answered that he thought Mrs. Ondreas did murder Stefan.

"But why?" Matt interjected.

"Because it has been common knowledge that Stefan and Stasha were having an affair, and that the only thing that I can surmise is that she became pregnant and Mrs. Ondreas found out about it."

"I find that hard to believe, Jozef," Matt said, shaking his head in dismay. "Jon and Stasha seemed to be very much in love. Wasn't she supposed to join him soon in America?"

"Yes, but she's a young beautiful girl, and Stefan pursued her relentlessly, from what I heard from other army officer friends of his."

"Are you sure this is all true?"

"Yes, all except that she is with child. That I'm only surmising."

"Has anyone asked Mrs. Ondreas if she is pregnant?"

"No."

"No? What do you mean no?" Matt asked, shaking his head again in disbelief.

"When Mrs. Ondreas was found she was in her kitchen sitting in a chair, staring into space. I had a doctor examine her and he said she was in a state of shock."

"From what?" Matt asked.

"The doctor said that maybe she witnessed the murder, or she committed the murder."

"What do your superiors say about it?"

"They don't know. I was able to keep it from them. The only one that knows about it is my father, who found the body at the entranceway to the barn when he came on a routine visit to talk with Stasha and Mrs. Ondreas about a letter he received from the Maliks in America. He ran into the house and found her sitting on a chair completely out of it. He had a message delivered to me here and then had Dr. Dombrosky examine her. The doctor has no love for the Magyars and because the messenger who is one of the men sworn to secrecy in our plot to free Mikhail, we have been able to keep the information from the Magyars."

"What did you do with the body?"

"We weighed it down with some stones and tossed it into the mountain lake near the ledge that overlooks Dubrovica."

"What about his horse?"

"We just turned it loose out in the countryside with the hope that some farmer will find it and keep it for himself. So far, it hasn't shown up."

"Will Mrs. Ondreas ever come back to reality?"

"The doctor said that is was hard to tell, some do and some don't. He said he saw the same trauma in soldiers that were in combat."

"Where is she now?"

"With my father."

"Well, where do we go from here, Jozef?"

"We will go on as planned. Mikhail is still imprisoned at Kapusany guarded by only three soldiers. They pull three eight hour shifts. While one is sleeping, two are awake. Do you have the weapons?"

"Yes."

"Good. We will deal with Stasha later."

CHAPTER 32

When the mass ended, Mrs. Novak introduced Jon to some of the families that were milling about outside the church. The women nodded hello shyly and the men hugged him heartedly.

"Are you hungry, Jon?" Maria asked while she clasped her soft left hand to his already calloused right hand.

"Yes," he answered, rubbing his stomach in a circular motion.

"Good. We'll go to the saloon. They serve a scrumptious breakfast on Sunday mornings. Of course, they do a lot of drinking, and by afternoon most of the men are drunk and dancing wildly with the women. "Come on," she said, "let's get there early before the craziness begins.

Splintered wood, chunks of glass, and two flying bodies crashed through the saloon window at the feet of Jon and Maria. Jon pulled Maria behind him and watched the two men roll over and over, exchanging Slavic curses. Suddenly both men were on their feet circling, waiting for an advantage to overcome the other. Jon rushed between them and ordered them to stop. They looked at him and told him to get the hell out of their way. By this time a crowd was gathering. Some looked on with crass indifference and others took sadistic pleasure in the spectacle, as if it were a Roman arena event.

"What's the problem," Jon asked, turning his eyes from one to the other, determined to find out why two Slovak men were fighting.

"Leave them be," a gruff voice shouted. Jon turned and saw a big burly red-headed man standing at the entrance to the saloon, speaking in English with an accent that was similar to Clancy's.

"And why should I," Jon answered in his best-broken English Irish accent.

For a second, the big red-headed man stood there with his mouth agape and his deep green eyes sparkling with laughter, and then finally asked with a broad smile on his face. "And who may you be?"

"I am Jon Valen," he answered, continuing his best Irish brogue.

"And from what clan be you?" the Irishman asked, continuing the charade.

Jon paused for a moment and then said, "I guess it would be correct to say that I am from the Slovak clan. The two combatants just stood there dumbfounded, not understanding a word of the conversation.

Extending his hand to Jon, he said, "I am Patrick McDevitt. Have you had any breakfast yet?"

"No," Jon answered emphatically while motioning to Maria to follow him into the saloon.

The two fighters and the crowd just stood there motionless as if they had been struck by lightning. Before Jon closed the door behind him, he shouted to the two men to come in and that he would buy them a drink. They looked at one another, shrugged their shoulders, and headed for the door.

"Just give me a few minutes to prepare you breakfast," Patrick said as he directed them to a dining room area that consisted of eight square tables with four chairs a piece. The two men headed straight to the bar that was located on the opposite side of the room.

Jon was surprised to see the polished mahogany bar with brass foot rails and spittoons. Large gold framed round mirrors were displayed on the walls, adding a touch of elegance to the interior. To the left of the bar near the entrance were six wooden barrels with wooden planks nailed to them, creating a bench for weary miners when the stools at the bar were taken.

"Nice place Patrick," Jon said as he pulled a chair out for Maria to sit on.

"It wasn't always like this. When I bought this place it was a dump. Little by little I added on. I got the bar for a song and a dance from some hunky that was going back to the old country to shoot his promised woman. He found out she was screwing some other lad. I gave him just enough money for the voyage back and extra so he could purchase a decent gun.

"Well, that was big of you," Jon answered, shaking his head in disgust.

"You can't really blame him, Jon," Maria interjected, shaking her shoulders matter of factly.

"Who? Patrick or the man whose woman shamed him?" Jon asked, puzzled by Maria's remark.

"The man, of course," Maria answered, laughing.

"Here's a man going back home to kill his fiancée, and you think it's funny."

"No, I'm not laughing at that. I was laughing because you thought maybe I meant that Patrick was fair in what he did when he took advantage of the man. Do you think it was right for the man to go back and kill her because of her infidelity? What would you do if your woman would do that, that is, if you had one?"

Jon paused for a moment and then said, "I don't know. I never really thought about it. I do remember being upset when my Stasha hadn't written to me for a few months."

"Stasha, who is she?" Maria asked, obviously upset.

"She is my promised woman."

"Woman!" Maria repeated. "How old is she?"

"She was seventeen this past July."

"Are you in love with her or is it just one of those usual old country traditions where the parents pick who will marry whom?"

"Yes, but we were already attached to one another since she was thirteen and I was seventeen."

"What do you mean attached?"

"I guess you could say we developed strong feelings for one another. We used to run off alone into the mountains where we had a secret hiding place. We would swim naked under the stars in the cold mountain lake."

"Did you do it?" Maria asked boldly.

"Do what?" Jon answered naively.

"Have sex with her?"

"No, of course not," Jon answered, wrinkling his forehead. "We were only children at the time, or at least she was. What the hell does this have to do with Patrick taking unfair advantage of the man he bought the bar from?"

Before Maria could answer, the two men at the bar shouted in unison, "Where the hell's our drinks?"

"Keep your pants on," Patrick shouted. I'll be with you as soon as I tell the cook to get their breakfast going. How about pirogues with cheese and some eggs and potatoes fried in bacon?"

"Sounds good to me," Jon replied, and then turned to Maria and said, "Is that alright with you?"

She nodded her head yes. Patrick went back into the kitchen and instructed the cook what to fry up, and then went to the bar and poured two fingers of whiskey for the two impatient men. They picked up their glasses and turned to Jon and said, "To our new arrival," and then slugged the whiskey down in one gulp.

Patrick was about to pour them another drink when Jon interrupted and said, "Before you have another drink on me, tell me what you two nice young Slovak boys were fighting about."

"Not only are they Slovak," Maria interrupted, "but they are also brothers."

"Brothers," Jon repeated, shaking his head in dismay. "But, why?"

"Let me explain it to you, Jon," Maria said. "You see Leo, the younger of the two is single, and Peter is married with three children. He continues to work in the mines in spite of the strike because if he didn't, his family would starve and be without shelter."

"Why doesn't Leo help him out?"

"He can't afford it because he hasn't worked in three months, and he has used up all of his savings."

Jon sat there for a moment and said, "Look, Leo, I am going to be doing some repairs on Maria's boarding house and I'll have to replace the window here you two just destroyed. How would you like to be my helper? I'll pay your room and board for one month at Maria's. Meanwhile, you can look for other work, or maybe I can get in touch with my cousins who went down river to work in the iron smelting mills, and see if there's work there. Is it a deal?" Jon said, extending his hand.

"How can I say no?" Leo said, grasping Jon's outstretched hand, shaking it vigorously, sealing the deal.

By the time they finished breakfast and were in the middle of finishing a couple of Irish coffees, the saloon was beginning to get rowdy. It was hard to believe that these were the same men they attended mass with. The atmosphere was filled with the smell of bad liquor, foul language, and women of ill repute.

"Come on, Maria, let's get out of here," Jon said, pulling her by the hand. "This is no place for a lady. Patrick," Jon shouted, who was busy behind the bar, serving shots of whiskey as fast as the men could throw them down their throats. "Where's the bill, Patrick? What do I owe you?"

"Nothing, this one's on me. Jon, visit me later on this evening. I'd like to hear more about where you learned to speak with an Irish brogue."

"Okay," Jon responded, waving goodbye as they exited the saloon.

CHAPTER 33

Roman inserted the five-round magazine into the butt stock of the Springfield rifle, pulled the bolt rearward and fired. He directed his aim at a scarecrow that was set up in the center of a cornfield outside Dubovica. All five of the bullets ripped through the cloth covered wooden stakes. One by one, fifty men took their turns until Roman was able to pick out the most accurate of the shooters. The remainder of the group were dismissed and assured that they too would play an important part in his scheme to free Mikhail. The next three days were spent in honing their marksmanship. Five hundred rounds of ammunition were expelled before Roman ordered them to stop. The remaining one thousand rounds would be saved. The spent cartridges were gathered up and taken to Mr. Sokolosky's blacksmith shop to be refilled with lead and ready to fire again.

It was early Sunday morning in the village of Kapusany where everyone was attending mass when Roman and Matt arrived mounted on two magnificent chestnut stallions that Roman brought from Poland. The crisp morning air was a refreshing reminder that summer was slipping away into that forest of the orange red death that would soon bring that knife called winter. They kept their horses at a slow trot and then kicked them into a gallop as they headed east. The fiery sun blinded them every step of the way until it vanished behind the mountain peaks that stood like sentinels over the castle that lay in ruins from a century of neglect. It stood in shambles on a high mound of dirt and rock at the edge of a dense green forest. They stumbled upon a steep dirt path that winded its way up to the rear of the castle. They dismounted, tied their horses to a tree, and then proceeded to climb to the top where they could get a clear view of the layout. When they reached the top, they were confronted by an old stone wall that was cracking and deteriorating from ages of pouring rain and ice cold winters. Roman had Matt boost him up on the top of the wall where he could get a strategic view of the grounds.

"What do you see?" Matt asked anxiously.

"I see barred windows. We're not going to be able to dynamite the dungeon wall without injuring Mikhail. Jozef said that he is the only prisoner being held captive. We are going to have to overcome the guards. That should be easy, seventeen men against three. We shouldn't have a problem, but escaping to the Polish border will be difficult. I have a plan that should help us."

"What exactly are your plans, Roman?"

"We will be back next Sunday evening just before sunset when the villagers are less alert from their Sunday drinking and dancing. We can do our maneuvering while there is still daylight and then by the time we're traveling north the sun will be sinking in the western horizon bringing the darkness that will help cover our escape in the event that we are being pursued by the Magyars. When we get back to Dubovica, I want you to ask Father Marin to make the church basement available to us where we can meet so that I can instruct the men what their duties will be. On the way back we'll stop at Sabinov and see if Jozef has any more information for us".

The church bells echoed faintly behind them as they raced at full gallop back to Dubovica where the decisions of Roman Polasky would determine the fate of Mikhail Yankovic.

Jozef was sitting behind his desk doing routine paperwork when the sergeant announced their arrival.

"I thought Sunday was a day of rest," Roman said jokingly to Jozef.

"Not in this business," he answered, looking up and then asked how things went for them at Kapusany.

"I think our venture will succeed," Roman answered empathically. "Overcoming the guards shouldn't pose too much of a problem, but getting to the Polish border might take some doing."

"Have you heard anything from Stasha?" Matt asked.

"No, nothing."

"How is her mother doing?"

"No change in her. The doctor's working on it. Look Roman, I was informed that a regiment of soldiers arrived in Presov yesterday. It might just be a routine army transfer, but I would like you to keep that in mind."

"I already have that worked out. I'm going to send another peaceful march to Presov similar to the one Mikhail organized, but this time to plead for the release of Mikhail. It's just a little diversionary tactic to keep the soldiers busy with them."

"We will make sure that the authorities at Caraffa Prison are made aware of the march so that they get the soldiers ready to confront them when they arrive. If by some misfortune they send soldiers to Kapusany, we will have seventeen repeating rifles aimed down their throats. We can make our escape down the path that leads to the forest where we can disappear and then head for the Polish border. Matt and I will have a horse ready to ride for Mikhail. Fifteen sharpshooters that I hand picked will stay behind and cover our escape. The soldiers will be easy pickings for our rifles that shoot five rounds of bullets from each magazine that can be replaced quickly by another."

"Sounds good to me Roman," Jozef said, reaching out to shake his hand. "See you in church next Sunday. After mass we will have a meeting in the church basement where I will give final instructions to the men."

When they arrived in Dubovica, Roman went to Andrew Valen's home where he was invited to spend the night. Matt stopped to see how Stasha's mother was faring. Dr. Dombrosky was attending to her when Matt entered the house.

"How's she doing Doc?" Matt asked anxiously.

"Still the same, I'm afraid," he answered, shaking his head.

"Have you heard anything about Stasha?"

"No, I haven't, but I did find this letter in Mrs. Ondreas' skirt pocket. It's a letter from Stasha. Here, read it," Doc said, handing the letter to him.

Matt unfolded it and began to read.

"Dear Mother,

Please forgive me. I'm sorry that I got myself in such a mess, I never intended for this to happen. It all started when I was looking to get Stefan to help get Jon's father and his friends out of prison. I really don't know what came over me. Father Marin forgave me at confession and now I hope that you too can forgive me. Please don't blame Stefan. He only did what I allowed him to do. Stefan will be taking me to Budapest to be married and then we will be going to Vienna where he will be stationed with the army until his enlistment is up. By the time that happens your grandchild will be two years old. Please write to Jon and tell him that I will not be coming to America."

CHAPTER 34

"Jon, why didn't you tell me about Stasha before?" Maria asked sheepishly as they were walking back to the boarding house.

Jon thought for a moment before he answered and said, "I don't know. It's been so long since I've heard from her," he paused for a moment and said, "I really don't want to talk about it, Maria, okay?"

"Of course Jon, I'm truly sorry. It was impolite of me to nose into your private life. Please forgive me."

Jon lowered his head and then looked up saying, "Oh hell, Maria, don't worry about it." He took her hand and said, "Let's hurry back to your place and I'll start working on some of the repairs I promised you I would do. I want to fix that front door and seal the windows before the cold winter comes. Meanwhile, you can get a fire started in the stove so that you can prepare some rice and ground pork wrapped in cabbage leaves and serve them for supper."

Jon opened the dilapidated door and entered the boarding house where they were greeted by a few of the boarders that were resting their weary bones from the long, tedious hours in the deep, dark, damp underground.

"Men," Jon shouted, "today Maria will be serving holubky. Supper will be on me tonight, so get some rest and be ready to eat at . . ." he looked over to Maria for confirmation.

"Three o'clock. It will be ready at three o'clock," she repeated, smiling and then she retreated into her bedroom.

Being a woman of her word, Maria started serving the meal at exactly three o'clock. Jon surprised the men by removing three bottles of homemade wine from his clothing bag that he brought along from the Maliks. The boarders were baffled by Jon's generosity and thoughtfulness.

After everyone had their fill of the delicious holubkies, Maria filled the miners' glasses with wine and raised her glass and said, "To Jon Valen" and then everyone shouted, "Jon," raising their glasses, emptying them in one swallow.

Jon just stood there, seemingly embarrassed by the reaction of the men. He composed himself and then shouted in a Clancy manner, "You can get off your lazy asses now and help Maria clean up the mess we made."

The men laughed at his orders and then began to collect the dishes and piled them up in the washtub that doubled as a dishwasher and for scrubbing the miners clothing.

After all was tidied up, the men lined up in single file and thanked Jon with a handshake and a hug in the Slavic fashion and then went outside to enjoy what was left of the last Sunday of the summer.

Jon bid the last man good bye and then asked Maria where the coal bin was.

"Out back," she replied. "Why?"

"Well, you're going to need coal for the stove and water from the pump."

"Why?" she repeated again.

"Because you are going to need to fill up the tub with water and then boil it so I can wash the dirty dishes."

"You wash the dishes? That's my job. That's why you pay me rent." Maria stood there dumfounded. Never had she met such a caring, respectful man.

"I'm going out back to get the coal while you fetch the water. Oh, Jon," she said before leaving, "there is a bucket behind the stove with a shovel that you can use to scoop the coal out of the bin. The bucket holds enough to fill the stove."

By the time Maria returned with the water, Jon already had the stove fire burning. "Here, let me help you," he said to Maria as she struggled to pour the water into the tub.

When it was filled, Jon lifted the tub onto the top of the hot stove. Maria could not believe her eyes as she watched this little man place the tub filled with dishes and water effortlessly onto the stove.

"I must have this man, and Stasha be damned," Maria thought as the blood raced to her face.

"What's the matter?" Jon asked, turning to her after he set the tub down.

"Nothing, why?" she stammered.

"Your face!"

"What about my face?"

"It's all red. Aren't you feeling well?"

"Don't be silly," she said, raising her eyebrows. "It's probably from the wine. That was powerful stuff."

"Yeah, I know. I'm still a little numb from it too. I never was much of a drinker. Hell, I still feel that Irish coffee I had at breakfast."

"Jon," Maria said, looking him straight in the eyes as she removed the large comb that held her hair up in a twist, and let it fall recklessly on to her shoulders, and then down to the middle of her back.

Jon's eyes were fixed on hers and softly he said, "Your eyes are so blue and your hair is like gold."

"That's the Polish in me. My mother is Polish." Before he could speak again, she said, "Jon, I have a problem. The front leg of my bed is broken, and it is so tilted I almost fell out of bed last night. Can you look at it while we are waiting for the water to heat up?"

"Sure"

Maria grabbed his hand and led him into her bedroom, closing the door tightly behind her and slid the door bolt to lock it.

Jon immediately got on his knees to inspect the damage. He could find nothing wrong on the right leg so he crawled on his hands and knees to the left side and found no broken leg there either.

"Maria," he shouted, turning to see where she was. "Maria," he whispered, "what are you doing?"

She was stripped down to her undergarments. Jon started to rise slowly as she pulled her left bra strap down off her shoulder exposing her breast.

"No," he pleaded.

Maria ignored his pleas and soon stood naked in front of him. He was flabbergasted as she stepped forward and touched him between his legs ever so gently as her wet lips caressed his, bringing him to a hardness that he never had known.

"You don't understand," Jon said shaking, his speech slurred. "You may not believe this, but I have never had a woman."

Maria's eyes sparkled. She grinned slyly and said, "Don't worry, I will show you how." She pulled him down on the bed and placed his hands forcefully onto her breasts. She reached down and unbuttoned his pants and removed his pulsating manhood and directed it into that fire that was burning like a churning volcano since the death of her husband.

Only thirty seconds had passed when both their bodies exploded prematurely, but with great satisfaction. It had been a long time coming for both. They lay still for a moment, trying to catch their breath and regain their strength.

Suddenly, there was a loud knocking on the door.

"Mama, Mama, are you in there?"

"Yes," she answered feebly.

"Mama, your water is boiling over."

"The children are back from visiting their aunt," Maria whispered, frantically grabbing for her clothes.

"I'll be right there, girls. The bedroom door has been sticking, so wait a moment. Mr. Valen is trying to fix it right now.

As soon as they were dressed, Maria asked the girls to pull on the door from the outside and then she held onto the doorknob slightly, making it feel like it was stuck. She waited for a few seconds and then let go of the knob, instantly swinging it open. Maria embraced her daughters and said that she was glad to see them.

"Now let Mr. Valen finish fixing the door while I clean up the floor."

As she turned to look for the mop, her hair disheveled and her blouse partially unbuttoned, a feminine voice snickered, "Well sister, you look like you've been having a roll in the hay."

Before Maria could respond, the front door flew open and a young boy shouted frantically, "Mrs. Novak, where are the men?"

Jon rushed out of the bedroom and said, "What is it, young man?"

"The men from the Nanticoke Colliery are on their way to the saloon."

"What for?" Jon asked curiously.

"I guess because most of the men here are working during the strike. They have clubs and some of them are carrying guns."

"Maria, you stay here with the children," Jon ordered, opening the door to leave. Before he closed it behind him, he said, "Maria, if you have a gun, load it."

When Jon arrived at the saloon, the men were shouting, "Scabs, Scabs," in several different languages. The mob was composed of Slovaks, Italians, Welsh, Hungarians, English, Irish, and Germans

Patrick was standing at the entrance of the saloon, and with a cool defiance said, "Now how can I help you lads? If it's a drink you need, you're all welcome to come in and have one on the house."

Jon shook his head, smiling at the sheer audacity of the Irishman. Jon pushed his way through the crowd and stood aside Patrick, and then shouted to the mumbling mob in reasonable English that he would pay for a second round of drinks.

The mob was nonplussed; their anger neutralized by the indifferent behavior of the tall red-headed Irishman, and the short stocky built Slav. For a moment they stood still and quiet, and then slowly they entered the saloon single file. When all the seats were occupied, Patrick brought out several more folding chairs from the back room, and then he told some of the men to step up to the bar and take a pitcher of beer to their respective tables.

After everyone was served, Patrick lifted his mug of beer and shouted, "To the success of the strike."

Jon stood there once more in amazement as the angry mob subsided to an attentive audience. Patrick waited until everyone drank a few rounds, and then called again for their attention and said, "Now what was it that you gentlemen wanted? You, young man," Patrick said, pointing to the table directly in front of him.

The young man stood up abruptly and said with defiance, "We are here to ask the men from this mine site to stop working so that we can apply enough pressure on the mine owners to give us what we have earned: better safety precautions, hospitalization benefits, and money for widows to have a decent burial for their husbands and children who die every day somewhere in the mines."

Patrick stuck his lower lip out and shook his head in agreement and said, "That sounds fair enough, lad, but clubbing the scabs won't get you what you want. That will only make things worse. You must sit down and talk with them. Here at my side is a newcomer. His name is Jon Valen."

Jon nodded his head to the crowd and then looked at Patrick as if to say now what. "Go on lad," Patrick said, turning to the young man that had previously spoken. "Tell Jon what you want."

"Only one thing . . . stop working. Then you can join us and help break the owners' backs for a change. Without coal production, we will hit them where they will hurt the most . . . in their bank accounts."

Jon listened attentively and then answered, "And what about the families who cannot subsist without having a paycheck? Who will provide rent for them and food for their children?"

"No problem, Mr. Valen. If they quit working we will all chip in and provide for those who need help."

"In all due respect," a voice spoke from the middle of the crowd in Slovak. "I know that you have only been here a short time, but by now you too must realize the terrible conditions we have to contend with."

"Yes, I agree that something must be done.

"But, what?"

"I will see to it," a voice rang out from the entrance door.

Everyone turned to see who had spoken.

"Father Karnovsky," Patrick said, "come up front and have your say."

As the Father worked his way to the front, "It's a Priest," reverberated through the whispering crowd. When he arrived at Jon and Patrick's side, he wasted no time and shouted, "Tomorrow morning we will all march to the mine headquarters in Wilkes-Barre and make our demands clear." He paused for a moment and then brushed his blonde wavy hair back that had been disheveled by his wild harangue and said in a deadly whisper, "If we cannot solve it peacefully, we will use force."

Before he left, he asked all to kneel and pray for God's help in their quest for fairness and equality as American citizens. "You men from Nanticoke, I will see that you have places to sleep tonight. You may use the church basement, and I am sure Patrick will find room for some of you right here in the saloon."

The orange red moon hung like an omen over the mining patch as the men rested, packed like canned sardines, in their assigned sleeping quarters.

CHAPTER 35

One by one, the men entered the candle lit basement of the church in staggered intervals so as not to arouse suspicion of Magyar spies that might be lurking in the village. Father Marin greeted each one of them with a pat on the back and told them to be seated.

After a half an hour, all the marksmen were accounted for, along with five men who were called to represent the marchers.

Roman directed himself first to the marchers and said, "I asked you men to be present here today so that I can explain my plans and how they have to be coordinated with me, Matt, and the fifteen men I have picked out to accompany us to Kapusany Castle. Matt and I spent time last Sunday afternoon at the castle to study the layout. There is a mountain path behind the dungeon entrance that should allow us to go unnoticed, giving us a chance to overcome the three guards without too much trouble.

"One guard will be sleeping while the other two are outside securing the front entrance, and covering the rear. We will try to free Mikhail without firing a shot. Gunfire might attract the attention of the villagers, or maybe Magyar soldiers in the area. I must assume these possibilities if we expect to escape to Poland. Now, you five men and the rest of your marchers are going to be a very important part of the plan. You will first be a diversion by getting the attention of the authorities at Caraffa Prison. Jozef told me last week that at least two hundred soldiers from Kosice marched into Presov and set up camp along the Torysa riverbank. Maybe it is just a routine army transfer, or they are onto our scheme. Whichever, we must assume the worst. So when you arrive at Presov, you must send two men with fast horses to keep watch on the army camp. If something suspicious looking comes up, like soldiers on horseback heading in the direction of Kapusany, one of the horsemen must try to beat them to Kapusany to warn us. The other would return to Caraffa where ten more men will be waiting to ride at full gallop to attack the Magyars' rear."

"Hold on Mr. Polsky," a voice shouted, interrupting Roman. "You said we are to attack the Magyars from the rear?"

"Yes, that's what I said."

"With what, if I may be so bold to ask."

"With your pitchforks and shovels," Roman answered laughing. "No, young man, you will all be supplied with a belt of dynamite sticks that will be buckled around your waists, and when you arrive there unnoticed, what a surprise it will be to the Magyars when your dynamite sticks are blowing their arms and legs off. All you have to do is light the short fuses and toss them in the midst of soldiers in close formations. Go now. You have three hours to prepare and get on with the march."

"Gods speed." Father Marin prayed, blessing them as they left to the sound of the church bells reminding the villagers that it was God's day of rest.

Matt put the Blahut brothers, Edward and William, in charge of the march. They were both high school graduates and strong of body from working the fields from the day they could walk. He gave them last minute instructions, kissed them on the cheeks, and sent them on their way to fight not only for the freedom of Mikhail, but for all the Slovaks that were imprisoned by some conqueror for a thousand years.

Before they marched off, Matt handed Edward a sealed envelop and asked him to take it to the Gypsy camp and see that it was delivered to Emile.

The streets of Presov were so quiet when the marchers arrived at Caraffa Prison; it made goose pimples stand up on their skin.

"Something's not right," the Blahut brothers said almost in unison. There wasn't one guard present at the main entrance.

"What will we do now William?"

"I'll knock on the door," William said, "while you go through the ranks and tell the men to be prepared for the worst and send a messenger to the Gypsy camp and ride swiftly to Kapusany to warn Roman and Matt."

William headed for the main gate while Edward gave instructions to the men. He told them that if there was any gunfire from the soldiers they should flee into the city streets and disperse in different directions and head for the Gypsy camp at the river.

"Do not use the same streets to escape." he repeated. "It will make it more difficult for them to fire at us if we are not crowded together."

William continued knocking on the main gate door, but to no avail; no one made their presence known. He turned and shouted to his brother to send someone back to the Gypsy camp and have the men ride as fast as they could to Kapusany. "Tell them not to forget the dynamite sticks."

The mountain peaks were rising swiftly in the west in their quest to hide the sun and bring the darkness that would cover the escape of Roman and his freedom fighters.

Roman sent Matt along with six other men to work their way to the front of the castle dungeon and then halted while the remaining nine climbed the dirt trail to the rear where Mikhail was secured by two guards.

Matt was instructed to send one of his men to approach the guard that was covering the front entrance and divert his attention while Roman and his men overcame the guards that were covering the rear. Once the rear guard was overwhelmed, Roman would force him at gunpoint to call for the other guard and then when both were disarmed, they would be led to Mikhail's cell where the third guard was sleeping.

"Halt!" the guard shouted, pointing his rifle at the lone figure that appeared suddenly from the steep stone step that led to the cracked marble floor of the courtyard.

"Don't shoot," the man shouted in a poor accented Hungarian. "Please," he continued, "all I need is water. I've been lost in the mountains for days."

The guard stood pensive for a moment and then slowly lowered his rifle with his right hand while he pointed with his left to a water pump that stood in the center of the courtyard. The man approached the pump, removed a tin cup that was hanging on a handle and filled it to the brim and then emptied it in one long swallow. It impressed the guard enough to ask him how long he had been lost.

"At least four days," he answered, while pretending to catch his breath.

"When's the last time you ate?"

"A couple of days ago."

"Wait a moment," he said, resting the rifle against the stone wall of the dungeon. He disappeared behind an iron gate that led to the inside. A short time later he arrived with a plateful of chicken paprika. When he looked up at the lost man, he found the barrel of a gun aimed straight at his face.

He made a gesture to shout, but the lost man pulled the bolt back on the rifle and pressed it against his forehead. The guard froze.

Roman snuck behind the guard and wrapped his left arm under his chin and then pressed a knife into his right kidney and whispered into his ear in his best Hungarian that if he moved he would rip his guts out.

"Now get me to Mikhail's cell," Roman commanded.

A short walk to a corridor led them to the cell where another guard was sleeping on a cot. Roman snatched the key to the cell that was hanging on a hook above the sleeping guard.

"Get up!" Roman shouted, shaking the guard violently. Soon Matt arrived with the front guard. All three were bound at their wrists and ankles, and then set side by side on the cot.

"Matt? Matt Sokolosky?" A weak voice called from inside the cell that was dimming from the rapid decent of the sun that was painting the sky black as it plunged into the liquid darkness of the infinite universe.

"Give me the damn keys!" Matt shouted as he pulled one of the guards by his hair off the cot.

"Calm down Matt," Roman said, pulling him away. "Here are the keys." The dungeon cell was dark, damp and slimy, smelling from human waste.

"Where is a lamp? Goddam, where is a lamp?" Matt shouted again impatiently.

"Right here," Roman said, as he removed it from a hook on the wall.

Matt raised the lamp at eye level and walked to the extreme corner of the cell where he found Mikhail naked, his body covered with bleeding sores and dirt so imbedded in his skin that it would have to be soaked and scrapped off with a knife. He was emaciated. His beard trickled down to his chest in a twist of filth and debris from all the days he spent in this bowel of hell.

Matt fell to his knees and pulled Mikhail up from the cold stone floor and embraced him and said, "Pleases forgive me. You put me in command and I failed you. I should have come after you sooner."

"No, Matt. There was nothing you could do. They already decided to take me prisoner and release Mr. Valen and his friends. Someone had already convinced the Magyars that I was the dangerous one."

"But who," Matt interjected.

"Father Marin," Mikhail answered sadly.

CHAPTER 36

The early morning miners' work whistle awakened the slumbering strikers.

"Come on, get up," a short burly built Italian man shouted as he ran about the church basement, arousing the men. "Hurry, don't you hear the work whistle?"

Suddenly, Father Karnovsky appeared and said, "Please stay calm. We will try to persuade the men to join us."

Five minutes later, in spite of Father Karnovsky's insistence on staying calm, the strikers were screaming, "Scabs, Scabs" as the miners were preparing to enter the cage that would bring them to the miserable, slimy, creaking gangways below.

Father counted thirty men and then asked if any one had gone down yet. They all shook their heads no. "Good then," Father said, relieved and then asked if they would join them in their quest to fight for better wages and medical care and whatever else was fair and required to improve their way of life in America.

"Isn't that why we came here? To find a better way of living than we had in our native lands?"

"But Father," a voice shouted from the cage, "I cannot do what you ask. My family needs my wages. We have debts at the general store. They will not supply us with food until we catch up. We have no food to feed our children."

"I know," Father responded, "and I promise you that everything will be taken care of. Your family will have food and shelter if need be."

The men looked at one another for approval and then said, "Okay, but . . ."

"Trust me," Father said, looking them straight in the eyes before they finished their sentence.

Twenty minutes later, Jon and Patrick caught up with the marchers, each carrying an American flag.

"On to Wilkes-Barre!" Patrick shouted, waving the flag back and forth in the cool morning air.

Women and children that were rummaging for coal on the culm banks cheered them on shouting, "We are Americans, not slaves!"

The sun was lifting itself out of the mountaintops, casting brilliant rays of light on the road before them. By the time they reached the city limits, their numbers grew to about three hundred men, women, and children. Maria also arrived brandishing a rifle. Jon gave her a stern look and snatched the rifle from her hands and asked her what the hell she was doing here.

"You told me to load my gun if I had one."

Jon just looked at her, shaking his head, and then ordered her to go to the rear where she would be safer.

She just smiled and said mockingly, "Of course, my dear," and then walked away laughing.

Jon just scratched his head and then turned to look for Patrick and found him with a wide grin on his face and asking what that was all about. Jon snapped, "Nothing."

Before Patrick could respond, a voice was heard screaming in the distance, "Go back! Go back!"

"What is it lass?" Patrick asked the young girl when she arrived out of breath from running.

"The coal and iron police are waiting for you. Please stop and go back."

"No, we cannot and we will not young lady," Father Karnovsky said, interrupting. "We are here to try and settle this peacefully."

She was surprised when she noticed the Roman collar around Father Karnovsky's neck. "You are a priest!"

"Yes I am, and hopefully my presence will assure the authorities that we are hear only to negotiate without violence. I'm tired of the injustices done to our miners. God willing, we will get our fair share. There will be no compromise, I promise you that." With that, he snatched the American flag from Jon's hands and shouted, "Justice for all Americans!"

Fifteen minutes later they arrived at the railroad station where the coal and iron police were lined up all along the loading platform with their rifles trained on the threatening marchers.

"Patrick, go home," a lone voice rang out.

"Who is that?" Jon asked curiously.

"My cousin Sammy McGovern."

"What the hell is he doing with the police?"

"He said it beat the hell out of crawling under the ground every day of his life."

Sammy leaped off the platform and walked along side of Patrick and Jon as the crowd continued to move in the direction of downtown Wilkes-Barre where the mining headquarters was located.

"What the hell are you doing here, Patty?" Sammy asked and then added, "Are you crazy? This is no concern of yours. You don't even work in the mines."

"What do you mean, lad? It is a concern of mine for two reasons: the first being it is wrong for the owners not to pay a decent wage and provide medical care and two, from a business point of view, I stand to make more money if the miners have more money to spend. Now get out of my way lad."

"Patty, please listen to me. We were given specific orders to fire on you with the slightest provocation."

"We came here to negotiate peacefully."

"Then why are some of the men carrying firearms and clubs?" he asked, his eyes searching the crowd.

"I guess they don't trust the son of bitches. Now get out of my way and don't worry about me. I'll be all right."

Sammy just shook his head and climbed back onto the platform and watched the crowd disappear into the city streets.

A few minutes later the county sheriff appeared backed up by a hundred state guardsmen and coal and iron police. Father Karnovsky put his hand up, signaling the marchers to stop and then walked forward and met the sheriff face to face. For a brief moment there was silence.

The sheriff finally spoke and said, "Look, Father, it is my job to keep the peace in this county."

"Fine," Father responded, "then you can first start by persuading the mine owners to come out and hear what we have to say."

He paused for a moment and then said, "Okay, but then you will march your people the hell out of here." The sheriff turned and walked to the mine owners headquarters.

Five minutes later, the sheriff arrived outside, accompanied by a well-dressed man. Father Karnovsky approached him with his hand extended. The man responded by shaking his hand and asking what he could do for them.

"We came here to ask for fair wages, medical compensation, and safer working conditions, for starters."

"Give me some specifics," the gentleman asked.

"A 15% wage raise and the right to pay and pick their own doctors, compensation money for widows so that they can at least pay the burial expenses for their family members who die in the mine accidents."

"All right, Father, I will relay this to my superiors and be back as soon as possible with their reply."

Fifteen minutes later, the gentleman was back and informed Father Karnovsky that his bosses would consider their demands only if they went back to work in the meantime."

"With all due respect, sir," Father said, with venom, "tell your bosses to go to hell. We want an answer now."

The gentleman turned abruptly with no reply and hurried back into the building.

"Well, what are we going to do now, Father?" Patrick asked.

"We are going to stay right here and not move until we get what we came for."

"Patty! Patty!" an excited voice shouted.

It was Sammy pushing his way through the crowd, begging his cousin to move out.

"I can't, lad. We came here with no thought of compromise."

"Well, will you at least let me escort the women and children out of here?"

"Yes," Jon said. "Do it now."

"Please, Patty, don't do anything foolish," Sammy pleaded as he turned to round up the women and children.

"Me? Do something foolish? Don't be silly," Patrick said with a big grin on his face, and then began to laugh as Sammy shook his head on his way to the rear of the crowd where the women and children were placed for their safety.

A half hour passed and still there was no word from the mine owners. Father Karnovsky's patience waned, and then suddenly he picked up an American flag and ordered the men to follow him to the main entrance of the mine headquarters. The sheriff and a dozen of the coal and iron police officers blocked the entrance, training their Winchester repeating rifles at the threatening crowd. The sheriff approached Father Karnovsky, wielding a handgun. He was soon pushed aside forcefully, causing the sheriff's gun to fire accidentally, hitting a miner between the eyes, killing him instantly.

CHAPTER 37

"What the hell was that?" Matt shouted as he helped Mikhail to his feet.

"It sounded like a gun shot," Roman answered as he helped Matt lift Mikhail.

"Can you walk?" Matt asked anxiously. "Are you strong enough? Look, put your arms around our shoulders. We will drag you if we have to."

"Hurry," Roman commanded, "the shots are getting closer."

The man that was the decoy at the front entrance came running into the dungeon shouting that the Magyars had both the front and rear covered.

"What will we do now, Roman?" Matt asked.

"I don't know. Let me survey the situation out there first. Meanwhile, take Mikhail to the rear where we had planned to escape. Give him plenty of water and see that one of these guards finds him something to eat. He has to get his strength up."

Roman went to the main gate and climbed a ladder that was attached to a wall that surrounded the castle that was originally built to keep invaders out. The only way to the wall was up a deep incline that also circumvented the castle. Roman estimated that there were at least a hundred Magyars carrying repeating rifles. In spite of the odds, Roman felt that they could hold off the soldiers long enough for the men at Presov to arrive as planned.

Matt came up beside him and asked what they would do now. First, Roman sent ten of the fifteen marksmen to the rear, and the rest up front. "We want our strength concentrated on the rear where we must escape under the cover of the forest and the darkness. Look Matt, the sun is going down fast," Roman said, pointing to the western mountain ranges that were fading in the glare of the sun. The men were placed in strategic positions on the wall and waited for the Magyars to attack.

A half hour passed and still no aggressive moves were made. "What's going on?" Matt asked anxiously.

"They know that they will lose a lot more men if they attempt to climb the incline, so what the hell, they'll just wait us out even if it takes a night or a week."

"Now what?" Matt asked, seemingly puzzled by Roman's no-care attitude.
"We'll wait too!"

"For what?"

"For our men in Presov to come to our rescue. While they're keeping the soldiers busy up front, we will concentrate all our fire power in the rear and hopefully encourage them to run."

"And if they don't?" Matt responded.

"Well, then I'll have to think of something else. Trust me, Matt, I will get us out of here alive and well."

The luminous moon rose, casting its light on the restless soldiers' camp beyond the castle wall. Fires dotted the encampment, and men could be seen dancing to traditional Hungarian music around the glowing embers.

"Matt," a voice whispered from the darkness.

"Well, Mikhail, you look a damn sight better," Matt responded.

"Yes, I feel better since I've eaten and drank water, but I think I was most replenished from the fresh air."

"Mikhail, are you sure it was Father Marin who betrayed you?"

"Yes, unfortunately."

"But why?"

"I don't know, Matt, I just don't know."

"Mikhail," Roman asked, "do you know how to fire a gun?"

"Yes, of course. I spent two compulsory years in the Magyar army."

"I want you to go back to your cell where we have the guards tied up and confiscate their guns and ammunition and go up front and help out."

Matt looked at Roman with disapproval and said, "Do you think that he is up to it?"

"He better be if he wants to get out of here alive."

Matt shrugged his shoulders and left to assist the men in the rear. The Magyars made several attempts to climb the incline, but were picked off cleanly by the marksmen. Realizing the futility of it all, they decided to wait. Roman and his men had a distinct advantage. They could observe their every move.

Suddenly, out of nowhere, came the sounds of gunshots and screaming men. One by one, they watched the Magyar soldiers running for their weapons as bullets rained down on them from every direction.

"What is it?" Matt asked Roman as he ran up front.

"I don't know. It can't be the men because all I hear is gunshots, and all they were equipped with was dynamite. Whoever it is, we have to take advantage of the situation. All of us will go to the rear and open fire down the hill and see if we can break their ranks, then we can get out on our own.

Eighteen men with repeating rifles stood at the top of the hill, firing nonstop for ten minutes. Bodies were falling backward down the incline from the spray of bullets, and then suddenly everything grew quiet.

Roman called for a cease-fire and then waited in silence to see what was coming next. Suddenly, a voice rang out from the darkness shouting to Matt.

"My God," Matt spurted out incredulously. "It's Uncle Emile. Yes, Emile, I'm here. What the hell are you doing here?"

"One of your men came to the camp and said they felt that you were in danger here, so I got a band of Gypsies together and we came to rescue you. Now, come on down and get going. Meanwhile, we will cover your backs."

The sound of dynamite exploding could be heard as the men made their way down the incline.

"Listen! The men are here! Let's move fast while the Magyars go looking for their body parts," Roman shouted as he led the men to the woods.

When they reached the bottom, they were met by Emile who immediately embraced Matt. When they released one another, Matt was embraced again, not knowing who it was, he stepped back.

"My God, Jozef, what are you doing here?"

"I'm going with you and hopefully to America to be with my brother. Sooner or later, the Magyars would catch up to me. It is time for me to go."

"Come on, come on, get moving fast," Emile shouted, waving his arms and pointing to the woods.

Roman led the way, with Jozef and Mikhail following close behind. Matt was stopped momentarily by Emile.

"Good bye Matt," Emile whispered in his ear as he embraced him heartily and before he released him said, "Don't ever forget where you came from and remember, a Gypsy was not born to be a slave".

CHAPTER 38

A cacophony of gunshots, breaking glass, screams of men, women, and children filled the air. The coal and iron police fired at random from the rooftop of the five-story Miners Headquarters building. Patrick relieved the sheriff of his handgun as he lay wounded in the shoulder from the reckless shooting of the police.

Father Karnovsky snatched the American flag from Jon, who stood paralyzed in disbelief. Miners were falling like autumn leaves in a wind storm all around him.

Father Karnovsky turned to the panicking crowd, raised the stars and stripes and shouted for justice, and raced towards the headquarters building, galvanizing the miners to follow him with wild abandon.

Seconds later, clubs were smashing windows as the miners climbed through the jagged glass onto the main floor in search of bloody revenge.

The police were racing down the stairway hoping to cut the miners off from reaching the rooftop where most of the police were strategically placed to wreak havoc on the mob. Patrick and Jon tried to keep some semblance of discipline. Patrick sent some of them through the main entrance, and Jon directed others to the rear of the building where they hoped to find stairs that led to the roof. Meanwhile, the police vacated their position on the roof and raced down the stairs to the second floor where they intercepted the miners, sending volley after volley of gunfire from the repeating rifles. One by one the men tumbled backward down the stairway, leaving the bottom a pile of torn and bloody bodies.

Jon and his men arrived too late to prevent the onslaught, but now the miners had the advantage and attacked the police viciously with axes, hammers, and clubs, sending them cascading down the stairway on top of the dead and wounded miners.

Father Karnovsky was outside caring for the wounded when Jon exited the building shouting, "Father! Over here!"

Father waved from the middle of the chaos. "What is it, Jon?"

"It's Patrick. He's been shot up pretty bad."

Patrick was slumped over the stair rail bleeding profusely from his neck and upper back. They gently lifted him off the rail and carried him to a sofa in the lobby and set him down flat on his stomach. Jon immediately began applying pressure to his neck to quell the bleeding while Father attended to his back wound.

"Jon," a voice called.

Jon turned to find Maria, accompanied by a large group of women.

"Maria!" Jon snapped. "What the hell are you doing here?'

"I came here to help. It's our fight too," she said, pointing to the other women. "Every one of these women you see either lost a husband or a son in the mines.

"Mrs. Novak," Father Karnovsky called, "I'm putting you in charge of attending to the wounded. Jon, you see to removing the dead. Transport as many as you can to the outside. Maria, set up a makeshift hospital here. Meanwhile I'll send someone out with a wagon to pick up as much medical supplies they can from the local drug stores and from the mine sites. Jon, get as many able-bodied men as you can to help you move the dead. But first, I want you to get the men to gather up all the guns from the coal and iron police that are lying dead or wounded. When that is done, I want you to go down to the basement with your newly acquired repeating rifles where I am sure you will find the mine owners and their associates cringing in a dark corner. Then we will make our stand using those fine gentlemen as hostages. One more thing, Jon, send a few men out with wagons and bring in as much food and water that they can muster up. I'm sure by now the Pennsylvania National Guard has been notified by telegram and will soon be on their way."

CHAPTER 39

"Emile." a voice shouted from the darkness in the woods.

"Over here."

A moment later one of Emile's men appeared, out of breath from moving at a fast pace between the trees.

"What is it?" Emile asked frantically.

"At the edge of the forest the open field is swarming with Magyars."

"Well, what do we do now?" Matt asked, slamming his fist against a tree.

"Don't worry," Emile said, patting Matt on the back. "I have another plan worked out." He took a deep breath. "It will cost a lot of money though."

"No problem," Jozef said, pulling a wad of money out of his jacket pocket. I've been saving for a long time. What did you have in mind Emile?"

"By the way," Matt said, interrupting them, "this is my Uncle from Presov."

"Pleased to meet you," Jozef answered, extending his hand.

"Well, aren't you surprised, Jozef?" Matt asked, baffled by his casual response.

"About what?" Jozef replied.

"About my uncle being a Gypsy."

"No!"

"You mean that you knew all along?"

"Of course, didn't you know that I served in the army with your father? He told me the whole story about the night at the dance hall where he first met your stepmother."

While Matt shook his head in dismay, Emile told them what he thought was a good plan. "First we must get back to Presov and wait for the right moment. There you can be dressed in Gypsy clothing so you don't draw the suspicion of the Magyars and then we'll head south to Budapest with a Gypsy caravan. There we will arrange for you to take the orient express to Paris and then to Calais where you will take a ferry across the channel to England where you can get a ship to America out of Liverpool."

"How the hell are we going to get by dressed like Gypsies?" Matt said laughing. "We'll be thrown in jail before the train leaves the station."

"I have that all worked out. Matter of fact, it just came to my head. First, I want you to strip the two guards of there uniforms, and then when we get into the encampment, I want you to strip the uniforms off of a couple dead Magyars. When we get to Budapest you can get on board as Magyar soldiers. I suggest that you look for a couple of dead officers."

"Uncle Emile, you are a genius!" Matt said, throwing his head back laughing.

The Magyars were laying in a bloody mess all over the encampment. Those that were still alive were in agony from the loss of limbs from the dynamite that the peasants tossed indiscriminately into their midst while the Gypsies' repeating rifles decimated the chaotic flight of the remaining soldiers.

Matt and Jozef, in their search for Magyar uniforms, found three officers hiding in one of the tents.

Jozef politely asked them to remove their uniforms and then told them to turn around. He shot them in the back of their heads.

Matt just stood there stunned, surprised by the cold blooded assassination of the officers.

Mikhail didn't seem shocked at all. Seeing the look on Matt's face, he said, "Matt, it had to be done."

"Why?"

"Because if they recognized Jozef, it would put our escape in jeopardy. Now no one will know that he helped me escape."

The Gypsies were waiting on the outskirts of Kapusany with a caravan of wagons that transported Jozef, Matt, Mikhail, and Roman to their camp in Presov.

CHAPTER 40

Father Karnovsky was attending to Patrick's wound when he heard a clamor of loud voices and stumbling men. He turned and found a few of the men that he had sent to search out the mining officials in the basement pushing and pulling them through the lobby.

"Enough," Father shouted at the men and then he pointed to a sofa and several chairs and told them to sit. "You fellows can leave now," he said, looking at the miners who had to be restrained from further physical damage to the officials. They stood silent for a moment, staring menacingly until Father once more commanded them to leave.

When the last man had closed the door behind him, he turned to the four officials and said, "Look around you. Look at Patrick here. All of this bloodshed because your bosses will not give the miners a fair wage or medical compensation and a pittance of money to bury their loved ones in a civilized manner. Loved ones who die in mines every day because of lax safety precautions. Tell me, sir, do you really think this treatment is fair and just?" Father asked, addressing the man who he first negotiated with outside.

"I'm just doing my job," the man answered.

"What is your name, young man?" Father asked, extending his hand to the young man who seemed genuinely stressed.

"My name is Hopkins. Jonathon Hopkins," he answered as he shook hands very gently with Father Karnovsky. "I know the conditions of the mines, I have been through them. I agree wholeheartedly. They are hell on earth. I would not work in them for a fair wage. But what can I do? I am employed by them and I have a family to support, too."

"Are you a Christian?" Father asked.

"Yes, I am," he answered firmly.

"So then you believe in the teachings of Christ, do you not?"

"Yes, of course, but sometimes it is difficult to abide by his teachings."

"Yes, especially when the comfort and well being of your life is threatened," Father added sarcastically.

Jonathon jumped up from his chair and said, "Father, I understand what you are saying, but I don't have the courage that you have. Do you realize what a predicament you are putting yourself in? We know that the Archdiocese Hierarchy in Philadelphia does not approve of the Catholic Clergy getting involved in the labor affairs. Are you aware that you can be excommunicated from the church for your actions?"

"Yes I do, and I am willing to risk that in the name of justice, and to the presumption that all men are created equal in the eyes of God and the Preamble of the Constitution of the United States of America. That is why we came to this country dammit, to escape from that kind of tyranny. All I am asking you to do is to convince them that what we are asking will not only be fair, but that in the long run they will make even more money. It will give the miners more incentive to work harder and be more productive."

Jonathon sat down slowly and said, "Alright, I will approach them with that argument. It sounds reasonable and I don't think my loyalty will be questioned when I present it to them in that context. What do you think, gentlemen?" Jonathon asked, turning to his other associates. They bowed their heads in approval.

The hours passed by quickly while the men and woman labored at caring for the wounded and piling the dead into wagons to be taken back to their respective mining patches so that they could be given a decent Christian burial.

The sun escaped beyond the western horizon without the slightest notice. The late autumn air brought cold winds into the embattled scene, forcing the men and woman to look for a place to keep warm. Those who found blankets covered the wounded men and the children that had joined in to help. Little by little, miners and their families arrived from other mine sites to pitch in.

Father Karnovsky greeted them with open arms and "God bless you." As the evening wore on more of the wounded died from lack of proper medical treatment and medicine. Most of the wounds were bound with material that was cut from the women's undergarments.

Around nine o'clock, a man rushed into the headquarters building, shouting that the telegraph office received a message that the National Guard would be arriving here before midnight.

CHAPTER 41

It was early December and the snow was falling graciously on the already frozen Danube River. The streets of the inner city of Pest were clamoring with young women dressed in their Sunday best and elegant gentlemen parading in their fur-collared great coats. Horse-drawn carriages crowded the avenues while an occasional black lacquered sleigh drawn by black horses with silver tackle cramped with passengers wrapped in fur lined blankets raced past with reckless abandon. Christmas was in the air, infecting the populace with gaiety and joy. Buda's view across the river with its great designer buildings and magnificent bridges most surely earned its comparison with Paris.

Stasha stepped down from the carriage onto the soft snow-filled street. It was ten in the morning and the inner city was bustling with merriment of the shoppers.

"I'm sorry," the coachman half-whispered as Stasha closed the door of the carriage, and then with one lash of the whip the horses dashed off and disappeared into the gusty wintry day. She stood frozen for a moment to absorb the magic aura that permeated Vaci Street, where the shopping district sparkled with its array of fashionable stores that sold the finest goods from London and the sweet-scented smells of Paris's fancy-cut bottles.

The snow had ceased, but gusts of wind raced wildly through the streets, blowing frozen snow dust like particles into Stasha's face. Her broad peasant skirt slipped across the snow above her ankle length black boots as she walked swiftly, looking for a place to escape the cold.

"Thank God!" she shouted as she saw the sign for a coffee house hanging over an entrance.

"May I help you, young lady?" a voice asked politely as Stasha entered the waiting room.

"Yes Ma'am," she answered with her teeth chattering.

"Come, miss, and sit here at this table and I will bring you something hot to warm you up."

Just as she finished removing her black-soaked kerchief from her head, the waitress set a cup of hot chocolate down on the table and then asked her what she would like to eat.

"We are still serving breakfast. How about an egg omelet sprinkled with paprika?" she suggested.

Before she could respond, the waitress scurried off into the kitchen. Stasha just smiled and decided to remove her wet shawl and handbag that was strapped to her shoulder. She opened the hand bag and reached deep into the bottom and scooped up a handful of coins which she hoped would be enough to pay for breakfast and have some left for her train fare.

The coffee house consisted of round metal tables that sat four chairs around, hugging both walls from front to back. The greater percentages of customers were men dressed in dark sack suits and donned black derby hats that were the fashionable dress of early nineteen hundred Budapest. While Stasha's eyes surveyed the scene, the waitress appeared with her omelet, set it down and said, "Enjoy."

Stasha lingered as long as she could, giving her body a chance to warm up for her trek to the train station that was several blocks away.

"Will that be all, miss?" the waitress asked, while Stasha was putting on her shawl and kerchief.

"Yes ma'am," she answered while at the same time handing her a handful of coins that she had retrieved from her handbag earlier. "Will that be enough to pay the bill?"

"I guess it will have to be, won't it, young lady?"

"Oh no," Stasha replied, digging into her handbag, searching for more coins. All she could come up with was one lone coin. She reached out to hand it to her, but was interrupted by the waitress's hand pushing her away.

"It looks like you need it more than me. You keep it and God bless you." With that said she walked away and disappeared into the kitchen.

The street traffic was getting busier by the minute as Stasha made her way through the walkway that led into the various shops that lined Vaci Street on both sides. Walking became easier as the shopkeepers shoveled the excess snow onto the street. Occasionally, gentlemen tipped their derby hats and greeted her "Good morning." The shop display windows that presented the latest fashions from London and Paris slowed her progress. The cannon shot from the Citadel exploded, reminding the populace that it was noon just as Stasha arrived at the West Railroad Station.

People were milling about, waiting for their scheduled trains to arrive. She found a seat close to the ticket booth, removed her shawl and kerchief and then sauntered over to the ticket booth and inquired as to when her train would be departing for Presov. He informed her that it would be leaving on track two at two o'clock.

"Two at two," she thought to herself. "Well, that should be easy to remember." She sat down and was suddenly overcome with fatigue. Her eyes closed and her thoughts raced back into time . . . into a time that was filled with one calamity after another. Her mind drifted back to the days that she and Jon spent on the ledge and then the night Stefan walked her home after her sixteenth birthday party.

"How weak and stupid I was," she said out loud.

"Stupid? Why young lady, you sure don't look stupid to me. In fact, you appear smart and also beautiful."

Stasha opened her eyes and found a handsome young man of about twenty-five years grinning from ear to ear.

"Excuse me sir, but I don't think that we have ever met," Stasha snapped indignantly, her dark eyes flashing from the sunlight that peered through the waiting room.

"Forgive me, miss, ah Miss . . . ."

" . . . Ondreas," Stasha answered, filling in the silence.

"I just couldn't keep my eyes off of you when you were at the coffee shop."

"You followed me from the coffee shop?" Stasha said, raising her eyebrows and throwing her head back, causing her blue-black hair to tumble down onto her shoulders.

"My God, you have beautiful hair."

"Enough, whatever your name is."

"My name is Gabor, Karol Gabor, Miss Ondreas."

"You can call me Stasha," she answered, her voice softening to a more civilized tone.

"Stasha Ondreas," he said. "Hmm, that most certainly is Slovak. I knew at first sight that you weren't Hungarian. Not with that dark black hair and that poorly accented Hungarian that you speak. Tell me, Stasha, where are you traveling to?"

"To Presov."

"Wonderful! because that is where I am going. I'm visiting my brother and his wife who is Slovak. Look, allow me to purchase the tickets for us and then I will keep you company."

Stasha thought about it for a moment. "Why not?" she answered.

CHAPTER 42

The men and the women labored through the cold black December night trying to bring some sort of semblance into the insanity that beset them. Dead bodies were piled two and three rows high, forming a barrier that would act as a buffer between the oncoming national guardsmen and miners that were placed strategically on the first floor of the headquarters and on the rooftop.

The sun was leaking through the crisp thick morning mist when the roar of the steam engine could be heard breaking the deadly silence as it slithered into the railroad station like a prehistoric serpent. Guardsmen clad in dark blue uniforms and donning garrison hats hustled in disciplined unison onto the street. Two hundred men strong gathered, forming lines of ten from front to rear. It was a formidable sight placing fear and doubt into the miners.

"Father Karnovsky, they are here."

"Yes, I see. How many?"

"I would guess about two hundred or more, and all with repeating rifles."

"Have you seen any cannons?"

"No, but they could be back at the train station on flat cars."

"Mr. Hopkins?"

"I'm over here, Father."

"Are you ready to negotiate?"

"Yes!"

"Remember, no compromise."

"I have written down all of your demands," Mr. Hopkins said, leafing through his notebook.

"Good!" Father said enthusiastically, slapping him vigorously on the back and then turned and shouted, "Mrs. Novak."

"Yes, Father," Maria replied as she turned while replacing a blood soaked bandage on one of the wounded.

"When you are finished there, I want you to go outside and inform the mine bosses that we have Mr. Hopkins and his associates in here and we would be very pleased if they came back with you to discuss our demands."

Maria finished attending to the wounded miner and then hurried out the front entrance where she found the guardsmen standing in military readiness, poised to fire their rifles upon command. Hundreds of miners' wives and children surrounded them in intimidating silence.

Fifteen minuets later, Maria returned with a dumpy little moon-faced man dressed in a black suit and a silver tie accompanied by two grotesque looking giants, each with their hands in their pistol pocket.

"How can I be of service to you, Father? Maria told me that you wish to negotiate a fair deal policy. Oh, let me first introduce myself, my name is Pennypacker. You may call me Henry."

"Pleased to meet you sir. Now why don't you sit down over here with Mr. Hopkins, who I am sure you are familiar with, and begin with the negotiations."

"That won't be necessary, Father. We've come here to take Jonathon and his assistants off your hands. We will take him to the president of the Mine Owners Association and discuss your demands with him and then we will get back to you with our decision."

Father just looked at him, shaking his head angrily in disgust and then snatched the notebook from Mr. Hopkins hands and said, "Here, Henry, examine these now. You go to your bosses and tell them they have until noontime to reply."

"I don't think so," the two bodyguards replied in unison, drawing their pistols.

"I think so," Jon Valen whispered as he pressed the barrel of the rifle on the nape of the little man. The two ogres spun around to answer the threat, but were met with two more rifles staring them in the face.

"Now drop your pistols and get your asses out of here and do what Father asked of you. Move out now," Jon shouted, while several rifles were trained on them. As they entered the streets, they could sense the chaos that was brewing between the guardsmen and the families of the miners.

CHAPTER 43

The train arrived in Presov at 5:00 PM. Stasha and her new gentleman friend were making their way through the station exit onto the street that was fading into the dusk. Men with long poles were stretching their arms high to light the gas lamps that lined the main avenues.

"Where to now, Stasha?" Karol asked, taking a deep breath.

All the way to Presov they had partaken in idle conversation. Stasha appeared to be preoccupied and Karol, being the gentleman that he was, politely tolerated her unsocial behavior. Karol suggested that they find a place to dine. Stasha shook her head in agreement and then he hailed a taxi.

Fifteen minutes later they stepped out in front of one of the most elegant restaurants in Presov. Stasha balked for a moment, complaining that she didn't think that she was dressed properly for such a fancy place.

He replied that her beauty would surely distract onlookers from noticing her lack of proper attire.

"You're certainly intent on charming me into submission. But let me warn you, I have had enough of men. So please don't waste your time."

"Maybe you had the wrong kind of men."

"Well, yes and no. I had one good one and one bad one. Like the idiot I am, I let the bad one destroy me."

"Where is the good one?"

"In America waiting to get financially settled before I join him."

"So, you will be going to America to be with him?"

"No, I don't think so. I am no longer worthy of him. I love him too much to do that."

Karol just raised his eyebrows, shaking his head and said, "I find it difficult to believe that you could have done something so bad that you feel unworthy. What did you do that was so terrible?"

"You don't want to know, believe me, you really don't."

"Come right this way," the hostess said, interrupting their conversation, quickly leading them to a table.

Karol was right about Stasha's peasant attire being no distraction. Men were stretching their necks and straining their eyes, much to the chagrin of their ladies to get a more examined view of the dark-haired beauty.

Stasha noticed the attention and took it with mixed emotions. She never really gave much thought about her looks. Jon and she had been attracted to each other at a very young age. They enjoyed one another's company at a time when physical appearance wasn't a factor.

Of course Karol was ecstatic over the attention she was getting. It was a feather in his cap. He was the envy of all the men. Just as Stasha made a gesture to speak, Karol called to a boy at the entrance to come over to the table.

When he arrived, Stasha noticed that he was carrying a bundle of newspapers.

"I'll have one," Karol said, snatching a paper off the top of the pile, at the same time tossing him a few coins that the boy deftly caught in midair. "Wow! Look at this," he said, turning the front page towards Stasha so that she could read the headlines.

It read: Band of Gypsies and Chief of Police break political prisoner out of jail at Kapusany Castle.

Karol began reading the story out loud to Stasha.

"Jozef Valen, Chief of Police of Sabinov was the apparent mastermind of the escape of Mikhail Yankovic, who was being held prisoner at Kapusany Castle. He was aided by a band of Gypsies. The authorities were informed of the plan to free him by the pastor of St. John, the Baptist Roman Catholic Church in the village of Dubovica. He named Jozef Valen and a Polish patriot by the name of Roman Polsky that was hired by Chief Valen to help in training a handful of peasants to accomplish the task."

"My God!" Stasha gasped.

"What is it Stasha?"

"Jozef Valen is my fiancé's brother. What else does it say?"

"Well, let's see. Oh yes, here is where I left off. A trap was set up at Kapusany. A hundred soldiers were sent to there and the plan was to allow them to enter the dungeon area and then close in on them where they would be hopelessly outnumbered. Everything was going as planned, when suddenly out of nowhere sticks of dynamite were tossed into their midst and a barrage of bullets from their rear poured into their ranks, killing most of the men. Some of the survivors pretended to be dead and overheard the conversations between the Gypsies and Roman Polasky's men. One of the men also witnessed the cold-blooded killing of officers by Chief Valen. Late last night the Gypsy camp in Presov was raided by the local police, but none of the guilty men were to be found."

"Enough," Stasha pleaded. "You must get me to Dubovica now, please Karol."

"Yes, of course," he said without hesitation. "Waiter, my check please," he shouted.

Five minutes later they were outside hailing a cab. It was pitch dark with the clouds covering the Milky Way like a shroud. The snow had ceased. But the wind was cold and icy, making traveling arduous for the horses that pulled the carriage. Karol convinced Stasha that she should spend the night at his brother's house and he promised to get her on her way at the crack of dawn after a hearty breakfast.

CHAPTER 44

Clancy was sitting down at one of the tavern dining tables reading the Sunday morning newspaper when he heard a knock on the door.

"Yeah, come on in," he hollered, "the door's open."

When Paul Malik and his wife Ana entered, Clancy showed no surprise at all. He pointed for them to sit at the table and then said, "Well, what are we going to do now? According to this morning's newspaper, the miners have twenty-four hours to release the hostages they are holding or face the consequences."

"What can they do to the miners without placing the hostages in danger?" Paul asked.

"I think that they are counting on the priest that is in charge to back down because he wouldn't think of risking human lives."

"What do you think, Clancy?"

"I think that before this priest decided to take charge he was fully aware of the consequences. I'm sure that he is prepared to fight to the death and that the men following him feel likewise. I've seen priests like him in Ireland."

"Clancy," Ana interrupted, "what can we do to help Jon?"

Before Clancy could reply there was a knock on the door. Paul got up and opened the door and saw the carriage driver that brought them from the ferry.

"Oh my God, young man, I'm so sorry! I completely forgot about you. Please bring the luggage in," Paul said apologetically. After the job was done, Paul tipped the man generously.

"Well," Clancy said, shaking his head, "when are we leaving?"

"You have exactly an hour and a half to get packed and get to the train station," Paul answered as he looked at his pocket watch.

At twelve noon, the train pulled away from the station huffing and puffing, the whistle screeching as Ana stood and watched with tears running down her cheeks. Clancy had convinced Paul that their quest to help Jon would be too dangerous to take Ana with them. He further argued that it would be better for Helen not to be left alone.

New York City evaporated behind the eastern horizon as the train engine struggled to reach its top speed. For the first half hour they exchanged pleasantries, and then got down to the business of Jon. Clancy pulled out a handful of letters from his coat pocket that Stasha had sent Jon from Budapest. Of course, Clancy was curious as to what that was all about.

"What was Stasha doing in Budapest?"

"All I can tell you, Clancy, is what my brother wrote to me, and I'm sure there is more to it than meets the eye. According to my brother, Stasha got pregnant from Stefan Nagy, a Magyar army officer. Her mother found out and murdered Stefan. When they found Stasha's mother she was in some sort of coma state. She's conscious, but her mind won't accept the reality around her. Meanwhile, Stasha disappears. They put finding Stasha on hold until they pursued the task to free Mikhail from Kapusany Castle, which I was told was made possible by your generous monetary contribution. They thank you, and I thank you," Paul said, exuberantly while he embraced Clancy.

Embarrassed by all the praise, Clancy shouted, "All right already, so what about Mikhail?"

"The last I heard was that they spent a day scouting the place and then made the final plans to free him."

"Well, that explains why the letters were coming from Budapest."

"Clancy, Jon is going to be crushed by the news of Stasha. How are we going to tell him?"

"Before we say anything to him, let him read the letters first. Okay?"

"Yes, that's a good idea, Clancy."

"Your tickets gentlemen," a deep baritone voice asked.

They looked up and were confronted by a tall black man dressed neatly in a black uniform. Paul reached into his pocket and handed the porter both of the tickets, but before that he punched them, he noticed that there was an extra one.

"You have one too many tickets here, sir. Is the other gentleman with you? Perhaps he went to the restroom?"

"No, no," Paul replied, reaching and snatching the ticket from his hand, "No, this ticket was for my wife, and at the last moment she had something important come up and couldn't come along. What do I do with this ticket now?"

The porter reached into his inside pocket and handed him a New York-Pennsylvania Railroad lines business envelope.

"Put the ticket in here and then write your address on the envelope and I will take care of the rest."

"Don't bother porter. I'll take the ticket a voice rang out."

"Well, Doctor Ginsberg. Where the hell are you going?" Clancy asked laughing.

"With you. From what I've been reading there is a lot of wounded people that need medical attention. I'm also concerned about Jon."

"Thank you porter," Doc said taking the ticket from him. "Now, could you give us any information on what's going on in Wilkes-Barre?"

"The last I heard, sir, was that the National Guard was called in and will attack the building if they don't send the hostages out before the nightfall today. It's possible that our train will not be permitted to unload passengers if there is any fighting going on when we arrive. More than likely we will have to drop the Wilkes-Barre passengers off at Ashley, just outside the city. Trolley cars can be dispatched to transport you into Wilkes-Barre."

"Ashley," Paul shouted. "Why, that's where Jon's mine site is located and where he lives. Surely someone there can tell us where we can find him."

"How long before we get there?" Clancy asked, turning to the porter.

"About four hours. We should arrive right around sundown."

Heavy snow was battering against the windows of the rocking passenger cars when the porter's voice rang out that arrival time in Wilkes-Barre would be in fifteen minutes.

Paul and Clancy looked out the windows and watched the artist of winter paint the black culm banks with wind-blown streaks of white snow, giving the viewers a false impression of the ugliness that hid behind its superficial beauty.

CHAPTER 45

Stasha was welcomed with open arms after Karol introduced her in Slovak to his sister-in-law, Francine. She offered her a chair to sit down in and then asked her where she was from.

"Dubovica," she replied.

"Dubovica, My God!" she shouted, slapping her hands briskly on her thighs. "Why, I am from Sabinov, only a short distance from your village. How old are you Stasha?"

"I was just seventeen this past summer."

"Well, that explains why I didn't know you when I was growing up in Sabinov. Hell, I was married the year that you were born. I once had a terrible crush on a boy from Dubovica. I found out years later that he became Chief of Police in Sabinov."

"What," Stasha responded, flabbergasted. "You don't mean Jozef Valen, do you?"

"Yes, I do. Why, do you know him?"

"I'll say I do. He is my brother-in-law to be, or more honestly was."

"If he was half as handsome as Jozef, I grieve for your loss. What happened?"

"It's a long story. Let me just say this; it was my fault and for now let's just leave it at that. Right now I have more important things on my mind. Friends of mine from Dubovica are in great danger with the Magyars, and I must do what I can to help them."

"What did they do?" Francine asked curiously.

"Here, read this," Karol said, handing her the newspaper.

After reading the story, she set the newspaper down on the mantel of their warm glowing fireplace and said, "I remember reading about this Mikhail person. They said that he was a revolutionist that was trying to gain complete freedom from the Empire."

"Not exactly. All we want is to be able to speak our language and keep our traditions intact. Mikhail, who was one of my teachers in high school, told us that when the language is gone, so goes the culture, and then in time the Slovaks will be a dim light in history."

"I don't believe that," Francine snapped. "I'm married to a Magyar and since then my quality of life has vastly improved."

"Well, Francine, I would rather be a simple Slovak peasant girl working in the fields than be an arrogant Magyar woman."

There was fire in Stasha's eyes, encouraging Karol to step in between them and change the subject.

"Look Francine, I would really appreciate it if you could provide a sleeping room for Stasha tonight. We will be off to Dubovica long before you awaken."

Francine took a deep breath, composed herself and said, "Of course, dear brother-in-law, anything for you. Follow me," she said to Stasha calmly.

Just as they turned to climb the stairs, the front door opened and there stood a Magyar soldier shouting, "We caught the ring leader, Roman Polsky. He was trying to sneak back into Poland. Wait until you hear this, my darling wife. That fellow that you had the hots for before you knew me was witnessed killing a couple of our officers."

"Not Jozef Valen, darling?"

"Yes, police chief of Sabinov."

Stasha passed out fully clothed. Even her deep sleep would give her no rest from her tormented soul. Her dreams floated back to the cool crisp mountain lake where she and Jon bathed in the luxury of childhood innocence.

The sky suddenly grew dark and there were no sparkling stars or incandescent moon to warm her heart. There was only the darkness where evil lurked.

She saw a black horse mounted by a Magyar soldier laughing fiendishly as he rode off into the bowels of hell with tongues of flames surrounding him as she bid him farewell with, "Remember, I still love Jon."

CHAPTER 46

Paul, Doc, and Clancy got off the train carrying two light bags that contained changes of underwear and articles for shaving and of course their toothbrushes. Doctor Ginsberg also had his medical bag gripped firmly in his right hand. The snow contributed to slowing down the negotiations. For the soldiers to attack now would be suicide. Visibility was non-existent and clearly on the side of the miners that were holed up in the headquarter building.

"Hey lad!" Clancy shouted to a soldier that was standing at attention as they reached the street.

"Yes sir," the soldier snapped, "how can I help you?"

"Well, first of all I would like to know what's going on. Has there been any progress in the negotiations?"

"No sir, the miners are being stubborn. It looks like we are going to have to get after them when the weather clears."

"Where is the building located?"

"Just down the street two blocks, and then take a right. You can't miss it. But I wouldn't advise you to go down there now."

"Are there many wounded?" Doc asked.

The soldier glanced down and noticed the initials M.D. printed on the side of Doc Ginsberg's bag.

"Well, I'll tell you this, Doc, you're going to need a regiment of doctors to tend to all the wounded. There are bodies lying all over the place inside and outside the building. Goddamn Doc, someone has got to stop this. I have two brothers in the building. My mom lost our father in the mines. She couldn't bear to lose one of her sons too. Hell, that's why I joined the Guards."

"We'll see what we can do soldier," Clancy said, patting him on his shoulder.

After a grinding walk down the two blocks of deep snow and blowing winds, they finally arrived at their destination. The snow settled down to a light fall that improved visibility. They couldn't believe their eyes. Bodies were strewn all over the street that led to the headquarters building.

Someone shouted for them to halt. Another guardsman appeared and asked them what their business was.

"Well," Clancy replied, "if you could direct us to the man in charge, we might be able to put a stop to this bullshit."

"Yes sir," the guardsman snapped, holding back laughter at the brashness of the Irishman as he led them to the main tent where Colonel Smith was having a meeting with the mine officials.

"Colonel Smith, sir," a voice shouted from outside the tent, "there are three gentlemen here with me that said they could be of some service to you in the negotiations."

There was silence for a moment, and then he said to send them in. The colonel and two of his military aides rose as they entered, and invited them to take a seat aside of the two mining officials. After everyone shook hands and introduced themselves, the colonel asked them what they had to offer.

"No," Clancy shouted, "what do the mine owners have to offer? All you have to do is compromise. If you give those miners half of what they are asking, that would be a vast improvement. For chrissake laddies, what the hell is the big deal? How much goddam profit do you have to make? You're all living like kings now in your fancy mansions with the miners' sweat and blood. Just give them a fair wage."

"And let them have access to medical treatment," Doctor Ginsberg said, interrupting. "Look," the Doctor said, "while you are having this discussion, may I please leave here and attend to the wounded?"

"Of course," the colonel responded. "the guardsman that brought you here will show you the way."

After Doctor Ginsberg left the tent they continued to try and solve the problem.

"Gentlemen, may I ask what concern is this of yours. Who sent you here? Are you from the union? Are you government men?" With that said the colonel sat down and waited for an answer.

"This may come as a surprise to you, but we are here because we have a mutual friend that is part of this strike," Paul answered. "Like my friend Jon I came here to better myself to find a future that I would never have had in Slovakia.

"All right," one official shouted, "fine, sign and seal the agreement, and you deliver it."

CHAPTER 47

Stasha sat across the kitchen table staring with disbelief at her mother. Her eyes were wide open but oblivious to the presence of her daughter, who had been absent from her life for months.

Stasha walked around the table and embraced her and said, "Mama, Mama. What have I done to you? I'm so sorry, please forgive me."

"Forgive you for what?" Karol asked as he entered the kitchen.

"Look at her."

"Yes, I see that she is in some sort of hypnotic state. But what does that have to do with you?"

"Do you remember the story I told you why I was out on the streets in Budapest?"

"Yes, you told me that you were running away from a wealthy Hungarian family that you were serving as a housemaid because they treated you cruelly."

"Well, I lied. The truth of the matter is that I became pregnant by the son of this wealthy family, while my fiancé, Jon Valen, was in America waiting to send for me as soon as he was financially able. He was only gone a few months when I gave in to the sexual advances of Stefan Nagy, a Magyar soldier, not once but a multitude of times until I became impregnated with his child." Stasha halted for a moment to catch her breath.

"And then what?" Karol asked.

"Well, then my mother found out just about the time that I had told Stefan that I was carrying his child, and that I wanted to kill it and myself. He convinced me that I had no right to do that because it also was his child. He said we would be married as soon as possible before anyone took notice. I agreed and that I would have to tell my mother. He insisted that he would tell her after we were married and living in Budapest with his parents. We told Father Marin, my pastor, about our predicament, and then he married us secretly one late night in the rectory. From there, Stefan transported me to Budapest with his family, and then went to see my mother, told her about our marriage, and that she would soon be a grandmother. My mother became outraged and went to the kitchen cabinet where my late father kept a loaded pistol and emptied all the bullets in his body. Jozef Valen investigated the case and could find no proof of who committed the murder, or at least that's what he told the Magyar authorities. I suspect that he knew all along, but was covering up for her. Stefan was long overdue in coming back from seeing my mother. One late evening a Magyar officer arrived at the house to inform his parents of what had happened.

"'Where is his body?' Mrs. Nagy pleaded.

'We don't know. The person upon discovering the body reported it to the chief of police of Sabinov, who happened to be in Dubovica visiting his family. When they came back to the house, the body was gone.'

"I suppose when Jozef saw the state my mother was in, he realized that she murdered Stefan."

"What about your child?"

"I had a miscarriage," she lied. "When I was strong enough to walk, they packed my bags and had their carriage man drop me off in the middle of Pest. They gave me an adequate amount of money to tide me over until I could get work and told me never to return, or harm would come to me."

"Does Jon know about all of this?" Karol asked, shaking his head in dismay.

"I suppose by now he received my letters. I wrote him a letter weeks ago telling him everything."

"Well, what are you going to do now?"

"Take care of my mother."

"How will you support her?"

"I'll move to Presov and get a factory job, or maybe be a waitress in a dance hall."

"If I asked you, would you come and live with me? I have a big house that was left to me in Buda by an old maid aunt who always favored me. You could each have your own rooms, and while you are out looking for a job, I can look after your mother. Meanwhile, we can become friends and enjoy each other's company."

"I can have my own bedroom?" Stasha answered. "And being good friends is all you're asking us to be?"

"Of course, but I am hoping that the future could bring us closer than just friends. What do you say?"

"Okay, it's a deal."

Stasha led her mother into the living room and put wood in the fireplace.

"You sit here Mama and warm yourself. I'll be in the kitchen if you need me." Just as Stasha entered the kitchen, there was a sharp knock on the door.

"Hello?" a voice rang out. "Anybody home?"

Stasha opened the door and found Mr. Valen and Father Marin standing there. Before Stasha could greet them, Mr. Valen shouted angrily at her saying, "How could you do this to Jon? He trusted you. You know how much he loved you. It's a good thing that your mother killed that Magyar bastard because if she hadn't, I would have burned him over a slow fire the same way that they tortured your father to death. My God Stasha, when my son finds out about it, it will kill him. What were you thinking?"

"Calm down, Mr. Valen," Father Marin said, stepping in front of him.

"And who are you, young man?" Mr. Valen spat contemptuously. "Another one of her lovers?"

"No sir, my name is Karol and I am only a friend."

"Look Mr. Valen," Stasha interjected, taking a deep breath. "I couldn't agree with you more. I am no longer worthy of Jon's love, and I wrote to him and told him everything. Can't we just leave it at that for now? I am concerned about your Jozef, Matt, and Mikhail. I read the newspaper in Presov yesterday that they've captured Roman Polsky."

"Don't worry about them," Father Marin answered. "They are on a freight train that came out of Russia. They are on their way to Hamburg, Germany to go to America. People are leaving by the thousands from European countries every day. For what reason, I do not know. I do not approve."

"What world are you living in Father," Stasha asked incredulously.

"Thanks to the Gypsies they were able to escape," Mr. Valen said, speaking a little less disturbed.

"The Gypsies?" Stasha said, wrinkling her forehead.

"Didn't you know that Matt was half Gypsy?"

"No. Mr. Valen, I'm sorry and I know that's not enough. I know you will never forgive me, and neither will Jon. I don't deserve to be forgiven."

"Don't say that, child," Father said, "God has already forgiven you."

"Maybe so, Father, but God forgiving me doesn't give me Jon back."

"Let's leave now, Monsignor, I said what I came to say."

"Monsignor!" exclaimed Stasha.

"He was ordained Monsignor last month."

"Well, congratulations Father, I mean Monsignor," Stasha said, embracing him.

As they were walking away, Stasha said once more, "I'm sorry Mr. Valen. You'll never know how sorry I am."

CHAPTER 48

"My God, what the hell are you doing here, Clancy, and Paul?" Jon shouted with sheer joy and surprise. "Don't you realize the danger you have put yourselves in?"

"Of course, that's why we came. The newspaper has been keeping up with the events here and from what we've been reading the last few days, it looks like they have you miners up against the wall with no place to go."

"You're right, and all the more reason that you shouldn't be here. This could end up with a fight to the death. Many have already died."

"We know, Jon," Paul said, "we saw the bodies all over the streets. Your friend Doctor Ginsberg came along too. He's outside seeing what he can do to help the wounded."

"Ha, that makes me laugh. The miners don't get paid enough to feed their families, let alone pay for medical bills. All we are asking those sons of bitches is to give us a fair wage, some free medical aid, and more safety measures that will cut down on accidents. Hell, Doc will end up in the poor house."

"Like hell he will," a voice boomed from the other side of the room.

Everyone turned and saw Father Karnovsky walking toward them at a fast pace.

"Get the men ready, Jon. Make sure they have all their weapons loaded and plenty of back-up ammunition."

"Hold on Father," Paul said softly, "that won't be necessary. Clancy and I have already convinced the mine owners to give into your demands. We have it here in writing, signed and delivered."

"Jon," Father snapped, "go get Mr. Hopkins now."

Jon unlocked the door that led to the cellar where Jonathon and his aides were being kept hostage and hollered down to them to get up here.

"Yes, Jon?" Jonathon asked as he arrived at the top of the steps.

"Father wants to have a word with you."

"What is it, Father?" Jonathon asked as he approached the group of men.

"Here, look at these papers and tell me your opinion."

"After thoroughly examining the documents," Jonathon said, "I believe that everything is in order except for . . ."

"Except, for what?" Father snapped.

"Well, I would ask them to have it notarized to make it legal."

"Good thinking, Jonathon, and God bless you."

Jonathon sent one of his aides to deliver the papers to be notarized and then everyone sat down and waited impatiently for the reply.

"While we are waiting, Jon, why don't you sit down and read some of the letters I brought for you that Stasha sent."

"My God, Paul," Jon said, tearing the letters from his hand, "I had given up on her."

"Sit down Jon and read the letters. Here is the last one sent to me. Read that first," Paul said.

Jon sat down, tore the envelope open, unfolded the paper and read:

> "Dear Jon,
>
> I'm sorry that what I have to tell you will hurt you badly. I'm going to get right to the point. I have become pregnant by Stefan Nagy, and I am to marry him and move to Budapest with his family. I know that saying I'm sorry will never be enough. I can only say that I will always love you and I wish you all the luck in the new world. I'm sure you will find a woman more worthy of you than me. Goodbye and God bless you. All my love forever in this world and after, Stasha."

Jon set the letter down slowly on the table and sat silent for a moment, and then suddenly went into a rage, snatching the letter and crumbling it in his hand.

"No, no," he cried, tears flowing freely from his eyes.

"What is it, Jon?" Paul asked, cradling him in his arms like a baby.

"Here, read this," he said, handing him the ball of paper.

Paul unraveled it and began to read it when one of the miners burst into the room, saying that all the coal and iron police, and the guardsmen were lining up outside ready to fire on the building.

"It looks like they are double crossing us," Clancy said, shaking his head.

"Maybe asking them to notarize the document wasn't such a good idea after all," Jonathon said apologetically.

"Listen, Jonathon," Father Karnovsky said, "you and your men get your asses back down in the cellar. There's going to be a lot of bullets flying around here shortly."

"Of course, whatever you say, Father."

"Jon," Father shouted, "get all the men together and place them at strategic positions inside the building. Make sure you have the rear of the building covered and the roof. There must be close to a thousand men out there and we have only two hundred, more or less. The building will help even up the odds. If they attack, they must do it in the wide open, making them more vulnerable to our line of fire."

A half hour later, all the miners were in their positions, waiting for the attack, when a soldier with a white flag attached to his bayonet walked towards the main entrance.

"Let him in," Father said, motioning to Jon. "What is it, soldier?" Father asked as he met him at the door.

"Father, sir, Colonel Smith says I am to tell you that you have one hour to lay down your arms and surrender, or be prepared to be annihilated by not only rifle fire but by cannon shot also."

Father Karnovsky thought about it for a moment then said, "Soldier, tell him that I said, even though it is unfashionable for a priest to say, to go to hell."

"Yes sir, Father, I mean," the soldier snapped and then fled out the door laughing.

The colonel kept his word and exactly an hour later bullets were raining all over the headquarters building. One formation after another lined up in rows of ten and twenty deep, and then moved to the rear to leave fresh riflemen take their places.

After a half-hour, the firing stopped, and in the silence a voice rang out warning the miners that if they did not surrender now they would have to contend with cannon fire. They were given another hour to make up their minds.

Father got the men together and asked them if they wanted to surrender. They took a vote and the majority wished to fight till death if need be. He told those who wanted to give themselves up could do so with no bad feelings and with God's blessing.

Father decided to wait the full hour out, giving the men more time to change their minds. Meanwhile, he checked to see how the wounded were fairing. He took Clancy to see Patrick who was recovering amazingly well from his wounds. When this was all over, they pledged to get together with one another. After checking in with everyone, Father noticed that most of the women were absent.

"Jon, where is Maria?"

"I don't know. I've been busy."

"She left about an hour ago. Just about the same time the soldier was here with his ultimatum," one of the women said, that was busy changing the bandage of one of the injured miners.

Once more Colonel Smith kept his word and exactly one hour later ordered his men to continue firing, but he delayed using the cannon fire. The miners responded, letting Father Karnovsky know that there was no change of mind.

One could almost hear Patrick Henry shouting, "Give me liberty or give me death" as the bullets tore through the windows, sending broken glass onto the already shattered miners that lay helpless on the floor. Men on both sides were falling dead and wounded, but it would only be a matter of time when the overwhelming odds would overcome the miners who were being decimated by the tens and twenties.

Jon stood at one of the windows firing at will with no concern of being hit by the continued volley of bullets that sprayed on all sides of him.

"Jon, for chrissake, will you get down before you get your head blown off!" Paul said, pulling him to the floor. "What the hell's the matter with you? Was it that letter from Stasha?" Paul reached in his pocket and pulled out the crumpled paper and finished reading the letter from Stasha. Paul shook his head and said, "This is terrible, but you can't throw your life away for a woman. You sacrificed too much. Do you understand Jon? No woman is worth that."

Before he could respond, the firing came to a complete stop. The silence was deafening. Father Karnovsky went to the front door and flung it open and to his dismay found hundreds of miners' wives and children lined up in front of the building.

In the midst of the silence, a feminine voice shouted, "If you want to take the building, you will have to get past all of us. That is to say if you are all cowardly enough to kill women and children."

Colonel Smith listened and then gave the orders, ready aim fire. A volley of rifle shots pierced the air only to go over the woman and children and crashed harmlessly into the already brick-riddled building.

First one soldier and then ten, finally a hundred lowered their rifles. Colonel Smith demanded one more time, ready aim fire, followed by a volley of bullets that poured into the rows of women and children, maiming and killing a great number of them.

The soldiers who had refused to fire upon them turned and defended them by shooting at their fellow guardsmen and iron police.

After several volleys and many dead and wounded, Colonel Smith called for a cease fire.

A half hour later, a notarized document was delivered that granted the miners their demands. There was only one catch; Father Karnovsky would have to surrender himself and go to trial for creating a riot that led to the loss of lives.

PART 3

THE BLOODY SIXTH

CHAPTER 49

The miners, receiving all they had asked for, still fell short of a fair exchange. The compensations never equaled the physical effort and danger that encompassed them every moment of their laborious task in the bowels of the earth.

Father Karnovsky's valiant effort was also repaid with a prison term of ten to twenty years where he would act as chaplain. The Catholic Church also unceremoniously defrocked and excommunicated him. Jon Valen pledged that he would make every effort to have him released from jail.

Clancy and Paul went back home to take care of business after a week. They stayed long enough to see that the mine owners did not renege on the agreement. Jon stayed to clean up the mess that they left in the battle at the headquarters building. Bodies had to be identified and mass funerals had to be performed. It would take weeks, if not months, to bring sanity and order to the mining community.

A month had passed since Father Karnovsky was found guilty and sentenced. The trial was a mockery to justice. Jon's hands were tied for the moment. What would he do now? He was devastated by the turn of events with Stasha. Maria and Patrick did everything they could to console him. They came up with the idea of having a three-way business partnership. The negotiations now permitted them to have their own general stores. They talked about having a combination general store with a bar and restaurant, and sleeping rooms for the miners. Maria, of course, would run the sleeping quarters and the general store while Patrick and Jon attended to the bar and grill. Clancy was willing to put up some capital to help them get started. The plan was to build onto Patrick's place. That would take some costly building material. Jon said that he would like to mull on it for a while.

Jon was sitting at Patrick's bar with a bottle of hard whiskey in front of him taking one swig after another. In between swallows, he would read Stasha's letter. Patrick just shook his head when he saw him in such a calamitous state.

"Enough Jon," he shouted with his Irish brogue. "You don't need to do this to yourself, lad. No woman is worth the pain. Stasha is not the only woman in the world."

"Yes Jon, Patrick is right," Maria said as she entered the barroom. "I can be more to you than she ever could be. We can be many things to one another, business partners, lovers, and if you wish, marriage partners."

Jon just stared at her, saying nothing. Maria, seeing that he was too drunk to reason with, pulled him up from the chair and led him home to the boarding house and put him to bed.

The next morning, Jon woke up to the sound of whistling March winds banging against the windows.

"Well, good morning Jon," Maria whispered as she saw his head rise from the pillow. "You look terrible."

"Jesus, Mary, and Joseph," he groaned in Slovak, "I feel like I got hit on the head with a rock."

"Here," she said as she handed him a cup of hot steaming coffee.

"I'm sorry, Maria, if I acted like a fool last night."

"That's all right, Jon. You aren't the first man to be betrayed by a woman. There are multitudes of them in the Bible. But now, you must get over it and I will help you. Trust me, I have loved you from the very first day that you walked into this room. The night I seduced you was out of love for you, not just lust. I want you to know that."

After a week had passed, Jon still couldn't come to grips with himself. He told Maria and Patrick that he would like to spend some time in New York with Clancy and Lucas. Maria started to speak and Jon cut her off saying that this was for the best right now, and he would give lots of thought to making a decision.

"I think the world of you Maria. I have great respect for you, but I do not love you."

"You can grow to love me!"

"We will see." Jon walked in on Clancy at his busiest time of the day. Clancy spied him as he entered the door and smiled, quickly shouting, "Get your ass to work!"

"Yes, Master Magyar," Jon answered while he put on an apron and started waiting on tables.

"Jon," a familiar voice called from behind him as he was cleaning a table. He turned, and there to his present surprise, stood Helen. For a moment he did not recognize her. She had grown to full maturity since he saw her last. Her shy demure was replaced by a scintillating aura of confidence. The scar across her neck did not mar her exotic beauty in the least. In fact, it added intrigue and mystery to her Gypsy persona.

"My dear Helen, it is so wonderful to see you. You have grown up so much, I hardly recognized you. Come here and give me a hug." After Jon released her he asked what she was doing here.

"No one knew that I was coming here today. You were visiting Clancy and by sheer coincidence I was here."

Helen put her head down and said, "No Jon, I am working here and living in your old room." Jon stared at her in obvious disapproval.

"I'm sorry!" she said, on the verge of tears.

"Hey, you two, get back to work. You can chat later."

Just as Clancy went to lock up at closing time, Lucas popped through the door and stopped dead in his tracks when he saw Jon. They hugged and kissed and slapped each other on the back until they had to sit down.

Helen came over and said, "Hello Uncle Lucas," then kissed him on the cheek.

"Will you two please tell me what the hell's going on? Lucas, do you know why Helen is here?"

"Well Jon," Lucas said, pursing his lips, "you'll have to ask her that question."

"Well Helen?" Jon asked, impatiently.

"Jon, I thought that when I came to America, I would be free form prejudice. Ever since Ana enrolled me in school, a day hadn't gone by when I wasn't ridiculed calling me Cigan as you well know means liar and thief in Slovak. The only friend that I had stopped associating with me. So when Ana and Paul left to see you, I packed my clothes and went in search of my parents in the city. I spent many nights sleeping in the streets and with Gypsies that I met. Not one of them knew of my parents' whereabouts. Finally I decided to come here to see if Clancy would put me back to work."

"Ana must have been worried to death," Jon said, shaking his head in disgust.

"I left her a letter telling her not to worry. I lied and told her that I knew where my parents were and that I would be in touch with her as soon as possible. Last month they came to visit Clancy and found me here. We keep in touch. She wants me to come back and try again. She said that she had a talk with Mother Superior. Jon, I know how much you wanted me to get an education. I'm sorry! Do you forgive me?"

"Yes child, but you must go back to school, if not here, somewhere else. I'm going to get in touch with my cousins back in Pennsylvania."

"You're not going back to the coal mines?" Lucas said, interrupting.

"No, no Lucas. They are working in a town near Philadelphia. They have a job where they smelt iron. They say the city is very progressive and jobs are plentiful. Well, I'm tired as hell," Jon said, removing his apron. "I came here from the train ride. Is my room still available?" he shouted to Clancy who was behind the bar cleaning up.

"No, but you can have Helen's old room."

"Lucas!" Jon shouted, slapping him on the back. "Tomorrow is Sunday, March 7, and my birthday. What do you say we head on down to the Slavic club we used to go to. Helen, you come celebrate with us. We'll need you along to see that we get home safe and sound."

"But I thought you were tired," Helen said.

"I am, but partying will relax me and make me less tired."

Helen just laughed and said, "Give me a moment to change my clothes."

CHAPTER 50

The early morning, March winds whistled through the cracks in the box cars of the slow moving freight train. The men were in separate cars from the woman and children huddled in close proximity trying to contain some of their body heat. The smell of body waste permeated the air. There were two makeshift toilets for fifty people. Jozef, Mikhail, and Matt were sound asleep, sitting shoulder to shoulder against the side of the sliding door. Suddenly, bodies were thrown forward as the train came to a stop.

"Wake up," Jozef shouted, shaking Mikhail, then patting Matt on the face, gently arousing him from his much needed rest.

They had been on the run for weeks, trying to avoid capture by the Magyars. The original plan went down the drain when Roman was captured and tortured into revealing where they might be found. Emile learned about a train that was loaded with Jews fleeing from Russia that was crossing Europe on its way to Hamburg, Germany where they would board the first ocean liner to America. The fare was minimal and open to anyone regardless of nationality.

After the train came to a complete stop, the doors were slid open, allowing the miserable masses to rush outside into the bitter cold, but clean smelling air. The early morning sun was slowly sending its light into the joyous crowd that was inhaling the fresh air, as if it was just sent from heaven.

People with similar Slavic languages greeted one another. They were Russian, Polish, Slovak, Czech, Latvian, Lithuanian, and Estonian. There were peasants mixed with Jews and Gypsies from all the represented countries. The peasants' life had been one of hard labor in the fields with no chance of improving their status, but compared to the Gypsies and the Jews, their quality of life was at a much higher plane. The Gypsies and the Jews were in constant threat of harm, not only by the higher authorities, but also by the common people. They were tortured and killed indiscriminately; the Gypsies because of the darkness of their skin and nomadic lifestyle, and the Jews because they were seen as the killers of Jesus Christ. They were sure that this attitude would change when they came to America, the land were a man was free to worship as he pleased, and where all men were created equal.

A man dressed in a dark uniform with the words *S.S. Hamburg America* emblazoned on his cap, approached the crowd and said, "Everyone pick up your belongings and follow me." After a brisk walk of about fifteen minutes, they arrived at a building with the name *Hamburg American Line* painted in large white lettering across the wide main entrance. The harbor was visible where several ships were anxiously awaiting to stuff as many immigrants as they could into their steerage compartments.

"I want everyone to enter the building and form two lines where your passage money will be collected. The fare is forty dollars, and when you arrive in America you must have another twenty-five dollars before you are permitted to leave the ship. When you are done paying your fare, you are to proceed to the room on your left where you will be examined by a doctor."

When Matt stepped forward to pay his fare, the collector told him to get out of line and leave the building immediately.

"What's the problem?" Matt asked in a low tone, not wishing to draw attention.

"No Gypsies aboard the *America*."

"I'm not a Gypsy," Matt answered, raising his voice slightly.

"You look like one."

"After traveling in a freight car stuffed like sardines, your clothes would end up looking like this too."

Before the conversation went on any further, Jozef stepped forward, pushing Matt aside and asked whet the price of a ticket was "forty dollars!"

"Here, this is for the three of us." Jozef counted out one hundred and twenty dollars, and then counted out a separate sixty dollars and said, "Here, this is for you. Will that take care of the matter?" The ticket man just looked down at the money for a moment and then scooped it up and said, "Next!"

After their examination, which consisted of checking for trachoma and any disease that could be spread, they wandered out into another area next to the examination rooms, where they were greeted by the ticket man.

"Now what do you want?" Matt snapped. "You're not getting anymore money."

"Look, I appreciate the money, that's why I'm advising you to get a change of clothes, or you will be sent back when you arrive there. Just last week they returned a boatload of Gypsies. We won't be shipping out until late this evening, so you'll have plenty of time to run into town and find a change of clothes.

"Thank you for the information," Mikhail said, extending his hand. "By the way, where did you learn to speak Slovak so well?"

"In Nitra, the town of my birth," he answered proudly. "I applied for this job because I am fluent in most of the Slavic languages, and I also speak German. Like your families, my family is also struggling to make ends meet."

"What did you do for a living back in Nitra?" Mikhail asked, curiously.

"I was a school teacher."

"I knew it!" Mikhail shouted joyously.

"How did you know?"

"Because I am a school teacher. I guess it takes one to know one, as the old saying goes."

"Please excuse me now, I must go. Lot of luck to all of you in the 'Land of Gold.' If things work out well for me, I may run into you somewhere in America."

As he turned his back to leave, Mikhail asked, "What is your name?"

"Jozef, Jozef Urban," he answered before he disappeared into the oncoming crowd of immigrants that were waiting impatiently for their voyage to the "Land of Gold."

CHAPTER 51

The club has improved considerably in the past two years that Jon had been away. The concrete dance floor was covered with wood that was now fit for dancing. One could slide along with the slow waltzes and the fast polkas. The band now had a stage to sit on overlooking the floor. The cafeteria-style tables with long benches still hugged the outer walls, but circular tables were placed on the floor, stealing some of their dancing space.

When they arrived, the festivities were just beginning. The band was tuning up their instruments and people were rushing to find a table close to the dance floor. Lucas and Jon were headed for the wall benches when Helen got their attention and directed them to a table. They were soon waited on and Jon ordered a pitcher of beer for them and a glass of wine for Helen. The place was filling up rapidly while the band played a lively polka.

"Come on Jon, let's dance," Helen said as she attempted to pull him up from his chair.

"No, no. I can't dance."

"How about you Uncle Lucas?"

"I'm sorry, but I don't dance either."

"How about me, beautiful?" a voice beckoned from behind. "Would you care to dance with me? Of course, with your permission," he said turning to Jon.

Jon hesitated for a moment and then said, "Yes you may, if she wants to."

"Yes, yes I want to," Helen said, excitedly. Soon they were twirling frantically to the music. Helen's long, full, multicolored skirt was almost touching the floor. Her blouse, that matched the skirt, was festooned with green, read, and white beads that complimented her obvious Gypsy attire. Even her cloth shoes matched. The polka music stopped and slowed to a waltz that had them gliding with such precision one would think that they were long-time dance partners. Soon they drew the attention of the people that were drinking and chatting at tables. Other dancers also stopped to watch them.

The waltz ended, and as they walked back to the table, they were showered with a hearty round of applause. The young man pulled her chair back and sat her down in the most gentlemanly fashion. Jon and Lucas just sat there stupefied.

"Where did you learn to dance like that?" Lucas asked Helen.

"Remember, I am a Gypsy. We were born to dance."

"You're what?" the young man asked.

"You heard right," Jon said menacingly. "Do you have a problem with that?"

"Um, no, not really."

"Well then, sit down and have a drink with us. What would you like?"

"A glass of beer will be fine."

"Waiter," Jon shouted, "bring us another glass" When the glass arrived, Jon filled everyone's glass and raised his saying, "To the dancers!"

After downing his beer, he turned to the young man and asked him his name and where he came from. His accented English seemed to be Hungarian.

"Sandor Lukas and I am from Budapest," he answered proudly.

"I knew it," Jon said, laughing.

"How did you know it?"

"Well, you don't have a Slovak accent."

"Do you have a problem with that?"

"With what?"

"That I'm a Magyar."

"No, not really," Jon answered, laughing again. Helen listened patiently and when they were done said,

"I think it is time for us to dance again. How can we resist the Hungarian waltz?" The gentleman helped Helen up from her chair and then they glided gracefully onto the floor and disappeared between the dancers.

Jon and Lucas started to sip on their beer as if it were wine. They had consumed two pitchers of beer in a very short time. They were so content in being with one another again that they reached across the table and squeezed each other's hands in pure affection.

"Well Jon, what do you have planned for the future?" Lucas asked curiously.

"Like I told you back at Clancy's, I'm going to Arland City. I'll see if I can get a job smelting iron and save money to open a business."

"Doing what?"

"I don't know yet. I would like to get into the building business. I am a carpenter. Patrick wanted me to go into the bar business with him and a widow named Maria, who runs the boarding house that I lived in. Patrick wanted to combine a boarding house, general store, and a bar."

"That sounds like a profitable proposition to me. What was the problem?"

Jon took a deep breath and said, "Maria."

"What's the matter with her?"

"She wants to marry me," Jon said, exasperated.

Lucas just leaned back and started laughing.

"What the hell is so funny about that?"

"Is she nice? Is she beautiful?"

"Yes, yes, but,"

"But what?"

"What will I do about Stasha?"

"For Christ sake Jon, I know all about that whore of a fiancée of yours. Forget about her and thank God you have someone worthy of replacing her."

"But I still love her in spite of what she has done. It is probably my fault anyhow."

"Your fault? How in the hell is it your fault?"

"I shouldn't have left her back home. I should have waited longer and saved enough money to transport both of us."

"Look Jon, I feel sorry for you, but you must go on with your life. Bring Maria with you to Arland City, and together you can make a life for yourselves."

"She has two children."

"Do you have a problem with that?"

"No. I always thought that Stasha and I would have a lot of children."

"Well, now you have a head start if you take on Maria. And if you take Helen with you, she can be a great help to you."

Just as Lucas called the waiter for another pitcher of beer, there was a disturbance on the dance floor

CHAPTER 52

The March winds pushed the ship swiftly across the stormy North Atlantic Ocean. The heaving up and down motion of the ship brought the steerage passengers into a state of extreme nausea and diarrhea. The pounding waves and banging ship engine drove them into a traumatized semi-consciousness. Three days passed before the ocean calmed, leaving the passengers in a state of euphoria.

"My God," Matt gasped, still in the last stages of nausea. "I thought it would never end. I remember feeling this way when Uncle Emile gave me some of his homemade wine. At first I thought I was going to die, and then I was afraid I wasn't going to die. I never drank a drop of wine since, and I can assure you this will be my last voyage on any kind of water."

"Come on, Matt, let's get up on the deck and let the fresh ocean air bring you back to life," Mikhail said, as he helped him to his feet.

The deck rail was lined with people hanging over the side, vomiting, until there was only air left in their barren stomachs. It was high noon, the sun hanging desperately to the clear blue sky with no clouds in sight to rest its fiery flames on. The mighty North Atlantic still held winter in its mighty jaws, absorbing all the heat waves that the sun could emit, leaving the passengers shivering in a glorious sun-filled day.

"Come on, let's find something to eat," Jozef said, motioning to Matt and Mikhail to follow him. He led them down below the main deck where they found a long row of barrels loaded with pickled herrings. Lines were formed where paper plates and cups were handed out and then filled with pickled herrings and a cup full of water. They could have seconds and thirds of the herring, but the water was given out sparingly. Matt ate slowly and started to feel a little better.

The day lingered while the setting sun waited anxiously to slip behind the horizon and light up the other half of the world. Finally, after eight monotonous days, the passengers were told to be prepared to arrive in Ellis

Island. After everyone got their belongings packed and ready to go, the Captain of the ship called their attention and advised them to be sure that they had their twenty-five dollars. Without it they would not be permitted to disembark. Those who did not have the correct amount would be given the money by the ship's paymaster. It was cheaper to give them the money because the *American Hamburg Line* would be responsible at their own expense to transport them back to Hamburg, Germany. Giving the immigrants medical exams before they boarded was also a new procedure that saved the ship's company a great deal of money. Previously, people who did not pass the medical at Ellis Island were sent back to Europe at the expense of the shipping line. The ship's steward had to enter each passenger's name in a formal list along with information about each person. This was the ship's manifest document of records.

On March 8, 1903, Jozef, Mikhail and Matt stood on the deck observing the Statue of Liberty. It was a beautiful, crisp, bright, sunny morning as the steerage passengers boarded ferries headed for Ellis Island, where they docked in a slip next to the main building on Ellis Island. The gangplank was put down where they were greeted by a man shouting for them to pile their luggage here and then led the men in one direction, and women and children in another. Those who had not been examined by a doctor on board the ship were given medical exams in assigned rooms. Their garments were tagged with their manifest number from the steamship. The medical exams were primitive and harsh, sometimes giving great pain to the immigrants. One in particular was the exam for trachoma, which was done with a buttonhook, a metal instrument used to button gloves. Examiners felt that this was the best device in pulling eyelids back to check for eye infections.

"Jesus, Mary, and Joseph, am I glad that's over with," Mikhail said, rubbing his eyes that were running with tears. "Mikhail, Jozef, where the hell are you?" Matt shouted, stumbling around the room as if he was in the dark.

"Over here," Mikhail answered as he reached out to grab a hold of Matt's outstretched hand and led him into a nearby bathroom where he instructed him to apply water on his burning eyes.

"Come on," Jozef called, opening the bathroom door, "we are free to get on our way. There is a ferry waiting to transport us to the mainland."

As they made their way to board the ferry, there was extreme joy and misery all around them. The people who were passed through were ecstatic, and then there was a family whose young child did not pass the physical exam and were ordered to be taken back. When they were disembarking from the ferry, there were two men demanding the twenty-five dollars that they had been given by the paymaster so that they could be permitted to enter the United States.

Now they would enter this strange new country without a penny in their pockets. Still, they showed no fear. After all, they remembered being told that the streets of America were lined with gold. They were sure they would be allowed to scrape up a few carats to hold them over.

CHAPTER 53

Mariska opened the door and forced a smile when she saw Stasha and her gentleman friend. Stasha hesitated for a moment and then embraced Mariska awkwardly, sensing her aloofness. Just as she turned to introduce Karol to her, a feminine voice interrupted saying, "Oh Stasha, it's so nice to see you. It's been such a long time."

"I know Mrs. Sokolosky," Stasha said, lowering her head shamefully.

"Mama, would you please excuse me?" Mariska asked, "I have to finish washing the clothes."

"Before you leave," Stasha said, "I would like you to meet my good friend Karol Gabor."

"Pleased to meet you," Eva said, extending her hand. Mariska just nodded. Karol bowed graciously and kissed her hand gently, stood up and made a gesture to speak, but the words wouldn't come out of his mouth.

"What is it?" Stasha asked, seeing the bewilderment on his face.

"I think I know what it is," Eva said, laughing. "He suspects that I am Hungarian. What gave me away?"

"I suppose it was both you and your daughter's red hair and green eyes. I've never seen a Slovak girl look like that."

"Oh, that's not always the case. I've met a few Slovaks with read hair," Eva said, smiling.

"Well, maybe so, but your accent when you speak Slovak is similar to mine."

"Yes, I noticed that, but I didn't have to hear you speak after I learned that your name is Gabor. That's a common Hungarian name."

Mariska stood there dumbstruck by what she was hearing and finally said, "Mother, you never told me that you were Hungarian. Why not?"

"Because the Magyars are the Slovaks' enemies and rightly so. I was ashamed of my heritage. I was born in Budapest to wealthy parents; my father owned a copper mine where he had Slovak and Gypsy workers labor for only food and a place to sleep. Most of them were falsely arrested and turned over to my father. The police were paid well for their dirty work. In our mansion, we had servants that my mother had whipped for what she called disrespect."

Eva spent the next half hour telling her story about life in Budapest. When she was done, Mariska came to her and said, "Mama, I love you."

"Mariska, I never let it be known of your Hungarian blood because I didn't want you to be ridiculed by your classmates when you were growing up."

"Everything will be all right, Mama. Don't worry. Now let me get back to the wash. Pleases excuse me," she said, turning to Stasha and Karol.

"No, please stay." Stasha importuned. I know that you both heard about the terrible things that I did to Jon. I don't blame you for being cold to me, Mariska. I know that you were a good friend of Jon's. I remember him playing with you when you were a little girl, and Mrs. Sokolosky, thank you for your kindness. You have treated me better than I deserve."

"No Stasha. We all make mistakes. Look at the secrets that I kept from my daughter."

"You did that to protect her. What I did was out of weakness. Let's face it, I behaved like a whore."

"That's not true," Eva said. "Because you were with one man doesn't make you a whore."

"What does that make me?"

"It makes you a young lady who the Good Lord created to have children. You were at the peak of your sexual life when the man you were to conceive children with left you behind, leaving you vulnerable to any young man who took a fancy to you. If my Charles had not been such a gentleman, I may have fallen into sin too."

"Did I hear you call me a gentleman?" Charles said, as he entered the living room. "Well, hello Stasha. Good to see you. I have good news. Matt, Mikhail, and Jozef made it safely to Hamburg and should be arriving in America soon, if they haven't already. They are not sure that Jon received the letter about them coming, so they are going to try and find Clancy's place. Mr. Valen received a letter from Jon saying that he was on his way back to New York City."

"Of, that's wonderful!" Stasha said, with a broad smile on her face. "That's the reason I came here. I was really worried about them after reading the newspaper. What will you do now, Mr. Sokolosky?"

"Follow them to America as soon as Matt is set up financially. Maybe he can find a job as a blacksmith. And what about you, Stasha? When will you go?"

"You know that I can't do that."

"Yes, I know what happened to you and so does Jon, but he still wants you to come to be with him. He said that it was his fault for leaving you behind."

Stasha just sat there, shocked at what she heard.

"Oh," she said, "let me introduce you to my friend Karol Gabor. He has offered me and my mother a place to live in his house in Budapest until I find a job. We will stay there until I am able to get my own place. I can't see how I can refuse that offer. I made up my mind that I could never go to Jon. I am not worthy and I love him too much to burden him with me. I'm going to take my chances with Karol's offer because right now I must see to my mother. You know that she is not capable of taking care of herself. I'm the one who put her in that position and now I must take the responsibility of her. I know that you have heard many stories about me. The truth is that I had sex with Stefan Nagy several times and finally got pregnant. We told Father Marin, who married us. I went to Budapest to live with his parents. After Stefan was killed, I had a miscarriage and then when I recovered, they threw me out on the streets of Budapest never to return, or they said something bad would happen to me. They gave me enough money to buy a train ticket to Presov where I fortunately met Karol. Now you know the whole truth. When you get to America, please tell Jon that I am truly sorry, and that I'm sure that he can find a better woman than me. Goodbye," Stasha said, closing the door behind her, and then suddenly she stopped and said, "Mrs. Sokolsky? I need you to do me a favor."

"Yes, of course. What is it that you would like me to do?"

"Would you please look after my mother until I get settled with Karol in Budapest?"

"Yes, I will do that for you, for as long as you need."

Stasha hugged her gratefully and said, "Goodbye," adding, "God bless you."

CHAPTER 54

Jozef showed a young man a piece of paper written in English asking for directions to the corner of Pearl and Fulton Streets, where Clancy's tavern was located. Not able to speak Slovak, he pointed his finger straight down the street that led to the East River. He drew a reasonable map where the street they were on met the river. He drew a bridge spanning the river and then gesticulated to them to be on the lookout for the bridge. He wrote the name, Brooklyn Bridge, down on the paper and pointed to his eyes, telling them to look for it. There was a sign giving direction to the bridge when they would arrive at Fulton Street. He was sure they would recognize the printing on the sign from the one he spelled on the scrap paper. They thanked him profusely and went on their way.

It was mid-afternoon and the sun was warming the cool late winter air, making their walk comfortable. They took their time taking in the mystic of their newfound country. The designs and architecture of the buildings were a far cry from the Gothic architecture that stood for centuries in Slovakia and much of Europe.

"Look!" Matt shouted, snatching the scrap paper from Jozef's hand and then pointed to the Brooklyn Bridge sign on the corner at the end of the street with an arrow directing them to the left. Jozef and Mikhail looked at the sign and back at the paper and then laughed as they turned on Fulton, and had their first glance of the Brooklyn Bridge.

"Awesome!" Mikhail said, repeating it several times.

Fifteen minutes later they came to the corner of Pearl and Fulton, where the sign hanging on the front of the building was displayed conspicuously. Jozef checked the letter that Mr. Valen had given him with the name Clancy written in English, and verified that this was Clancy's.

It was around four in the late afternoon, but still a little early for the supper crowd. Only a few tables were occupied, and there were only three men sitting at the bar.

Mikhail walked over to the bar and said in his best English, "Clancy?"

"Yeh," a voice answered, raising his head from under the bar.

"Uh . . . uh," Mikhail stammered, trying to speak something that would make him understand.

Without hesitation, Clancy called out, "Helen, where are you? I need you."

"Coming," Helen answered, pushing the swinging door open from the kitchen. "What is it?"

"I have three men here that can't speak English, and I suspect by their accents that they are Slavic."

Helen greeted them good afternoon in Slovak, and then asked them how she could help them. Matt just stared in amazement; not only could she speak Slovak, but she was obviously a Gypsy. Mikhail introduced himself and told her who they were, that Clancy should be expecting them, unless he didn't receive the letter yet that they were coming.

Helen translated for Clancy, and without any further conversation he shook their hands and invited them to sit at one of the tables. Helen filled up four whiskey glasses and delivered them to the table where they immediately clinked them together and drank them in one swallow.

"Where is Jon?" Jozef asked.

Helen translated, but before Clancy could respond, the supper crowd arrived through the door in droves, prompting Clancy to ask Helen to take the men to her and Jon's rooms, and tell them to rest and clean up. When they were done to come back down and have a meal. He also instructed her to tell them that after the rush hour he would close early and then they would discuss Jon's whereabouts.

It was 7:00 PM when Helen saw the new arrivals enter the tavern from the outside back stairway. They all had a change of clothes and appeared well rested. There were a few stragglers at the bar, but all the tables were vacant.

"Come over here," Helen said, pointing to a table near the bar.

After they were seated, Helen said to give her a few minutes, and then she would bring them something to eat. True to her word, before five minutes had passed, she placed before them steaming bowls of hot ground beef and rice wrapped in cabbage leaves, along with potato dumplings, both indigenous meals of Slovakia.

They just looked at one another and smiled, and ate to their hearts' content. It had been a long time since they had a decent meal. They nearly starved on the ship. Helen finished cleaning up. Clancy locked the doors and directed Helen to sit at a table with him and the men.

"Well," Clancy said, directing his attention to Jozef, "there is no denying that you are Jon's brother. The resemblance is remarkable. You could pass for twins."

Helen translated. Before Clancy could continue, Mikhail interrupted, asking them where Jon was. Helen took a deep breath and said, "In jail."

"In jail! For what?" Jozef asked, jumping up from his chair.

"I'm sorry to say it was on account of me," Helen said, grimacing. "It happened last night at a club we went to for Jon's birthday. I was dancing with a gentleman that we met there. While we were dancing, someone made a remark to him about dancing with a Cigan. He asked him to apologize for his remark. He refused, so they began shouting at one another. Suddenly, there was Jon, pulling the man out of the chair, beating on him. Another man from the table tried to pull Jon off of him and then my dance partner got into it and soon the police arrived and hauled Jon, Sandor, Lucas, and the two other men that they fought with, off to the jail house."

When she finished, Clancy, assuming that she told them what had happened, ask her to tell them not to worry because he was bailing Jon and Lucas out of jail tonight and the young man who helped to defend her.

CHAPTER 55

Stasha and Karol stopped by the church rectory to say goodbye to Father Marin. He heard her Confession, gave her absolution, and then sent her on her way with a penance of reciting the Rosary every day for one month.

Mr. Sokolosky approached them as they exited the church and offered them a ride to the train station in Sabinov in his horse drawn wagon. They accepted the offer.

On the way, Charles turned to Stasha and said, "I have something to tell you. It's about Father Marin. I know that you have great respect for him. Up until now, so did I."

"What is it?" Stasha asked, puzzled by his remark.

"I hate to tell you this, but it was Father Marin who informed the Magyar authorities about the plan to free Mikhail."

"What! Why?"

"It looks like he made some kind of deal. Maybe that's why he was ordained a Monsignor all of a sudden."

"He must have had a better reason than that. I can't believe he would be that selfish at the expense of Mikhail and the lives of the villagers who helped free him. Why do you think he did it Charles?"

"I haven't the slightest idea. We haven't confronted him on it yet because we too are finding it hard to believe."

"I might be able to help you," Karol said, interrupting. "My brother is an officer in the Hungarian Army. I'm sure he can find out what the real truth is. When I find out I will inform you."

Less than an hour later, Stasha and Karol were sitting in his brother's living room, chatting with Francine, waiting for her husband to arrive. After a half an hour, Francine invited them into the dining room and served them lunch. While they were drinking coffee, Karol's brother Janos entered the dining room, fully dressed in his Magyar uniform.

"Well, this is a pleasant surprise! I wasn't expecting you back this soon. And what is Stasha doing here with you? I thought you were escorting her back to her village?"

"He did that, and then offered to have me live with him in Budapest."

"Don't tell me he asked you to marry him already!" Janos said, laughing.

"No, of course not. He is just being kind enough to give my mother and I a place to stay until I get on my feet, financially."

"Come on brother, there has to be more to it than that. You are attracted to Stasha, and you are hoping it will get to be the same with her in the future. Am I right?"

"Yes, something like that," Karol answered, somewhat embarrassed, and then said, "Janos, we are on our way to Budapest. We have to catch the next train. We stopped to see if you can tell us if you know anything about how the authorities found out about the plot to free Mikhail. We were told from a reliable source that a priest from her village by the name of Father Marin informed them.

"Yes, that is true that a priest informed them, but I didn't hear what his name was. How many priests are at the church in Dubovica?"

"As far as I know, he is the only one there. Isn't that so, Stasha?" Karol asked.

"Yes, our village is small and only warrants having one priest."

"Yes, then there is no doubt that it is Father Marin," Karol said, feeling sorry for her. Stasha sat there with a mixture of sadness and anger running through her body. Karol helped her up from the chair and said, "Come Stasha. We have a train to catch. When we arrive, I will send a telegram to Mr. Sokolsky informing him that he was right."

The train arrived at West railroad station just as darkness fell upon the already bustling streets of Pest. The smell of violets permeated the air as they were being hawked in the station and out on the streets. Karol reached in his pocket and handed a few coins to a young girl that was selling flowers. "Here," he said, handing the violets to Stasha, "this ought to help bring your good spirits back."

"Thank you," she said. "They are beautiful, but I'm afraid it will take more than violets to make me overcome the thought that Father Marin was responsible for Mikhail suffering all those months in that dungeon, and the torturing of Roman Polasky."

"I'm sure he had his own good reasons."

"How could any of his reasons be good when people's lives were at stake?" she snapped, furiously.

"Look Stasha, there is nothing you can do about it. I'm sure that Jon and Matt's fathers will confront him after they receive the telegram.

CHAPTER 56

The fire chief and some of the police officers that had befriended Jon after his heroics at the hotel fire and the incident with the local gangsters, they had used their influence to have Jon and his cohorts released from jail. There was a minimal fine for damages that Clancy gladly paid. Jon didn't have to serve anymore jail time, but he was once again advised to leave New York City.

Jon could hardly believe his eyes when he saw his countrymen waiting for him back at the tavern. It was enough to make grown men cry, and cry they did.

After they composed themselves they sat and had some serious talks. They filled Jon in on all the events that had taken place since he left the village, right down to their escape and voyage to America. Of course, Jon insisted on knowing the whereabouts of Stasha. They told him what they knew about her affair with Stefan, and about how he died. Jon found it hard to believe that Mrs. Ondreas murdered Stefan.

It was way after midnight when they were interrupted by Helen telling them that their makeshift sleeping quarters were ready. She had Jon and Jozef in Jon's old room, and Mikhail and Matt in her room. Meanwhile, she would stay with one of her Gypsy friends only a few blocks from Clancy's.

Tomorrow would be the day of making important decisions. Jon was determined to go back to Slovakia and bring Stasha and her mother to America. Jozef didn't think that was a good idea and hoped to talk him out of it.

Before Helen left, Matt approached her and asked when she would be coming back. She said she would be back to work early tomorrow morning. Matt told her that he was looking forward to seeing her.

She smiled shyly and said, "Good night and have a restful sleep."

"Oh," Clancy shouted as she headed for the door, "wait for me. I'll walk you part of the way. I'm going to my cousins in Brooklyn to sleep tonight. I'll depend on you to open up. Oh, and one more thing, ask this young lad here if he would help you out tomorrow. I got an idea that he may be taking Jon's old job."

Helen translated what Clancy asked, and then Matt replied in agreement with the nod of his head and a smile from ear to ear. "Until tomorrow morning, I kiss your hand beautiful," Matt said, with sparkling eyes and his heart pounding.

CHAPTER 57

Budapest was reaching its zenith in culture and world popularity when Stasha invaded the confines of Ancient Buda. Stasha stood exhilarated as she gazed at the rose-covered slope from the glassed in veranda.

"Well, how do you like the view?" Karol asked, smiling, noticing the look of awe on her face.

"It's breathtaking."

"Yes, one of the last vestiges of the Turks."

"I was taught in school that they were cruel and destructive."

"True, but it just proves that old adage, that one can find the best of us in the worse of us, and vise versa."

"Yes Karol, I am living proof of that statement."

"Oh, be quiet and stop being so critical of yourself. Now, if I may, let me show you to your sleeping quarters."

Karol led her by her hand through an immense living room that was a combination of exclusive wood that covered all the structured phases of the interior framing and enormous fire place that added grandeur to the already magnificent room.

"This will be your bedroom," Karol said as he opened a sliding door.

Once more, Stasha was greeted by artistry in wood of the finest texture and cut and to her pleasant surprise the ceiling had several windows that were projecting sunlight off the sparkling brass bed.

"Beautiful!" Stasha shouted, as she ran and leaped onto the white satin covered bed. "Oh, it's wonderful! I never had such luxury. What can I do to repay you?" she asked, turning as Karol slipped onto the bed beside her.

Karol looked into her eyes and made a feeble attempt to answer, but to no avail. Stasha pushed her body firmly against his and then kissed him softly on his lips, arousing the deep feelings in his heart that he had for her. Her advances became more heated. Her sexual proclivities were incited and Karol was getting lost in the fire.

She pulled her skirt up and started to wiggle out of her underpants when suddenly Karol jumped off the bed and shouted, "No! I cannot do this," and then repeated sobbing, "I can not do this." He fell to his knees aside the bed and said, "I'm sorry, please forgive me."

Stasha reached over to him and ran her soft hands through his hair and said, "You are right and as usual I am wrong. I must ask you to forgive me. Now let's get up and finish moving in. Karol, let's stick to our original plan. Let's see if time can bring us together."

After touring the rest of the house, Karol invited her to dine out at one of Pest's most luxurious hotel restaurants, *The Hungaria*. Stasha declined the offer, at first pleading that she didn't have the proper attire to go to such a fancy place. Karol offered to buy her any dress that she felt would be proper. She agreed, but only if he allowed her to pay the cost back to him when she earned her own money.

Dressed in the finest that the Parisian influenced fashion shops of Vaci Street had to offer, they sauntered down the Danube Corso. The hint of spring was everywhere. The bitter winter cold seemed to flee from the city leaving the sweet smells of lilac and violets permeate the air. They entered the hotel from Maria Valeria Street onto an awning-covered terrace. A slender dark-haired young man greeted them as Madame and Gracious Sir, as was the custom in a country of social classes.

After they were properly seated, a waiter dressed in an elegant black and white tuxedo arrived, bowing and asking them, "What is your pleasure?"

Karol, without hesitation, ordered the very popular Hungarian foges, considered the most delicate fresh water fish in the world. Stasha consumed chicken paprika, not a gourmet by any means, but more inviting to a Slovak peasant woman's taste.

Stasha attired in an evening gown of Vaci Street's most fashionable designer clothing store sparkled like a diamond in the rough. Karol's' impeccable appearance and manner put the final touch to the artists portrait of class and elegance.

After an evening of dining, dancing, and socializing, they returned home joyous and exhausted, to separate bedrooms.

Stasha fell off to sleep murmuring, "I still love Jon."

Karol stayed awake, vexed by the thought that Stasha still loved Jon.

CHAPTER 58

Jon dropped Mikhail off at the Maliks, and then boarded a train for Philadelphia with Jozef.

It seemed the smart thing to do for Mikhail. Paul and he had dreams of furthering their education and becoming professors at some prestigious university in America.

Matt was ecstatic when Clancy insisted that he stay on and work with Helen at the tavern. Helen remained in Jon's old room and Matt lodged in hers across the hall.

Jon and Jozef could feel the spirit of Ben Franklin roaming the streets of Old Philadelphia while meandering down Market Street looking for a place to eat and perhaps imbibe some Irish coffee.

Market Street, like Vaci, had the smell of spring in the air. It was noontime and the business district was swarming with shoppers. Philadelphia on the Delaware River, the largest fresh water seaport in the world, was inundated with ships. Sailors from all parts of the world were invading the taverns and various streets.

After half and hour of sightseeing at Independence Hall, they wandered into the Spirit of '76, a tavern that was constructed in 1776. An immense portrait of George Washington crossing the Delaware River covered the length of the wall behind the bar.

Having their fill of Irish coffee and pork sandwiches, they headed back up Market Street to the Reading railroad station where they boarded the train for Arland City.

The smoke of the steam engine painted the blue sky with streaks of ash as the train disappeared into a network of farmland and forest that were already beginning to show their plush green. The noon sun raced through the sky, keeping time with the train. After several local stops, they arrived in Arland City at 3:30 PM.

Cousins Francis and Stanley were waiting anxiously on the station platform. It had been a couple of years since they saw Jon, and at least ten years since seeing Jozef,

"My God!" Jozef said, beaming from ear to ear when he saw his cousins approaching.

"How wonderful to see you," Jozef said in Slovak. They balked for a moment, smiling, and then answered in Slovak that the feelings were mutual.

The railroad station was situated on the river on the lower end of the main thoroughfare of the city. Trolley cars and horses and buggies were in full swing in the late afternoon, ready to pick up the factory workers. Arland City was booming with business, thanks to the transfer of the silk industry from Patterson, New Jersey and the garment district from New York City.

Immigrants were pouring in from the coal regions looking for less dangerous work and better wages. The vast majority of the population was of German decent called the Pennsylvania Dutch, a culture that developed in the area since the end of the Revolutionary War. They weren't happy with the influx of the Micks, Dagos, Sand trotters, and Kikes and Hunks

The Irish arrived around 1860, running from the devastating results of the potato famine that decimated the economy of Ireland.

"Where to now, Stan?" Jozef asked, patting him on the back.

"To the 6th Ward, as soon as the trolley car arrives."

"The 6th Ward? What's that?"

"Well Jozef," Stan answered, "Arland City is divided into wards. This area is the 1st Ward. This is where the first settlers set up residence. As the population grew, the wards multiplied. We will be living in the 6th Ward, which is composed of foreigners, as the Pennsylvania Dutch calls us."

"Who are they?" Jozef asked.

"The enemy," Stan responded emphatically.

"Here's the trolley," Francis shouted from the corner of Hamilton Street.

Fullerton via the 6th Ward was printed boldly on the front of the trolley car. The doors were opened front and side, paying passengers from the front and departures from the rear. The aisles were narrow but the double seats were wide and comfortable.

They headed straight to the back where seats were still available. Stan led the way, and without warning was tripped by a seated passenger and fell flat on his face.

"How'd ya like that Hunky? Oh, I forgot. You don't speak English!"

While Jozef attended to Stan, Francis grabbed the Mick by his hair and pulled him up out of his seat and said in clear English, "Fuck you, you goddamn Mick! How's that for English?"

Just as a serious fight was to break out, the trolley conductor turned around and said, "If this bullshit continues, I will drop all of you off at the police station which is only a couple of blocks from here."

Jon was ready to go into one of his violent rages, but Jozef held him back.

"What did he say?" Jozef asked. Jon translated. Jozef, using his policeman's instincts, motioned for everyone in the trolley to calm down. After a couple of minutes, the conductor closed the doors and proceeded on into the jungle called the Bloody 6th.

CHAPTER 59

The trees of Ancient Buda were all dressed in their late spring green. Flowers of all species surrounded the rose covered slope.

Stasha gazed at the breathtaking view, but could not find any solace in its beauty. So many good things could not overcome the bad. Her mind was plagued with the thoughts of Jon. Just when she was finding some semblance of sanity, she received painful news about her mother.

Mr. Sokolosky sent a message with Emilie two weeks ago informing Stasha that her mother was arrested by the Magyars and placed in an insane asylum. Karol contacted his brother to see if he could help, but to no avail.

Stasha had just landed a job in a silk mill. With her free room and board, she expected to save enough money to eventually support herself and her mother. Karol offered to care for her, but she would not hear of it and if Karol did not have enough influence to free her mother, she would seek out someone who did.

"Hello," a voice rang out from the vestibule, "are you home, Stasha?"

"Yes Karol, I'm enjoying the scenery and thinking about how I made such a mess out of my life. First I lose the love of my life, my child, and then my mother."

"Yes, I know, and now you are about to make another mistake by not marrying me."

"Jesus, Mary, and Jozef, Karol. Will you give it up? You don't know when you have it good. I would make you're life miserable. You deserve better."

"I'll never find anyone as beautiful as you, nor as honest as you. Sure, you've made mistakes. So have I. Do you know why?"

"No."

"Because we are both young. Hell, you are only eighteen, and I'm only twenty-two. I have no excuse though. I come from a wealthy family. I had a first-class education. If it weren't for my late aunt, I wouldn't have all this luxury. I would like to succeed on my own, and with you as my wife I know I could do it."

"Yeah sure, with Stasha, the Slovak peasant girl with only a high school education and only experienced in picking fruit and vegetables."

"Stasha, please give it some more thought. Meanwhile, I will try to find out where your mother is. Now get dressed and we will have dinner at the *Hungaria*, and then we're going dancing."

—and dance they did, after a scrumptious dinner at the elegant *Hungaria* restaurant they whirled to contemporary waltzes in the adjoining ballroom.

They clicked their glasses together that bubbled with the finest champagne that Europe had to offer. Intoxicated by the spirits and music, they wandered down Vaci Street and stumbled into a small tavern where the sound of Gypsy music filled the room. A Gypsy girl slithered like a snake to the exotic beat, bringing groans to the men that leered at her sensuous body.

The guitarist's eye caught sight of Stasha. His coal black hair hung carelessly on his forehead. His eyes matched the color of his hair, adding an air of intrigue and mystic to his Gypsy persona. Stasha met his stare with defiance and then quickly melted to a sensuous smile.

Karol observed the flirtatious exchange and reached out and shook Stasha by her shoulder and said, "Woman, you are impossible. Can't you control yourself?"

Stasha looked at him and smiled, laughing hysterically. The music had stopped just as she made the outburst, allowing the patrons to hear her. Karol, embarrassed by her unruly behavior, pulled her by the hand roughly out of the chair and drag her out of the tavern. She continued to laugh as they walked down Vaci Street while Karol hailed a carriage to transport them home. When Karol opened the carriage door politely for Stasha, she stepped back and told him she would see him at home later. He just stared at her with hurt and anger in his eyes, then entered the carriage and ordered the driver to move on. Karol was sleeping on the living room sofa when he was aroused by Stasha calling for him.

"Where the hell have you been?" he asked, as he shaded his eyes with his hand from a ray of sun that was peering through the window. "My God, it's daylight already. Where did you sleep last night? Were you with that Gypsy?"

"That is none of you're business. Look, I thought we had an agreement. You offered to keep me and my mother here until we could go on our own."

"But . . . but," Karol began to stammer.

"Yes, yes, I know. You also hoped that in time we would be married. I told you that would probably never happen."

"Yes, you are right. I'll give it more time."

Stasha threw her hands up in the air, and with exasperation shouted, "You still don't get it! I will say it one more time loud and clear. I STILL LOVE JON!"

With that said Stasha went to her room undressed, took a long hot bath and then put on her bathrobe and walked out onto the rose-covered slope. She stood there for a moment with her eyes closed, facing the sun. Suddenly she removed her robe and stood naked and prayed to God to cleanse her sinful body and heal her soul.

"You are so beautiful," Karol said, breathlessly as he picked up her robe and covered her body. "It's Sunday," he added, "and I suggest that you put your Sunday best on, and then we will go to mass.

The May flowers inspired by the April showers engulfed them as the elegant Hansom carriage transported them to a place where God forgives the worst of sinners who truly beg forgiveness, and sends the rest to an eternal fiery death.

CHAPTER 60

One week after their arrival in Arland City, Jon and Jozef had already acquired jobs. The city was in dire need of housing to accommodate the massive influx of immigrants and businesses. The silk mills, iron and steel, and cement and wire mills were flourishing industries.

Jon had no problem choosing a career. He immediately applied for work as a carpenter in the home building industry. Jozef too decided to continue his career in police work. Francis took him to police headquarters to fill out a job application and have an interview.

After studying Jozef's credentials, the interviewer was impressed, but felt his inability to speak English would nullify his approval to be hired at the present time. Francis translated for Jozef and then turned to the interviewer and said that he had heard somewhere that the city wanted to set up a precinct in the 6th Ward.

"Yes, that's true."

"Well, then why haven't you already? Because of the language barrier?" Francis paused for a moment and then he pointed to Jozef and said, "Here's your answer."

After three months of on the job police training and classes in English, Jozef became headman in the 6th Ward precinct with a lieutenant's ranking and several bilingual men under his command. It wasn't an easy job because crime was rampant and the men under his command were getting paid a pittance. Some doubled up as firemen. When a fire was in progress, they had to drop everything they were doing and get to the site of the fire. Jon visited the Hibernia fire house that was located at the corner of Ridge Avenue, and Tilghman Streets, just a block away from where he was living. They asked him if he had any experience in the field. Jon just smiled and handed him the New York newspaper that printed his heroic story. They were impressed and told him that they were looking forward to seeing him in action.

Jon soon became completely involved in the building business that was engaged in erecting row homes in the more affluent parts of the city. Jozef was busy helping calm down the Union strikers. The trolley Transit Company was their target this time. They were looking for higher wages and time off. After a day-long picketing-without-violence, the strike was settled and everyone went home peacefully. Jozef's diplomatic approach contributed immensely to the calm conclusion. His superiors were very impressed. Not bad for a "dumb Hunky."

It was Sunday and Jon and Jozef were home resting when there was a knock at the door. "It's open, come on in," Jon shouted.

Jon's chair was facing away from the door and before he could get up to see who it was, two hands came from behind him and covered his eyes.

"Guess who?" a voice whispered.

The hands were soft and feminine. For one fleet second, Jon thought, "Oh my God, it's Stasha!" He jumped out of his chair and turned to find not Stasha, but Maria. For a moment he froze and showed obvious disappointment, and then quickly drew her close to him and said, "Oh Maria, it's so nice to see you. What a surprise!"

"I'm sorry that I didn't let you know that I was coming. I wasn't sure that you would want me to come."

"Nonsense," Jon replied as he invited her to sit down. "May I get you a cold drink? This has been one hell of a hot summer. Working outside has been exhausting, especially on top of roofs."

Jozef made a coughing sound to get their attention.

"Oh, I'm sorry, Jozef," Jon said, a little embarrassed, and then said, "Maria, this is my brother Jozef."

She extended her hand for Jozef to kiss, which was customary in Slovakia. He responded gracefully and said in Slovak, "I kiss your hand beautiful," giving the gesture a more respectful meaning.

Maria stood back to get a more studied look at Jozef.

"My God, you two could pass for twins," she said, smiling, amazed at their resemblance.

"That's why I grew this mustache. I got tired of people mistaking me for Jon," Jozef said, laughing. "I remember people coming up to me and asking me to fix this and that for them."

"Yeah, and I remember people asking me to come to the tavern and break up a fight," Jon retaliated, laughing.

"Yes, and how many times was I called to break up one of your fights?"

"Alright, enough," Jon said, and then directed Maria to sit down on the sofa with him. "How is my friend Patrick doing? Have you got together on your business venture?"

"No."

"Why not?"

"That's why I came to see you. Patrick wants to be my full-time partner."

"Well, with him putting up most of the money that ought to make you happy."

"No, you don't understand, he wants to marry me."

"Oh, that's wonderful!" Jon responded while he slid over to embrace her.

"No it's not and you know why. You know that I love you and that I want you to marry me. How could I possibly wed Patrick when I am in love with you?"

"And how could I marry you when I am still in love with Stasha?" Jon shouted back.

"After all the terrible things that she has done to you and you still want her?"

"It was my fault. I should have never have left her behind. I should have waited until both of us could afford to come together."

"Nonsense Jon, she was fooling around with that soldier only a few months after you left."

"Jon, she is right," Jozef said, interrupting. "Brother, I haven't told you half the things that she has done. I wanted to spare you that. My God, how lucky can you get to find a woman like Maria here? She loves you and she is also beautiful. I should be so fortunate."

"What will Patrick do without you?" Jon asked, trying to change the subject.

"I turned the boarding house over to my sister with the hope that Patrick and her will get together."

"Where are your daughters? Are they with you?" Jon asked curiously.

"They are with my sister temporarily."

"What do you mean temporarily?"

"Until I find a job here and get settled in my own house."

Jon just shook his head in disbelief.

Maria noticed his exasperated look and said, "Jon I'm staying whether you want me or not. Your cousins told me that there are plenty of opportunities here. I'll find a job, save my money, and when I can afford a decent place to live I will send for my children. If nothing else I want to make a better life for my girls. That's why we came to this country. Francis told me that you have an extra bedroom. Would you be kind enough to rent it to me? I can also be your cook and housecleaner."

"Do I have a choice?"

"No."

"Women," Jon shouted, throwing his hands up and then helped her out of the chair and led her to what would be her temporary bedroom.

CHAPTER 61

All through the summer Stasha kept a weekly routine. She was up early in the morning and then off to the factory where she worked hard for a miniscule wage. Karol offered money to add to her weekly wage, but as usual she stubbornly refused.

When the weekend arrived, she would dress in her finest and disappear into the labyrinth of Pest and not return until midnight on Sunday.

Karol bit his tongue for as long as he could stand it. Finally one Sunday night he went looking for her. He went to the elite *Hungaria*, *Carlton*, and the *Bristol Hotels*, assuming that she went out dressed to frequent the finer places of Pest, but to no avail. He went to the nearest coffee shop and sat down to contemplate where she might have gone, when suddenly it came to him. She went to the tavern to see the Gypsy that she flirted with the first night he took her out dancing at the *Hungaria*, ending up at the tavern.

Ten minutes later he arrived. He walked right over to the Gypsy guitarist and confronted him about the whereabouts of Stasha.

"Where is Stasha?" he shouted, almost in a rage.

"Stasha who?" the Gypsy shouted back, jumping out of his chair, poised to throw a punch.

"You know goddamn well who!"

"Hold up you two," the bartender shouted as he approached the table area. "Karol," he said, recognizing him, "I haven't seen you for a long time. What's the problem? Sit down, both of you and tell me what this is about."

"Andrew, do you remember the last time that I was here with a young beautiful girl?"

"How could I forget? She had all the men dazzled. It took along time for her not to be the topic of conversation around here."

"How many times did she come back to see this Cigan?" Karol asked, spitting his words out.

"Never, at least not on the nights I was tending bar. How about you?" he asked, turning to the guitar player, "when did you see her last?"

"Andy, I swear on my mother's grave, I never saw her since the last time she was here with him."

"Do you swear on your mother's grave that she didn't meet you someplace that evening? The night you were slobbering over one another?"

"I swear but I will be honest with you, I was praying that she would return. I must admit that she made my blood run hot."

A distinguished looking gentleman dressed in the latest fashions, wearing a Derby hat, spun around on his stool at the bar and said pointedly, "I saw her!"

"You did! Where?" Karol responded anxiously.

"On Magyar Street."

"Where all the whorehouses are?"

"Yes."

"How did you know it was her?"

"I was here the night you came here together. I must admit she made my blood run hot too."

"Did you see her going into any of the brothels?"

"No! She was just walking the street and wow, was she making heads turn. When I became aware of who she was, she disappeared."

Karol rose slowly from his chair, his eyes fixed with grief. He first apologized to the Gypsy, and then thanked the stranger.

"Give it up, Karol," the bartender shouted after him as he was leaving.

Karol turned before he closed the door behind him and said sadly, "I can't."

Magyar Street was inundated with the highbrow of Budapest society in search of a fling with the ladies of the night. The passing hours diminished the throng of gentlemen, lending a chilling silence to Magyar Street. Discouraged and angry, Karol returned home and waited.

Sunday evening, just before midnight, Stasha staggered through the door exhausted. She went straight to her bedroom, stripped, and then slipped into a steamy hot bath.

Karol had dozed off on the living room sofa and didn't hear her pass by. It wasn't until the clock chimed midnight that he saw the candlelight flickering in her bedroom. The door was left slightly ajar. He quickly got up and pushed the door open and found her clothes scattered all over the bed. His eye caught sight of a small leather case. Curious of its contents, he opened it and found a document of sorts that designated that she be required to get frequent medical checkups as long as she practiced prostitution in Budapest.

"What the hell are you doing Stasha?" he shouted, bursting into the bathroom with the document in his hand.

"So now you know," Stasha answered, seemingly relieved by his discovery, adding, "Don't worry about it."

"What do you mean? Don't worry?"

"Well, it's not like you can get a disease from me. We aren't having sex together."

"I know but . . . but," he stammered.

"I know," Stasha said exasperated, "you had hoped to marry me some day. Give it up!"

"Never"

"Well, I'm going to make it easy for you," she said, lifting her naked body up out of the tub.

Karol stood there gasping for breath at the sight of her voluptuous body. "This is not making it easy for me," he said, handing her a towel.

"Look Karol, I'm sorry. You've been so good to me, more than I deserve, and I love you but I'm not in love with you, so I'm moving on and making a life for myself."

"Prostituting!"

"Yes, but I'm not street walking anymore. I've been invited by Madam Rita Pilsey to travel to Moscow where I will get under the silk sheets with the aristocrats of tsarist Russia. She promised me that I would return with a small but adequate fortune."

"Oh, that's great! Do you know what the Russians call you ladies?"

"No."

"Hungarian girls of light morals."

"I'm not Hungarian."

Karol threw his hands up in the air in complete surrender and said, "Fine! When are you leaving?"

"Next Sunday at twelve noon from West Railroad Station."

"What about your job at the factory?"

"I gave notice last week."

Stasha's anxiety made the week drag on, but Karol's' was tantamount to the fire that erupted a split second after lightening struck. In spite of being angry with Stasha, he escorted her to the train station in his private Hansom carriage. They spoke not a word, but their silence translated their feelings. When they arrived, they were accosted by Madame Pilsey and her party of fillies, a name given to them by the Hungarians, more for their refined manners than for their feminine beauty.

"All aboard," a voice shouted from the railway platform.

Without further adieu, they embraced. Karol made one more attempt to stop her with a pleading look in his eyes, but Stasha stubbornly ignored it. Karol stood motionless as the train pulled out of the station like a rhinoceros charging through a herd of elephants. He ran to the edge of the platform and fell onto his knees in despair, tears clouding his eyes as Stasha slipped into a world of impropriety.

CHAPTER 62

It was early September 1905. Manhattan was bustling with the combined sounds of horse hoofs and the new horseless carriage, the automobile. Clancy told Matt and Helen that he was giving them two weeks paid vacation. He needed time to do some remodeling. It didn't take them long to decide where they would go. Clancy sent a telegram off to Jon informing him that they would be arriving by train on the first Sunday in September.

Matt and Helen were strolling hand in hand up Broadway, enjoying the last of summer's delight while they licked furiously at their ice cream that was dripping down their cones into their hands. They looked at one another and laughed and then together tossed their cones in the air. They embraced, kissing and licking the residue of melted ice cream off each other's lips, and then raced to Penn Station to board the train for Arland City.

Six months had passed since they met and fell in love. Matt fell in love at first sight, Helen when she found out about his Gypsy heritage. They spent a lot of their off time mingling with Gypsies that lived in Manhattan that had come from all parts of the world. A desperate search was made to find the whereabouts of Helen's parents, but to no avail. Finally at the advice of immigration officials that frequented the tavern, they checked the deported list at Ellis Island. To Helen's delight she found her parents' name. The reason for their deportation was because they didn't have the necessary twenty-five dollars that was required. Matt found that hard to believe and was sure that they were deported because they were Gypsies. Helen said she didn't think that was the case because her father and mother had given their share when she left the ship with the two men promising her work and a place to live. "They told my parent's that they would get back to them later. Instead they took the money from me and beat me up and if it wasn't for Jon and Lucas, only God knows what would have happened to me."

The train rolled over the New Jersey countryside, splashing the summer green with black smut that poured out of the fiery coal burning furnace that powered the engines. While Helen sat by the window enjoying the scenery, Matt fell into a semi-conscious state. His mind drifted back to the first day he laid eyes on Helen and how he fell in love. Slowly but surely Helen succumbed to his advances. Their relationship seemed perfect except for one curious item. They never had a consummated sexual encounter even though they had slept together in the same bed on several occasions. Was it because of the loss of her parents? Maybe, so he sent a letter to his Uncle Emile and asked him if he would try to find her parents who had lived in Presov for years before making the voyage to America.

Helen was thankful but still resisted his sexual advances. Matt was at the point of despair. He was hurt and frustrated. It suddenly came to him that Helen was a lady with morals, and that he should be thankful for that. He figured out how he was going to solve that problem. One Saturday night after work, he took her to one of their Gypsy night clubs. In the middle of the dance floor he got on his knees and proposed. The band stopped playing and people stared excitedly, waiting for the romantic scene to come to its Romeo and Juliet conclusion. For a moment there was a deadly silence, ending with Helen sobbing and running out onto the street. The next day she asked him to be patient with her, and that she needed more time. That was a month ago and still no progress. Maybe Jon could help her. He was like an older brother to her.

He suddenly was struck with another thought and opened his eyes and shouted, "That's it, isn't it?"

"What?" Helen responded, startled by his sudden outburst.

"The reason you have this fear of having sex is because of what happened to you in that alley. They did more than beat you. They raped you too, didn't they?"

Helen just stared at Matt, speechless.

"Didn't they?" Matt repeated, softening his voice. "Tell me please."

"Hey do you two have a problem here?" the conductor asked, leaning over and whispering.

"No—no sir," Matt answered, speaking in broken English. "Thank God we were speaking in Slovak," he said to Helen. "Don't worry, no one understood us. Look, I won't ask you about it anymore. You tell me when you are ready."

She looked at him with pleading eyes and said, "Please, don't think that I don't love you, because I do."

The conductor's voice rang out and said, "The train will be arriving in Little Steel City in about ten minutes. Get your suitcases and any other baggage ready to go. Thank you and enjoy your day. Eight minutes later, the conductor shouted that all should be ready to disembark.

Helen looked out the window and saw Jon waiting on the platform. The moment her feet hit the ground she raced towards him, her arms outstretched and then crashed bodily into him, almost knocking him over.

"Oh Jon!" she cried, tears pouring from her eyes. "God, how I've missed you!"

Meanwhile, Matt and Francis embraced and kissed. "It's been a long time Francis, at least eight years since you left Dubovica. You put on a lot of muscle. You're not that skinny little kid anymore."

"Yeah, a year in the coal mines did that to me. I was one of the lucky ones, I survived."

"Come on," Jon said, looking at his pocket watch, "the trolley will be leaving any minute for Arland City. We should be home in about a half hour."

When they arrived at the house, Jozef was at the door to greet them.

"I'll bet you people are hungry," he said, smiling and beckoning them to come into the dining room. The table was all set and they could smell the fresh smell of cabbage permeating from the kitchen.

"Well Jozef, I didn't know you could cook. It smells like you steamed up some holubkys."

"You're right, but I didn't make them."

"I did!" Maria shouted, bursting into the room with a bowl full of hot steaming halubkys in her hands.

Jon stood up and said, "This is Maria Novak. She used to be my landlady when I was working in the coal mines. Now I'm her landlord.

CHAPTER 63

Russia was not in a state of euphoria in the early nineteen hundreds. They had just lost a war with Japan and the reign of the Tsars was obviously in jeopardy. Demonstrators were gunned down mercilessly by the Tsarist troops. The populace referred to the infamous day on January 22, 1905 as "Bloody Sunday."

After a three-hour stopover in Kiev, the train steamed into Moscow's Kievskiy Station at 3:00 PM. They collected their luggage and waited to be picked up by private carriages that were sent by the nobility. Each lady was assigned to a particular nobleman.

Stasha's name was called out and without further adieu her luggage was picked up and strapped to the roof of an elegant hansom carriage. They rode swiftly down the main thoroughfare, trying to flee from the demonstrators that crowded the streets carrying signs that pleaded for justice and equality. Some were courageous, stating to do away with the tsars. These peaceful strikes led to promoting some reforms, such as elections being held.

Stasha covered her eyes with her hands as they entered into the Kremlin. It was like she had passed into a fairyland. The magnificent structures designed centuries ago by Italian renaissance architects were scattered majestically throughout the square. She removed her hand and realized that it was not a dream. One by one, the glorious cathedrals and palaces appeared like magnificent paintings against the cloudless ocean blue September sky. First in line came the great Kremlin palace with lavish stuccowork where state receptions were held. Its marble walls were inscribed with military heroes. The Cathedral of the Archangel that housed the tombs of the infamous Ivan the Terrible's family embraced Cathedral Square. Finally, they reached Trinity Tower and exited through the same gate that Napoleon entered in 1812, leaving one month later in a humiliating defeat.

After an hour passed, they arrived at the outskirts of Moscow where a mansion stood like a giant fortress on the western bank of the Moskva river. A high-iron fence surrounded the structure that was a mixture of Russian and Italian design.

Stasha was sitting motionless, taking in the breathtaking view when the creaking noise of the main gate swung open allowing the carriage to enter the lush green grounds that had a line of trees forming an avenue that led to the main entrance.

When the carriage came to a halt, the door was opened by a gentleman elegantly dressed.

"Welcome to the Wooden Palace," the young man said as he helped Stasha step down off carriage.

"Wooden!" she answered, puzzled because from the distance and up close, she was sure that it was made from stone.

"Oh, please forgive me!" Stasha said, bowing respectfully.

"No, no madam, I am only the humble servant of Count Malovsky. Please give me your hand and I will take you to him. He is waiting in the grand parlor."

Stasha couldn't resist rubbing her hand across the pillar that stood next to the main door.

"Yes, gracious madam. It is wooden. The paint is mixed with plaster and sand, making it appear to be stone."

"Amazing!" Stasha whispered, shaking her head.

Once more her breath was taken as she entered the open wide doors to this magnificent room. The chandeliers sparkled high above, connecting to a ceiling that was festooned with paintings and stain glass ornaments that hung like a myriad of diamonds in the infinite universe. The great Italian renaissance paintings flanked by long narrow stain glass windows lined the four walls. In the center of the rear wall, above a marble and stone fireplace, was an immense portrait of Tsar Nicholas and his family.

"Madam," a voice echoed through the mystified aura of Stasha's mind. "Madam, are you all right?" the voice persisted.

"Oh, yes. I am just enthralled by the luxury and the artistic beauty of your home. It reminds me of a museum I once visited in Buda."

Slowly, Stasha glided back to her senses and began to see the handsome young man that was addressing her. He was tall and slender with a well-barbered beard and a thick crop of dark brown wavy hair that sat on his head like a fields of wheat in a windstorm. "Madam, I welcome you with open arms. I have been waiting anxiously for your arrival. You're all that Madam Pilsey said you were," and then he added, "And more." He kissed her hand and led her into the library where they sat and had tea, getting acquainted with each other. To his pleasant surprise, the conversation was held in Russian. Stasha had studied Russian at the urging of Madam Bilsy. Stasha had no problem with the translation because after all, the Slovak language was the core of all the surrounding Slavic nations. This would prove to be a big advantage.

After unpacking and then dinner, they set out for a night at the opera at the palatial Bolshoy Theater, one of the most famous landmarks in the world.

A throng of people entered the grand black and white tiled vestibule. Magnificent staircases lined with white marble led up from either side of the vestibule to the spacious main foyer. The foyer extended around the whole of the front of the building on the first floor. Its vaulted ceiling was decorated with paintings and elaborates stucco works.

Situated in the center of the gallery, the royal box hung with crimson velvet, was one of over 120 boxes. The imperial crown stood majestically on its pediment.

The evening was a magic ride with fine dining, sophisticated entertainment, and waltzing to the music of one of the many unique Russian symphony orchestras. With all the elegance and beauty that presented itself in abundance, it still could not overshadow the sparkling presence of Stasha. Everywhere they appeared they were greeted with stares and whispers.

The count was ecstatic with the attention and paraded like a peacock through the throng of admirers. Stasha was more than ready for a night of ecstasy. When they arrived home, a maid opened the door and informed them that their bath was ready. A marble tub filled with warm water and saturated with exotic perfumes from every corner of the earth was at their beckoning call.

They went to their separate bedrooms. After donning in silk and velvet bathrobes, they entered the bathroom. He was attired in red velvet and she in white silk. For a moment they stood and gazed at one another and then Stasha slowly started to remove her robe at the top, revealing her voluptuous breasts, causing the count's heartbeat to rise. Suddenly she let her robe fall swiftly to the marble floor. He just stood there speechless and motionless.

Before he could gain his composure, Stasha stepped towards him with her dark Mongol eyes fixed hypnotically on his. She undid his belt and slipped her hand between his thighs and grasped his manhood that was as hard as a steel sword that was poised for battle. After a moment of soft caressing and heavy breathing, they submerged themselves into the warm steaming sea of luxurious bathing. They laid motionless for awhile, enjoying the comfort that was bestowed on them by the aroma and soothing heat of the water. Without warning, the count stood up and helped Stasha rise out of the water. They stepped out of the tub onto the tile floor and reached out for the bath towels that were conveniently set on a wheeled table. He wasted no time in drying her body softly but swiftly with tantalizing precision. Stasha was swimming in an exotic whirlpool oblivious to her surroundings, while he led her out of the bathroom naked across the hall that led to a giant golden door. Stasha was mystified as he opened the door to a room that was all mirrors, and in its center was an enormous four poster bed. Beside the bed was a mirrored top table with two glasses of Russia's finest vodka. Without further adieu, they clinked glasses, drank their contents with one swallow, and then swam into a pool of mirrorotic ecstasy.

CHAPTER 64

Autumn swiftly vanished into winter, bringing projects to a standstill. Arland City was still growing in leaps and bounds. Immigrants from the coal regions and Europe poured relentlessly into the 6th Ward. Slovaks, Syrians, Jews, and Irish were the predominant nationalities.

Jon had purchased several old, broken down vacant houses in the neighborhood. He would spend the rest of the winter remodeling the interiors to get them ready for rentals for the immigrants. Jozef was busy pleading with the city officials to recruit more policemen. The new arrivals brought conflict and violence between the different cultures. Language also caused problems in communication.

Finally one day, frustrated from the lack of cooperation form the city, Jozef decided to call a mass meeting at a local park along the Lehigh river. He had interpreters pass the word around from each nationality. They were also there to translate what he said at the meeting. To Jozef's surprise, almost everyone attended

The crowd quieted down as soon as Jozef stood up on one of the park benches. He paused for a moment to get his composure and then he shouted for all to hear.

"Everyone must stop fighting amongst one another. We all must concentrate on becoming successful American citizens. The rest of the city looks down on us as being inferior. We must prove otherwise. From this day on we must join together and have solidarity. Remember, after this day we will be only two nationalities: Americans and Sixth Warders.

The anxious crowd stood silent, absorbing the advice. Suddenly they threw their arms into the air in total agreement. They turned to one another, Irish to Slovaks and Syrians to Jews, shaking hands and embracing.

This generation would show their worth with physical labor, but their children would contribute with their intellect.

March 7, 1906 arrived and Jon celebrated his twenty-sixth birthday. Maria surprised him with a party that included all his close friends. Clancy,

Lucas, and Matt traveled from New York City, along with Mikhail and Paul. Jon was overwhelmed, but his biggest surprise was when Doctor Ginsberg arrived. He had decided to leave his charity work in the coal regions and start a more lucrative practice in the burgeoning community of Arland City. With the iron works, wire mills, and steel industry, injuries were running rampant. A shortage of doctors was indeed prevalent.

After an evening of wine and Irish coffee, they all settled in the living room and discussed the future. Clancy was talking about maybe retiring and turning the business over to Matt and Helen. Mikhail and Paul hoped to be teaching in a year or two. Lucas would be busy supervising the maintenance of the Hotel Royals that were being built in the resort areas of the Catskill Mountains in upstate New York, and in the thriving ocean shore tourist area of Atlantic City, New Jersey. When the party ended, Matt got hold of Helen's hand and led her out to the backyard where Maria had nurtured a rose garden.

"Perfect." Matt whispered under his breath.

"What's perfect?" Helen responded, flashing her eyes.

"Look at the beautiful garden. It couldn't be a more perfect place."

"For what?" she asked, perplexed.

Matt fell to his knees and pleaded with tears in his eyes for her hand in marriage.

Helen closed her eyes, gritted her teeth, and shouted emphatically, "No! I told you before that I will let you know when I am ready!"

"But, but . . . ," Matt stammered, "You've had six months to think about it."

"I know but please give me a little more time. I've been praying every day to the Blessed Virgin Mary. I have faith that she will enlighten me and remove the guilt from my soul. I recite the rosary every night kneeling on stones."

"What? Kneeling on stones? Are you out of your mind?"

"You don't understand. I must pay for my sin."

"What sin?"

"Oh! Here you two are," Clancy said, interrupting. "Matt, I'm sorry to break up this romantic scene but we have to get the midnight train back to New York. Don't be sad, Helen. You know we have a business to take care of and by the way, I was hoping that you would be coming back to the tavern soon."

"I was just discussing that with her."

"On your knees?" Clancy replied, laughing, and then said, "I'll give you love birds five more minutes, and then we're out of here."

"Okay Helen," Matt said, getting up off his knees, "I'll give you until June, and then I want an answer one way or the other. Do you understand?" he said, raising his voice.

"Yes, yes. I promise you, one way or the other."

As they were saying their goodbyes at the front door, Matt pulled Maria to the side and asked her if she would help him with Helen. "Of course," Maria answered, "but what's the problem?"

"I have asked her to marry me several times and even though she swears that she loves me she won't give me an answer. Look, I don't have time to explain, but you talk to Jon about it. He knows the situation better than anyone. Good bye and thanks," Matt said, and then kissed her on the cheek and left.

"What was that all about?" Doc Ginsberg asked, overhearing the conversation.

"I honestly don't know. We'll have to ask Jon."

"Ask about what?" Jon asked, entering the room.

"About Matt and Helen's problem. He asked me if I could persuade her to marry him."

"Sit down," Jon said, and then told them of that fateful night when he and Lucas rescued her.

"Was she raped?" Maria asked emphatically.

"I honestly don't know," Jon answered, shaking his head in frustration.

"Where is she now?" Maria asked.

"She went to the convent to do penance. She goes every night."

"Look," Doc said interrupting, "I can settle this with a vaginal examination."

"Let me talk to her first," Maria said. "It might be easier for her to talk to me about it because I am a woman. Now please excuse me, I have cleaning up to do in the kitchen."

"Well Doc, it looks like it's just you and me," Jon said, as they sat down on the sofa. "What are your plans now?" Jon asked.

"I've been in touch with other medical men that are interested in moving here. I went to medical school with most of them, so we know each other pretty well. It was a dream of ours to someday get together and have a practice. Where could a better place be than here in Arland City, probably the fastest growing city in America?"

"Where are you going to get all this money to finance this venture?"

"Our parents said that they would contribute most of the capital and hopefully we can get a bank loan to cover the rest."

"Hell, I can help you with the loan. I have recently made friends in the banking business. When I had immigrant buyers for my houses, they loaned them the money and put them on easy monthly payments. Look, tomorrow I'll set you up with a meeting with one of the loan managers."

"That sounds great Jon!" Doc answered excitably, rising from the sofa, shaking Jon's hand.

CHAPTER 65

April was just around the corner, but winter was still cold, harsh, and snowbound. Stasha received a letter from Madam Pilsey informing her that she was to leave Moscow as soon as possible and return to Budapest. Her train ticket would be paid for in advance. Stasha wasn't too happy about leaving the plush life that she had become accustomed to. The count was very good to her and obviously very much in love, but Madam Pilsey warned her of the dangers of the ensuing revolution. There would be violence committed to the aristocracy and anyone connected with them.

After finishing the letter she paused for a moment, absorbing what she had just read. She took a deep breath and said out loud, "Well, I guess I better get dressed. This will probably be my last night at the opera, and my farewell dance."

The bedroom door suddenly flung open, smashing against the wall and breaking the lock. "What is it?" Stasha shouted, alarmed at the violent intrusion. Misha, the young man that she mistook for the count when she had arrived handed her some clothing and told her to hurry and put them on.

"But, these are the maid's clothes," she answered, puzzled.

"Exactly! Now you are one of us."

"But why?" she asked, as she slipped on the dress.

"Because the peasants and factory workers are on their way. They have had enough of the inequalities the tsars have rendered on them for centuries. Equality is all we are asking for. Now, hurry before they arrive and please don't show any sign of pity for the count, or they will hang you alongside of him. You cannot show any sign of being royalty, or they will murder you too."

"What!" Stasha snapped, shocked.

"I'm sorry, but that's the way it is"

"But he is a good man."

"Yes he is, but . . ."

"But my ass," Stasha shouted, interrupting. "Where is he now?" Stasha demanded.

"In the study."

"Is he aware?"

"No."

"Then he must be warned and given a chance to escape."

"Go if you must Stasha, but I cannot help you. I would be a traitor to my people."

"Well, I'm not Russian. I won't feel guilty helping him."

She rushed out of the room and arrived just as the count was closing the door behind him. When he turned and faced her, he balked for a moment and then began to laugh and said, "Well, Stasha! I see that you are dressed to go dancing. Is that the latest fashion from Paris you are wearing?"

"Boris, listen to me and believe what I am saying. The peasants and the factory workers are on their way here to murder you. Do you understand what I am saying?"

"Yes," he answered, finally grasping the danger he was in.

"Then tell me, if there is a way you can escape without being seen?"

"Yes, there is. There is an underground passageway that leads to the river behind the mansion. There's a boat there that can get us down river. Here," he said, reaching into the cloak room closet for two warm fur-lined coats.

In a few minute they were stumbling blindly through the dark, damp, freezing passageway. They could hear the shouting and stomping of the invading mob above them. They finally arrived at the bank of the river where the count watched his wooden palace being ransacked and set afire. Stasha, seeing his pain, embraced him as his tears flowed freely from his eyes.

"Come Boris, we must go now," she said, pulling him into the boat, not realizing that it was stuck in the frozen river. Suddenly, Misha and a gang of peasants rushed out of the passageway exit; Stasha immediately stepped forward to plead with Misha to stop them. Everyone grew silent, ignoring her gesture as they watched the count race across the ice-swollen river. The moon was full, exposing the desperate fleeing figure of Count Boris Malovsky. They watched as he fell through the ice into the cold flowing undercurrent of the river.

"Who is she? His whore?" someone shouted from the midst of the mob.

"No, she is just his personal maid," Misha responded while he reached out to help Stasha out of the boat.

"Then why is she so upset?" a voice shouted. "She should be cheering instead of crying."

Stasha pulled away from Misha's grasp and shouted, "Boris was a good man. Just because he was a noble, doesn't make him bad. He treated all of us who worked under him with kindness and respect. Is that not true, Misha?"

"Yes, it is true. Now we must go before the tsar's soldiers arrive."

They worked their way back through the passageway and headed for the main door. By good fortune they were the last ones to arrive out of the tunnel. The soldiers had entered the mansion and were making an attempt to extinguish the flames that were racing furiously up the walls. Tsar Nicholas' family portrait was already destroyed. When the peasants appeared, the soldiers began opening fire on the onrushing mob. Misha quickly pulled Stasha back into the passageway, locking the door from the inside.

The hours passed slowly into morning before the sound of footsteps quieted down to an eerie silence. Misha cautiously opened the door and climbed the cellar steps that led to a secret revolving bookcase in the study. Slowly he pushed it open, and to his horror found the bodies of the peasants lying in a bloody mess all the way into the grand parlor.

He turned to face Stasha, who was in a state of hysteria and said, "Well, now what do you think of the nobles?"

Stasha stared in disbelief as they climbed over the bloody flesh.

"Come, Stasha, we must go now. Go to your room and pack some of your clothing. Put on your Sunday best.

"Where are you taking me?"

"To the railroad station."

"That's good, because Madam Pilsey has tickets waiting for me."

Red Square was buzzing with violent altercations about the massacre at the wooden mansion. Peasants were carrying placards denouncing the tsar while the soldiers kept a watchful eye.

Slowly Misha guided the horses through the square, trying to attract as little attention as possible. Stasha turned to take one final look at the glorious Red Square. She would never forget the experience, and would never stop mourning for the count that she grew to have respect and affection for. At one point in their relationship she contemplated whether she loved him. Of course it was no, because she still loved Jon.

It was also a sad departure when she said goodbye to Misha. He had been like a brother to her. She tried to persuade him to come with her where Karol could employ him. He thanked her but said that he could not desert his country at these crucial times.

"Good bye and God bless you," Stasha said, turning to Misha as she boarded the train, and then turned once more and said, "Misha, if you ever change your mind, please get in touch with me through Madam Pilsey."

It snowed all the way to Kiev, and then gradually disappeared as they approached the surrounding countryside of Budapest. Stasha wired Madam Pilsey from Kiev and informed her that she was on her way and would arrive at West Station at noon on Monday. When the train pulled into the station, Stasha glanced out the passenger window and went into complete shock at what she saw.

She raced out onto the platform screaming, "Mother, Mother!"

She looked at Karol and asked him where he found her.

"She was brought back to your house in Dubovica thinking you would be there to care for her. When you couldn't be found, they inquired throughout the village and found Mr. Sokolsky. He remembered promising you that he would take care of her until you got your life in order."

"Mother, are you alright?"

"Yes, I am, but who are you and why do you call me 'Mother'?"

CHAPTER 66

The year 1907 brought a flood of immigrants into the 6th ward bringing social changes and serious domestic problems. Jobs and housing became a burdensome task for Arland City's government body. Ironically the dilemma filled the pockets of Jon Valen. He was able to rent and even sell most of the properties he had acquired and remodeled. He arranged for his immigrant clients to make mortgage loans through a local bank that set up a branch in the 6th ward for the expressed purpose of accommodating the immigrants. It was Jon himself who persuaded the bank president to make the accommodations for them. He also reminded them how successful the loan they made to Doc Ginsberg worked out.

In 1909 Maria finally convinced Jon to marry her. It was a grand wedding at St. Mary's Irish Roman Catholic Church, the only Catholic church in the 6th ward at the time. Five years later, Jon would contribute a great deal of his profits to building a Slovak national church on Front Street just across from where he was in the process of building his first row of brick homes. By 1912 he purchased a piece of land from the city in the neighborhood that was originally planned to be a city park. He immediately began to build houses around the perimeter of the lot. He built six brick buildings on Tilghman Street, a road that would one day would be one of the main thoroughfares in Arland City. On the northeast corner, he built a three-story building with rental apartments on the second and third floors and a grocery store on the first floor that Maria worked. Next to the store, he built another three-story building where he also had two rentals and a hardware store that he leased to Jacob Rosenthal a Jew that had fled from the massacre of his people in Russia. Jon remembered him when he peddled fruit and vegetables in a pushcart on warm summer days and slept outside. In the winter he had tried finding jobs where he could sleep in the cellar. Somehow he survived. They would both become successful businessmen and life long friends. Jon and his family lived above the grocery store while the main house was being constructed just aside the hardware store. It was constructed with the latest modern bricks that were light golden brown in color that paled the surrounding red brick and wooden structures. It too was three stories high but because of its cathedral ceilings, it towered above the neighborhood like a Manhattan skyscraper

"Momma," a young feminine voice shouted as she entered the grocery store.

"Oh, it's you," Maria said, as she entered the store from the back room where all the canned goods were stored. "Where is your sister?"

"Rosemarie is down at the playground with her boyfriend."

"What boyfriend?" Maria asked.

"Tomas Brenkacs."

"You don't mean that Cigan," Maria snapped.

"Yes, Mother, the Gypsy. Do you have a problem with that? He's a very nice polite boy. He treats Rosemarie with great respect."

"She's too young to have a boy friend," Maria countered.

"Mother, Rosemarie is sixteen years old. She's no baby anymore. You were married when you were fifteen and had Rosemarie when you were sixteen!"

"Those were different days. In the old country that's the way it was."

Suddenly, their conversation was interrupted by Rosemarie bursting through the door with Tomas Brenkacs' arm wrapped around her neck. His face was cut and bruised.

"What happened?" Monica shouted.

"A bunch of Slovak boys beat Tomas up because he was with me," Rosemarie answered breathlessly.

"Maria reached out and said, "Let me help you get him to the kitchen sink. I'll clean the blood from his face and then she turned to Monica and told her to contact Doc Ginsberg and leave word that there is an emergency at the Valen's store. Monica cranked the telephone and asked the operator to call Doc Ginsberg and tell him to come as soon as possible to Jon Valen's store.

Fifteen minutes later Doc arrived all excited with worry.

"What is it?" he asked frantically. "Is Jon all right," and then he noticed Tomas slumped in the kitchen chair. "What happened to him?"

"He got beat up by some Slovak boys."

"Why?"

"Because he's a Gypsy."

"Yeah, I can relate to that being a Jew myself."

After a thorough examination he concluded that his nose and two ribs were broken and a cut above his left eye was deep enough to be stitched.

"I'll have to take you back to the clinic. Meanwhile, you get in touch with Jozef and have him investigate and find the boys who did this.

CHAPTER 67

Stasha was sitting in the West Railroad Station in Pest waiting for the train to take her to Presov and then hopefully have Karol's brother transport her to Dubovica

It was a little more than eight years since she had left Moscow. Karol had finally given up on her and ended up wedding Matt Sokolosky's sister. Mariska had came several times to visit Mrs. Ondreas and Stasha. Karol had been attracted to her the first time they met when he visited her home with Stasha.

Stasha was still working for Madam Pilsey, entertaining the rich and sometimes famous aristocrats of adjoining European countries.

After a half hours wait, her life was to change immensely.

Her thoughts were on Jon when suddenly a strong gust of wind tore the main door open, glass was breaking everywhere and falling onto the waiting room floor, and then without warning part of the roof ripped off showing a dark ghostly sky and then as quickly as the rage came, it calmed, leaving debris scattered everywhere.

Stasha instinctively crawled under the bench she was sitting on. She could hear people groaning in the sudden silence as she came out from under the bench.

Bodies were everywhere, some dead and others injured.

"What happened?" she asked a railroad official who was making an attempt to help survivors.

"I really don't know," he answered with a stutter.

Stasha wandered out of the station onto the streets of Pest where the storm had laid waste to many buildings, showing no mercy to the most classic of structures that blocked its path. It was learned later that winds of a hundred miles an hour was caused by an unprecedented tornado. The roofs of the Basilica in Pest and the Coronation Church in Buda including the Chain Bridge were damaged along with bringing death and injuries to the populace.

"Armageddon!" someone shouted, from amidst the scattered piles of bodies and structural pieces. Stasha, dazed and bewildered, shuffled her way through the chaos until she reached the great Chain Bridge. People were rushing by foot and by horse and carriage in panic as they left the devastation of Buda behind them. All Stasha could think of was her child that was taken from her by the Nagy's. No sooner had the thought entered her mind when she heard a voice call her name from where the crowd was exiting the bridge onto the Corso. "Stasha, Stasha," a masculine voice shouted.

"My God," Stasha said, breathlessly recognizing Sandor, the servant that dropped her off in the middle of Pest to fend for herself and never to see her new born son again. Through the years she tried to keep thoughts of her son out of her mind. She was warned that if she ever came near her son, they would have her killed. In those days of Magyar absolute rule, killing a Slovak was as common as slaughtering a lamb.

"Oh, Stasha," Sandor shouted happily and then he continued, "You can't imagine how I prayed that I would find you. There is a God after all." Just as Stasha was ready to embrace Sandor she felt a pull at her skirt and then a soft voice asked, "Are you my mother?" Stasha stepped back shocked as looked at a little boy and then she turned to Sandor and asked, "Is this my son?"

"Yes, this is your son Stefan," he said, smiling from ear to ear. "They gave him his father's name."

"My God!" she responded, pulling Stefan into her arms and almost squeezing all the breath out of him and then she stood back to examine him. His hair was black and his complexion was dark and his eyes had the Mongol look. "Yes, he is the son of Stasha and Stefan," she said to herself.

"Stasha, you can't imagine how much I prayed that I would find you. But to find you like this is miraculous. This storm was sent from God."

"Why do you say that?"

"If you only knew know how terrible it has been living under the rule of the Nagy's. They were cruel and treated us like slave animals and your son included. He was whipped for no reason. I only believe she did that because of his Slovak blood. I heard her curse her son Stefan out loud many times for fornicating with a peasant Slovak woman."

"That Magyar Slovak traitor bitch. I will kill her," Stasha screamed as she pulled her son close to her.

"You won't have to. The storm took care of that. The roof in their bedroom collapsed and fell crushing both of them to death."

"Thank you, dear God," Stasha said, looking up to the dust filled sky.

"What do we do now? Sandor asked.

Stasha looked across the Danube and observed that the storm winds had slit a narrow path causing destruction in the Water District and Castle Hill just south of the Margaret Bridge. "Come with me," she said, putting her hand out to her son to hold. "I live in the Ancient Buda district. It looks like the storm spared it."

There was no transportation available. The trolley cars shut down because the wires that provide the electrical power were cut down they say by the hundred mile and hour wind. After and hour's walk they arrived at Karol's residence where they were greeted by Karol, Mariska, and their five year old daughter Eva with obvious relief.

"Thank God, you survived the storm," Karol said hugging Stasha. "It is the weirdest storm I've ever experienced. In the distance we saw a huge funnel cloud spinning madly through Buda and then crossing the Danube at the Chain Bridge. And who is this young man?" Karol asked, bending down to get a closer look.

"My son."

"I thought you said he died in childbirth."

"I lied. I didn't want to face the fact that I would never see him again. They had threatened to kill me if I ever tried to see him. Tell him Sandor how cruel they were."

"Yes, she is right," Sandor said, as he shook hands with Karol. "I was their servant for twenty years. You can't imagine how many times we were whipped and sometimes even starved by those Magyar bastards."

"What is your name?" Karol asked, as he grabbed the little boy's hand.

"Stefan," he replied with a sad look on his face.

"I'll bet you are all hungry. Come everyone, Mariska will prepare us a hearty Slovak meal."

"Where is my mother?" Stasha asked, as they walked outside to the patio where they would imbibe some cool summer drinks while they waited for dinner.

"She's resting in her bedroom. The storm frightened her. I told her I would call her when all was clear. Why don't you go get her?

"What difference will it make who goes to get her? After all these years she still doesn't recognize me."

"Yes, true, but she is still your mother."

"Stefan, Sandor," she said, "I'll be right back. Meanwhile, you can get acquainted with one another. Oh, Sandor," she said before she left, "now you're going to find out that all Hungarians aren't Magyar bastards."

CHAPTER 68

"Good for the goddamn Magyars," Jon shouted in the living.room. "Look Maria," he said, walking into the kitchen where she was preparing breakfast. "One disaster after another. First the tornado in Budapest and now they're in a war that they can never win. Slovakia will finally be free. Thank you God," he said, looking up to heaven.

"What started the war?" Maria asked.

"Don't you remember last month reading about Archduke Ferdinand and his wife getting assassinated in Serbia? It was only a couple days before the tornado struck in Budapest."

"No," Maria responded unenthusiastically. "How's the construction of the church progressing?" she asked, changing the subject.

"Not so good. We're running out of money. Anyway, what the hell does that have to do with the war?"

"Plenty," Maria answered in anger.

"What do you mean plenty?"

"Now we will need the church to go to so we can pray for all the men that will be killed. Thank God, I have two daughters and our son is too young to be a soldier."

"Well, I'm not too young," Jon snapped.

"What are you going to do? From what I've heard, the United States is not interested in getting involved in European affairs, so what army are you going to join?"

"I don't know. Maybe the Canadian army. England has declared war on them and so has Russia. Either army will do."

"Wake your brother and tell him breakfast is ready."

Jon burst through Jozef's door with the newspaper in his hand. "Read this brother," he said, as he shook him from his deep slumber.

"What is it Jon, what's the matter? Is something wrong?"

"Read this," he repeated placing the newspaper in front of him.

Jozef rubbed his eyes and read the headlines. "England, Russia, and France declared war on Germany and Austria-Hungary."

"Come on, get up. Maria has breakfast ready."

Jozef continued to read the newspaper while drinking coffee. When he finished, he asked Jon what he thought they could do to help.

"Join the Canadian army or wait until the United States declares war."

"Don't hold your breath, Jozef," Maria said, as she set a dish of ham and fried eggs in front of him.

"I know. I read the news too. The United States is not interested in getting involved in foreign affairs."

"Maybe so but we are still Slovaks," Jon said with passion.

"No, we are not. We are Americans," Maria shouted.

"She's right, Jon."

"I know, but we still have relatives and friends in Slovakia getting their asses kicked by the Magyars. We must find some way to help them get free."

"Think about this, brother," Jozef said, getting up from the table. "Russia, Great Britain, and France have declared war on them. They are surrounded by the super powers of Europe. They haven't got a chance in hell to win." That said, Jozef plucked his policeman's hat from the clothes rack on the living room wall and said, "I'll see you tonight" as he closed the door behind him

Everywhere Jon went that day the air was filled with talk of the European crisis. He was crushed when most of the opinions of the Sixth Warders were to stay out of it. The summer of 1914 came to a swift halt as the war escalated. In October, Turkey and Bulgaria joined the central powers and Italy joined the allies later in May. Before it was over, twenty four world countries comprised the allies and only five Europeans remained neutral. When Jon read where all the major countries of the world allied to destroy the evil Magyars, his desire lessened to volunteer in the army. He would contribute with his money to the various Czech and Slovak organizations in America that were pushing for a Czechoslovakian nation to be created after the central powers were defeated. Little did Jon or the rest of the world dream that the war would rage on for four years. Meanwhile, he got busy with his buying buildings and then selling or renting them at an affordable price to the deluge of immigrants that were in pursuit of the American dream, "Justice for all." The Slovak church project was at a standstill. Jon had invested all his money in his real estate adventure. His new elected position as a Director at the local branch bank that was that was awarded to him because of his success with loans to the immigrants wasn't at an advantage at the moment. The bank made some bad stock market investments and was struggling to stay afloat. Just about the time Jon was ready to give up on the completion of the church temporarily, an executive from the bank stopped by his house to tell him that his account was filled with sufficient money to finish the building of the church and, "If my calculations are correct, you will have plenty of money left over for yourself."

Jon just sat there in a state of euphoria. "Where did it come from?" he asked, after he composed himself.

"We don't know. The donor obviously wants to be anonymous."

"What does that mean?"

"Whoever it is don't want you to know."

"But why?" Jon asked, bewildered.

"All I can tell you is that it was transferred from a bank in Manhattan."

"Now that makes sense. The only one I know that would do that for me is Clancy. He has no wife or children so he has always treated me like I'm his son."

Two hours later Jon was on a train to New York City to thank Clancy in person for his more than generous gift. When he arrived at the tavern, Matt and his parents were busy with the dinner hour. Jon couldn't fight the urge and pitched in to help serve the patrons. Matt and his dad just shook their heads and smiled. When the rush was over, Jon pulled up a chair with Matt as his mother and father cleaned up.

"Now tell me where is Clancy?"

"He went back to Ireland to visit family and friends."

"Damn it!" Jon shouted, disappointed.

"What's wrong?" Matt asked, concerned.

"I need to see him now"

"Why?"

"Because he donated a ton of money to help me complete the building of our Slovak church. He never mentioned it to me. When do you expect him back?"

"I don't really know. He didn't give us a specific time. Why don't you send him a cablegram for now?"

"Good idea. Would you do that for me?"

"Yes, no problem."

"Hello Jon, Mr.Sokolosky said in Slovak as he approached the table. How have you been?"

"I couldn't be better. I'm having lots of luck lately. Tell me, Charles do you know anything about Clancy transferring money to my bank account?"

"No, he never mentioned it to me."

"Charles, do me a favor and call my friend Lucas at the Royal Blue Hotel. Clancy has his phone number in a notebook under the bar. Tell him that I am here but that I have to get the early morning train back home."

"Sure thing. I'll call you as soon as I reach him."

When Charles left, Matt shook Jon by the arm and said, "You know I'm going to ask about Helen. Has she taken her final vows yet?"

"No, but I know that it is coming soon."

"Then it's not over for me yet."

"Give it up. It's been nine years."

"How many years did it take you to give up on Stasha?" Matt fired back.

"You're right and guess what, I was an idiot. I am now very happy with Maria. You can find another woman like I did. Don't get me wrong. I love Helen like a daughter but enough is enough where you are concerned."

"You're probably right, but I want one more chance to try and persuade her to leave the convent and marry me. Promise me that you will call me shortly before the day of her final vows arrives."

Just as Jon answered, "I promise," Charles shouted that he had Lucas on the line. He rushed over and grabbed the telephone from Charles and said, "Lucas I'm getting richer by the day." he told him about the money transfer to his account. "Hell, I didn't know Clancy was that rich." For a moment there was silence. "Lucas are you there?"

"Yes."

"What's the matter?"

"I don't know, but something is strange here. I too just recently was given stocks in the Royal Blue chain of hotels. My bank informed me that they were put in my account. I know that you are like family to Clancy, but I'm not. All I was told was that it was transferred from another Manhattan bank. Look, Jon, just go back home and take care of business. Meanwhile I'll investigate and try and track down the donor. I'm planning on visiting you on Thanksgiving Day. I will get in get in touch with you as soon as I find out."

The next morning Jon was at the Pennsylvania Railroad Station waiting for his train when suddenly Lucas appeared smiling from ear to ear.

"You found the donor."

"I think so. I contacted the bank yesterday. I gave them all them all the bank code numbers that I was sure would identify the person we are looking for. They called me back and said that they came up with the identity but said they were sorry but they couldn't relate who it was. I then begged them to see if the person would please contact us so that we could thank him or her and find out why we deserved this generous gift. A half hour later they called me back and said that the donor would have a meeting with us. You're not going to believe this—at Clancy's this afternoon at two o'clock over a bottle of champagne."

They were aware that there was plenty of time so they decided to walk. After a half hour or so, they arrived at Chamber Street where Lucas suddenly turned to Jon and asked, "Jon, do you remember that we came this way after the fire?"

Jon thought for a moment and then replied, "Yes, yes I do. The only thing that's changed is there are more cars than horses and buggies on the streets."

It was 1:45 PM when they entered Clancy's. Mrs. Sokolosky was there to greet them. "Well, hello Jon," she said in Slovak. "I was thinking this morning after you left that it had been at least fifteen years since I saw you. It was the day that you left for America."

"Yes, I remember that day well. Your son, Matt, and his sister were there to see me off. How is Mariska? Why isn't she here? She must be quite grown up now."

"Fortunately, she's married to a wonderful wealthy Hungarian gentleman and lives in Budapest and you are going to find this hard to believe but he was highly recommended by Stasha. I was told he pleaded with Stasha for years to marry him, but she refused, insisting that she was still in love with you."

Jon just shook his head in disbelief and asked, "Where is Stasha now?"

"No one knows. After the tornado hit Budapest, the Nagy family was killed while her son survived that she hadn't seen since birth. A servant found her by pure accident as he crossed the Margaret Bridge to Pest. It wasn't the first time that she disappeared."

"Well, hello!" a handsome young man with fiery red hair and dazzling blue eyes, shouted, holding out his hand. "My name is James McDevitt and I am the little boy you two saved in the fire. I'll never forget crashing into that rug after my mother dropped me from the balcony. You put your lives in jeopardy to save me."

"No, son, it was your mother who was courageous. She gave up her life for you."

"True, but you lived and I want you two to have a life of luxury which I can well afford to help you with."

"How did you find us?" Lucas asked, incredulously.

"One day I was sitting at home in our West Chester mansion when I realized how fortunate I was. It made me aware that without you two rescuing me I wouldn't be here. The first chance I got I inquired at the New York

Times about that day. They brought me a copy of the story where you not only rescued me but a multitude of people. From there I talked to my father about finding you. He hired a detective and here we are."

"My God," Jon said, "I don't know how to thank you."

"That's easy, just use the money anyway you want. I was told that you put some of your own hard earned money into building your church and now you have enough to finish it. And then he looked at Lucas and said, "Now you are more than just a maintenance man. You are part owner of The Royal Blue Hotel."

Matt came over and popped the cork on the champagne bottle, poured it into everyone's glass, clinked them together, and saluted the appreciative, generous young man.

"I have an appointment," he said, looking at his watch. "We'll be keeping in touch and we will have a grand party at my place in West Chester in the near future."

CHAPTER 69

Mariska and Karol were placed in a compromising position with the outbreak of the war. She wanted to leave and be with her parents in America. Karol reminded her that she was half Hungarian. She said that she never considered herself a Magyar and then she added that even her mother denied her Hungarian heritage. "I told you how my parents met. That should tell it all about my feelings."

Karol pointed out to her how he would lose his home and the love and respect of his brother who was the only living member of his family. "Think about it, Mariska, look around you. If we go to America, you will lose all of this luxury. We will have to start all over again. People have been leaving Europe for America because they had nothing to lose and everything to gain. Please think about it and sleep on it tonight."

Mariska reached out and held his hand gently and said, "Yes, my love, I will."

The next morning during breakfast Mariska said she gave it much thought and that she agreed with him. They would stay and when the war ended, they would go to America to visit her family and maybe look into settling there permanently.

"Compromise! Now that's what real love is all about!" Karol said, raising his coffee cup. Mariska smiled and raised her cup and said, "To our everlasting love."

"Well wasn't that sweet," a voice said teasingly at the entrance to the dining room.

"Stasha," Karol shouted, "where the hell have you been?"

"Living the life of luxury in Turkey and now I don't know what I'm going to do to earn a living. Madam Pilsey said I could go back to Russia. Things have cooled off for awhile since the war started, and how are you?" she asked, turning to Mariska and embracing her.

"Fine and how is your mother these days? I thought she'd be living with you by now. I guess it's hard for her to leave Dubovica."

"No, Stasha, she's not there. We got her off to America and thank God, just in time before the war started."

"Oh, that's wonderful! Your father must be so happy."

"We can thank Karol for that. He paid all her expenses to make the voyage."

"Are they living with Jon?"

"No, they are working for Jon's friend Clancy at his tavern restaurant in New York City along with Matt."

"Now, where is my mother?"

"She's in her bedroom. I hired a personal maid to care for her. She's probably having breakfast in bed."

"Is she any better? Has she got her memory back?"

"Sometimes, but then she falls right back into oblivion. Why don't we finish breakfast and then we'll talk later?"

"Yes, of course, good idea, then you can tell me what was going on with you two when I arrived."

"Mariska told her about the compromise and then said that they had some concern over Jon's father. They were hoping to get him to America. Because Jozef took part in the rescue of Mikhail, it put their father in jeopardy."

Stasha contemplated for a moment and then said, "I think I can solve the problem. I'm going to see Madam Pilsey today about assigning me to Russia. I will take Mr. Valen with me to America. I want to do this because I owe it to Jon," she said, getting up and then left to see her mother.

The next morning Stasha was off to Presov where she had previously rented a room for Sandor so he could tend to Stefan while she was away making her living. She visited Emile and asked him to transport Mr. Valen to Presov. A week later Emile showed up without Mr. Valen. He refused stating that he wanted to wait out the war's ending and be involved in the independence of Slovakia. He had been informed by Jon of the Cleveland Agreement document signed by Czech and Slovak Americans that was designed to set up a federal state of two autonomous nations. The Slovaks would have their own Diet and retain Slovak as their official language.

Cold November nights brought frosty mornings, reminding the populace that winter was just around the corner. Stasha knew that she had to move quickly before the weather made it difficult to travel. Madam Pilsey warned her that crossing into Russia would be dangerous if not impossible. Stasha chose the hazardous path with the help of Emile and his Gypsy band. They crossed the treacherous Carpathian Bow passageway into neighboring

Ukraine. Stasha thanked God that she had left her son with Sandor. The journey was brutal as they trekked through the snow and ice of the cloud piercing mountain peaks.

Miraculously they arrived in Kiev where she boarded a train to Kieviskiy railroad station in Moscow. Amen, she evaded the Magyar border guards; she spoke out loud to herself. This time there was no grand reception. She was on her own. Madam Pilsey decided that she would not betray her country by giving pleasure to the enemy. Her only hope was to try and contact Misha. Her other alternative was to take Emile's advice and accost the first Gypsy she encountered. He gave her a letter written in a language that only a Gypsy could translate. She had no luggage. All she had was the clothes on her back that was only fit for mountain climbing. Fortunately there was a break in the weather. The snowfall had subsided and the clouds vanished allowing the blazing sun to warm the Artic air that was invading Red Square.

After a long rest and a bite to eat at Kievskiy Station, she headed for the Moskva river where Gypsy bands usually camped. The winter brought early darkness exposing the campfires that helped guide her way. In spite of her common garb it did not distract from her beauty. All eyes were fixed on her as she entered the compound.

"May I help you?" a young Gypsy man asked in Russian.

Without answering, Stasha handed him the letter that Emile had written. After pondering its contents for a moment, he suddenly broke out into a wide smile and then began to laugh.

"Come," he said, reaching out to grasp her hand. Noticing that his Russian was not spoken well, she asked him if he spoke Slovak. Once more he smiled and answered in pure Slovak that he did. She asked what Emile had said in the letter. He answered,

"We were to give you a place to stay until you work things out." He also said that "you were a vengerk."

"No, I am not a Hungarian girl with light morals," Stasha shot back. "I'm not a Magyar whore. I'm just a Slovak peasant girl trying to earn a living."

Everyone in hearing distance burst out laughing.

After settling into her primitive but comfortable accommodations, Stasha went in search of Misha. Dressed in Gypsy attire she wandered the streets looking to give sexual pleasure to Russian soldiers that inundated Red Square. Compared to royal payment, her take was miniscule. After a couple of months she earned enough money to buy some fancy clothes. Now she would make her move to attract the aristocracy.

258   Thomas J. Lipovsky

The war did not distract the nobility from attending the ballets and operas at Bolshoy Theater. Stasha was dressed in the finest black gown money could buy and the Gypsy women added more brilliance with artistic decorative beads. Saturday night arrived and with the help of the Gypsy woman she dressed lavishly for a night at the opera. Marcel, the young man that greeted her when she arrived transported her to Red Square with horse and wagon. Approximately one block from Bolshoy Theater she asked to be left off. Her intention, of course, was to attract attention. Throngs of people entered the grand black and white tiled vestibule. The only change that she noticed was that almost everyone was arriving by motor vehicles. The hansom carriage was nearly obsolete. While her eyes were exploring the massive crowd a voice rang out, "Stasha, Stasha!"

She turned and to her shocking surprise there was Misha running frantically towards her with arms outstretched. They embraced with such vigor that they both ran out of breath.

"My God, Misha, I have been praying every day for the last several months that I would find you. What are you doing these days? I was worried that you might have been imprisoned or killed after that horrible night at the wooden mansion."

"Well, I'm doing what I've always done except now I drive an automobile instead of a horse and carriage. When did you come back to Moscow? Are you still in the same business?" he asked with a sly smile.

"I'm here a few months and yes and no to your second question. I came specifically to find a way to America. Do you remember me telling you about my son I had from a Magyar soldier and that I had him taken away from me?"

"Yes."

"Well, I got him back and I want to find a better life for him in America."

"Misha, where the hell are you?" a voice shouted.

"Over here, Sir and do I have a surprise for you."

Stasha turned to face the gentleman and suddenly her knees went weak. Seeing her distress, he put his arms around her and said, "Yes! Count Malovsky. I survived the fall through the ice."

Stasha just stood there petrified, unable to speak. "Come Stasha now we can start where we left off. Do you remember that last night we were on our way to the opera?"

"Yes, of course. How could I forget that terrible night?"

"Come," he said, reaching out to take her hand.

Misha smiled as he watched them disappear into the maze of people entering the grand black-and-white-tiled vestibule of Bolshoy Theater. This